DOLL FACE
A DI Tudor Manx Novel

Dylan H. Jones

Also By Dylan Jones

DI Tudor Manx Series
Anglesey Blue (Book 1)

Dedication

To my wife, Laura and daughter Isabella for their endless patience and cheerleading.
Also, to my nain (grandmother) Grace Jones, whose kindness and generosity was an inspiration.

PART ONE
PROVISIONS OF THE FLESH

Chapter 1

She was the lump in the throat, the shiver down the spine; the shadow that cast itself across a twilight street.

She was all these things, and he would christen her Lucy.

He recalled the name from a DVD he'd rented last year; another of those action movies he liked to watch when the static in his head crackled so much it hurt to even think. It had all started around this time, the inciting incident as he'd learnt to call it – the irreversible trigger that set everything in motion. The thought amused him as he doused the cloth in the baptistery water he'd collected yesterday and wiped it across the blade. He slipped the knife into the sleeve of his backpack and heard her voice call out to him from the kitchen.

'Will you be long? What about your dinner? Do you have your warm coat?' Questions, always questions. Lucy never asked questions. She already knew the answers; understood what was required.

Before leaving, he permitted himself a small vanity. He paused at the hallway mirror, admiring his creation. Lucy was every bit as beautiful as they'd promised; her online profile did her little justice. Her wide familiar eyes, the plump lips, her hair, equally familiar and soft; the way she chaffed against his groin shoving his junk where the sun doesn't shine. He could love her for that alone, but it was her purity that touched him the most. He stepped into the chilly March evening but felt no cold, just the ripple of Lucy pressing into him as if she were flesh itself.

Chapter 2

Sian Conway swept a pack of Embassy No 1's from the table and tapped out a single cigarette into her palm. *Last one*, she promised, but tonight they were all that stood between her and an inevitable descent into self-loathing. Bad news was like that; once it made itself known, it was relentless – a river in flood sweeping away all in its path.

She twisted the empty wine glass around her fingers and contemplated her choices. She could continue with the evening's usual trajectory and have nothing to show for it but a day-long hangover, or she could just leave now and avoid the whole clichéd ritual.

'Be the death of you,' Donna said. A tell-tale, glassy sheen had settled across her eyes as she struggled to keep her friend in focus.

Sian balanced the cigarette on the corner of her lips where this morning's lipstick had cracked and dried to a crust. 'I'll take my chances.'

Donna scrunched her forehead. She wasn't completely smashed, but it was a short ride to that destination; stone-cold sober to weepy-eyed drunk in three hours. She gulped at the last of her vodka and tonic, the ice cubes spilling from her glass and onto the floor. Sian's heart sank. She couldn't do this again, not tonight. She slid a tenner across the table.

Donna shoved it back. 'Thought we were out for the night?'

Sian bristled at the familiar whine of disappointment, though it bothered her less than usual tonight. Maybe she was acquiring a taste for disappointing people.

Donna's eyes widened as the funk-tinged chords of 'Staying Alive', the Bee Gee's classic, riffed through the speakers.

She grabbed Sian's wrist. 'Oh, just this one. Used to be your favourite, yeah?'

Sian extended her friend a tight, resigned smile. 'Next time, eh.'

'Suit yourself, got plenty of company anyway,' Donna said, smoothing down the front of her dress and adjusting her bust. 'Divorcees and Daiquiri Thursday, free drinks in half-hour. You're missing out.' She shoved past Sian and tottered, unsurely on her new heels, towards the dance floor.

Within the hour, Midnight Magic would be packed to the mirror-balls with students looking for a jump on the weekend and single women of a certain age, like Donna Robinson, looking to fill the emptiness that was slowly consuming them. Sian had seen this movie before, paid the price of admission many times over and resigned herself to the predictable ending that came with it. She watched for a while as Donna shimmied her declining wares to the amusement of the younger men, jostling like lions at the easy-pickings of the watering hole. She left a few minutes later, her heart a few grams heavier than when she'd arrived.

Outside, Bangor High Street was bathed in the milky hue of dim street lamps. A gang of university students staggered past her in full throated rehearsal for their next karaoke performance. She rolled the cigarette between her fingers and contemplated its allure before throwing it to the ground: *one nil to willpower,* she thought and plucked her zipper to the neckline. The night was cold, eight degrees at best. She'd feel better once the weather turned, she always did.

Inside the utilitarian comfort of her Nissan Micra she tuned to Heart FM and swivelled the mirror; she looked dog-tired, had done for weeks. She pushed it back and reached for her phone. She hesitated before dialling his number – one of only three in her favourites list. It cut straight to voicemail. That wasn't unusual, and anyway, she'd already made her decision, there were only the details to be discussed now, and they could talk them through tomorrow.

She pulled out from the car park. Behind her, another car did the same, following her at a safe, controlled distance.

Chapter 3

He stopped at the lights and glanced in the mirror. His breath caught in his throat as Lucy's reflection stared back at him. He was hard too, like an iron bar, but those sorts of urges would have to wait. There were more important priorities to attend to, like making sure the woman didn't notice she was being followed. But why would she? He'd seen plenty of movies that dramatized the exact same scenario: the careful pursuit of a suspect, keeping two or three cars behind, allowing other vehicles to edge in front every few minutes so the headlights changed shape. Planning and patience, that's all that was required.

An overwhelming sense of power surged through him as he imagined what the next few hours held for the woman. She was clueless, like most people were, not just about what fate had designed for her, but about the salvation she was soon to be blessed with. She would be his first: she would thank him, eventually. He glanced over at his backpack on the passenger seat. *Act one*, he thought, and permitted himself the faintest of smiles.

Chapter 4

Sian tugged on the curtain and looked out across the familiar tapestry of rooftops and postcard-sized gardens; the same mundane vista she'd surveyed for the last eight months. Satisfied his car wasn't parked nearby, she drew back the curtains and pulled the cork on a bottle of supermarket red. She was intending to save it for the weekend: *break open in case of emergency* she thought, and poured herself a generous measure. Wine was cheap enough these days, it was the hangovers that were becoming expensive.

Snapping the belt of her dressing gown around her waist she flopped onto the sofa and stabbed the TV remote in a resigned manner that suggested she held little hope of finding anything that would hold her attention. Within half an hour she was asleep, her wine untouched and the TV muted in the background casting a pale light over her body as she breathed.

Chapter 5

*H*e'd take good care of her, he told himself as he studied Lucy's reflection in the glass pane of the backdoor. A keeper? Isn't that what they called them? He'd never had anything or anyone to take care of before. His parents had forbidden any *'distractions'* as they called them. If nothing else, it had taught him discipline; the kind of discipline it took to see a plan through from conception to completion. It was like his father had always preached: *what kind of world would we have if God had lost interest halfway through the week?* No, a plan had to be seen through and executed with precision and skill.

A few gardens down, a dog barked and pulled hard against its chain. He waited for it to stop, reached into one of the large planter pots and picked up a hollow rock around two inches long embedded in the soil. *People were clueless,* he thought, as he slid back the cover to reveal the spare key. He'd followed her into the garden centre that day, watched her buy the item, even queued up behind her and bought the same one so he could practice extracting the key in darkness. The rest was easy. He pushed gently on the door and walked into the kitchen.

The faint glow of a computer screen blinked at him as he entered. He crept slowly down the hall towards the low murmur of the TV. A drop of sweat fixed into the corner of his eye. He took a deep, calming breath. *'And darkness was upon the face of the deep'.* The words from Genesis came to him as he cast his eyes over the length of her body. This would be his own, personal Genesis. He would deliver light into the darkness; purity to what was unclean; salvation to that which was cursed.

Chapter 6

She was sleeping. Her dressing gown had fallen open to reveal the pale round of her thighs and a thatch of pubic hair. *Women shouldn't be displaying their parts like that,* he thought as he stood close enough to catch the sickly aroma of her stale perfume. It wasn't right, not godly. But the flutter of excitement deep in his belly confused him. The woman's breasts, flopping lazily from her bra and swelling with the rhythm of her breath stirred another part of him – the part his mother had always warned him could never be trusted. He could easily have reached out, passed the back of his fingers over the soft flesh, but Lucy provided him with the strength to abstain.

After laying down his backpack, he carefully extracted the knife and felt its weight in his palm. He was set to begin the ritual when a loud musical ping from the kitchen startled him. He paused, waited for it to stop. It pinged again, demanding to be answered.

His first mistake: he should have unplugged the computer. Retreat was his only option. She was already stirring, wiping smears of saliva from her lips. Grabbing his backpack, he edged back into the kitchen, passed the urgent plea of the computer and into the bathroom.

Chapter 7

Sian stumbled, her eyes blurry with the remnants of sleep, into the kitchen. Donna was Skyping her.

'Hiya. What's going on?' she asked, rubbing her eyes.

Donna sniffed and ran the back of her hand under her nose. 'Didn't miss you, you know. Had a brilliant time.'

Sian yawned. 'You woke me up just to tell me that?'

'Thought we were mates,' Donna said, waving her finger accusingly at Sian. 'Shit mate you are, Sian Conway. Shit.'

Sian sighed. 'Go to bed, eh, you'll feel better in the morning.'

'Yeah? You a bloody doctor now too?' Donna sneered, and took a large gulp of what Sian guessed was neat vodka from a nearby tumbler; it was the only alcohol she kept at arm's reach.

'Haven't you had enough?' Sian said. 'Just go to bed for God's sake, it's after midnight. We've both got work tomorrow.'

'The night is still young!' Donna said, leaning closer and allowing Sian a clear view of the blood-red tributaries mapped across the whites of her eyes. 'But I'm not.' She laughed, a curt, rough cackle. 'What have I got to look forward to, eh? It's all right for you, never short of boyfriends. You know what my mam told me? *You're no looker, Donna luv, you've got to make the most of what little God gave you.* Imagine, a mother saying that to her daughter.'

'Yeah, cruel that is,' Sian said, having heard the story on more than one occasion. Donna continued anyway. Sian listened, hoping the booze would eventually shut her down.

Behind Donna's shoulder, Sian saw a shadow pass behind the glass partition followed by the sound of piss forcefully hitting porcelain. 'Oh, Donna, not again.' A wave of guilt rippled through her. She shouldn't have left her in that place, it was a meat-market.

'So what?' Donna said. 'At least I'm living my life, not like you, little miss stay-at-home. You want to know something? He's not interested any more. He's moved on, let it go for God's sake.'

Sian felt a prickle of concern as the shadow moved behind Donna and rapped its knuckles impatiently on the glass.

'Better go,' Donna said, scraping back her chair and wiping her mouth with the sleeve. 'He don't like the smell of it on me.'

'Shit,' Sian muttered to herself as Donna turned away, forgetting to shut down the camera.

Sian thought about what Donna had said. Maybe she was right; it had been a year now and he hadn't tried anything, not for months. She took it as a good sign but she knew better than to be too optimistic where he was concerned.

'*He don't like the smell of it on me*' – Donna's words had stuck in Sian's mind. There was something both familiar and disconcerting about the phrase. With the luxury of time she would have dwelled on it and finally made the connection. But there was no more time. He was already at her back, his warm, sour breath snaking across the hairs of her neck.

Chapter 8

Donna's kitchen was empty, illuminated by the faint spill of light from the computer screen. The only sound in the house was the rhythmic thrust of an old bed-frame slapping against the bedroom wall.

What happened next was a matter of timing; random and unpredictable. Donna would debate this for months to come, blame herself, but eventually would come to understand there was nothing she could have done. She would have been a silent witness to the act; a voyeur unable to avert her gaze from the events as they unfolded scene by scene in front of her.

Had she been sitting in her kitchen, watching, she would have felt the same knot of confusion Sian felt as the stranger's breath fell on the nape of her neck. Would have turned the same curdled shade of white as the expressionless face of a woman loomed over Sian's left shoulder. Would have looked on, unbelieving, as the knife slashed past the camera, drawing itself across Sian's neck with absolute precision. Only then might she have screamed; when the blood from Sian's neck splattered in thick, red blotches across the lens. And, as Sian's hair was pulled back and her body dragged from the chair, Donna might have had the presence of mind to call 999 and attempt to explain the nature of her emergency. But, she witnessed nothing. It was a slender sliver of mercy she would hold tight to over the next few weeks as if it were life itself.

Chapter 9

By eight o'clock that morning, he'd lost count of the number of times he'd emptied the contents of his stomach into the Irish Sea. He gripped a nearby stanchion and vomited another spit of clear, thin liquid.

'Better out than in, eh?' the coxswain said, patting Manx on the back. 'Old sailor trick is to keep your eyes on the horizon.'

Detective Inspector Tudor Manx wiped his mouth and looked eastwards as if he were searching for the lost continent.

'Big land mass right in front of you,' one of the volunteers said, gesturing towards the Snowdonia mountain range to the southeast. He was called Tom: one of those sea-faring macho types with a mandatory bush of seaman's beard and a habit of staring at Manx as if he were a hapless Sunday sailor they'd rescued from his upturned dingy. Manx took an instant dislike to the man.

He curled his fingers around the lifeline as the boat cleaved through the undulating swell. 'Remind me why I agreed to this?' Manx said, running the sleeve of the drysuit across his salt-sodden eyes.

'Your number came up, remember?' Frank explained. 'First prize in the lifeboat fundraiser? Three-hour joyride on the old girl before we trade her in.'

'What was the second prize?' Manx asked. 'Six hours?'

He had a vague recollection of the evening. It was one of those rare occasions when the Pilot Arms was stuffed from doorway to lounge with customers. The raffle had kicked off late in the evening when people were already several pints in and throwing a fiver at a pretty face in a too-tight RNLI T-shirt seemed like a bright idea.

The coxswain wiped a sop of condensation from the cockpit window and turned to Manx. 'Probably not the best day for it mind. Sea's swelling like a bugger but you're lucky, we don't usually take civilians out on training exercises. Your man, Canton, very supportive he was. Mentioned you were looking to be more involved with the community and that.'

'Is that right?' Manx said, imagining his chief inspector and the coxswain plotting the whole outing over a couple of pints. 'He mention anything else about me?'

'Not that I could repeat.'

Frank's shoulders shook as he laughed at a joke that only he was privy to. Manx didn't request the punchline; he'd probably heard it before anyway.

The lifeboat, a Tyne Class, was three miles out from Moelfre and tacking close to the north-easterly lee where the coastline was a sketch of inlets and sand beaches that had now soured to a muddy dark-brown in the flatness of the morning light.

It had taken Manx over an hour to quell his nausea, and while not exactly finding his sea legs, he took Frank's advice and steadied his gaze on the horizon where the sun was bleeding through in bursts of deep, promising orange. It would be a false promise as it turned out, but for now the day's early optimism was reflecting brightly across the ocean.

Manx felt a rare sense of calm as he looked towards the cliff heads and the neat rows of static caravans laid to rest like shoeboxes across the fields above. He took a deep breath. At forty-nine years old, a sense of calm was something he'd learnt never to trust.

Manx had arrived back on Anglesey six months ago, a swift transfer from the London Metropolitan Police Serious Crime Division. As his DCI, Ellis Canton, had explained to him at the time, 'Spend the rest of your career pushing paper in a back room in Scotland Yard or do some proper police work and make a difference. It's just another place, Manx, get over it.'

The fact that Manx had seriously considered the Scotland Yard option was testament to his reluctance to return here. Eventually, he'd rationalised his decision. Maybe he could make the most of his time on the island and gain some perspective on his life like some Buddhist hermit meditating on existence in the hope of finding enlightenment. Three weeks into his new posting a series of brutal murders and an epidemic of highly addictive methadone imported onto the island had almost got him killed and further estranged from his family. *So much for the quiet life.* But today, despite the queasy unrest of his stomach, he sensed he might be forging a cautious truce with the island. The thought troubled him. Hating the damned place outright was far easier – a black and white deduction that required little philosophising. Finding peace here? That was a different proposition all together and one he was far from ready to negotiate.

As the morning's false promise spread itself liberally across the sky, the ship-to-shore radio crackled to life.

'Copy that. No can do,' Frank said, throwing a quick glance in Manx's direction. 'Is that right? Shit on a stick. We'll send him in one of the outboards. Over.'

Frank eased the boat to a slow drift. 'They need you on land, emergency apparently. You can ride with Tom, he'll have you back at Moelfre in less than half-hour.'

'What kind of emergency?' Manx asked.

'Didn't say. Surprise seems like.'

'Never liked surprises,' Manx said, watching the grey clouds scuttle like locusts over the back of the mountains. 'It's like being mugged by bad news.'

Chapter 10

The 1974, Mk 4 Jensen Interceptor shuddered to a stop. The cold didn't agree with the car; it rubbed its electrics the wrong way, got under its rotting fuel line, squabbled with its carburettor until it whined with complaint. Manx's father, Tommy, had bequeathed him the vintage model decades ago; it was as world-worn and unreliable as the old man himself.

He was parked at the entrance of a housing estate on the north-west of the island, Gwalchmai – the sort of place you drove quickly through on your way to someplace else. *Bad memories,* Manx thought to himself as he recalled a cold and wet Saturday night at the local disco when he was a teenager. The DJ was playing the last song, 'Long After Tonight is All Over,' a Northern Soul classic, when some of the local kids took a dislike to him; maybe it was the way he danced or his hairstyle was too short or too long; – who the fuck knew? They were probably just bored and Manx, living all of ten miles away, was considered an out-of-towner and a prime target for a weekend shit-kicking. He'd been suspicious of the place ever since.

He checked out the scene. A handful of neighbours were already loitering their gardens, mugs of tea in hand and gossip radars calibrated to maximum. Their object of attention was number thirty-seven, where several service cars and a CSI van had surrounded the driveway. Behind the temporary cordon, a pack of reporters peeked over each other like curious meerkats and thumbed impatiently at their phones waiting for the action to unfold.

Manx stepped out – the air felt taut, as if it were preparing for a confrontation. PC Kevin Priddle stood at the front of the driveway, clipboard in hand and a practised seriousness applied to his face. It was a look he was still perfecting; his boyish features, as they always would, betraying his best efforts.

'Morning, inspector,' Priddle said, lifting the tape. 'Clear pathway's to the right. I'll log you in.' He scribbled Manx's name in the scene of crime log. 'I told them they shouldn't start before you arrived, like.'

'They listened?' Manx said, glancing over at the CSI van.

'Um, not sure.'

'Responding officer?'

'DS Nader. He's in the temporary incident room.'

Manx nodded. 'Enjoying a code ninety-nine no doubt.'

'I'll let the boys know you're here,' Priddle offered, tapping his radio.

'And ruin the surprise?' Manx said, brushing past the tall, beanpole figure of the PC.

'You'll need gloves and an over suit,' Priddle said, gesturing towards the van. 'Bevan left a pile of them out. Must be a bloody mess in there, aye?' He shuddered and pulled his face into a long, sloping grimace.

Chapter 11

Priddle's request to wait had been duly noted and unilaterally ignored. Ashton Bevan, Lead Scene of Crime Investigator, was in the kitchen, already ninety minutes into his evidence gathering.

Manx surveyed the scene. It was one of those modern starter-homes furnished with only the most necessary of appliances. Several half-empty takeaway food boxes were scattered across the kitchen counter, a squadron of flies already buzzing around the leftovers.

The kitchen chair was laid out on the floor, along with a white dressing gown. To the left, a wide smear of blood still glistening with damp ran across the linoleum and ended at the hallway where the carpeting began. Priddle was right; this was going to be ugly.

Ashton Bevan raised the crown of his balding head from the samples he was swabbing. 'You're late to the party, Manx, had to kick things off without you. Your boy out there, Prickle, or something or other, tried his best but when you're dealing with professionals, it's like Canute trying to hold back the tide.' Bevan smiled tightly as he held the inspector in his gaze.

It had been four months since Manx had last seen that smile; he hadn't missed a speck of its awkward insincerity. It was at Mickey Thomas's retirement party, if he remembered correctly. Bevan, and his wife, Sherri, had cornered him at the bar before they shuffled off to the dance floor. Manx had made his excuses soon after.

'Hardacre?' Manx asked.

'Bathroom. Take a vomit bag, three of my lads have spilled their guts already.'

'I'll pass,' Manx said, figuring he was already squeezed dry on that subject, and continued into the hallway.

In the bedroom to his right, one of Bevan's men was riffling through a chest of drawers and extracting random items of underwear, each of them a similar off-white colour as the walls. The next item the investigator pulled from the drawer attracted more interest: a long, steel knife. He slid it into an evidence bag.

As Manx edged towards the bathroom he felt the expected rush of anxiety that always accompanied the first few seconds of a fresh crime scene. It was a familiar feeling, and proof that despite three decades of police work, he still retained some vestige of humanity; for better or for worse.

Through the gap in the door he saw the coroner, Doctor Richard Hardacre, bent over the lip of the bath, his arms buried deep in the tub as if he were bathing a small dog. He pushed on the bathroom door. It swung open, slapping loudly against the wall. Hardacre jumped, bringing his hand to his chest.

'Jesus H. in Christendom, Manx, you nearly had another body on your hands,' he said, wiping his sleeve across his brow. 'Sneaking up like that on a man in my condition, what were you thinking?'

'I was thinking it's about time I saw what all the fuss is about.'

Hardacre huffed himself to standing. 'Be my guest,' he said. 'But this one's probably a lodger.'

'The lodger?' Manx asked. 'How do you know—'

'*A* lodger, Manx,' Hardacre interrupted, 'not *the* lodger.' He pressed the tips of his fingers to his temple. 'Takes up residence somewhere in here and you can't shake the bloody thing. Mercifully it's only happened a few times but still rattles the old nerves.'

Manx understood. He'd witnessed several of those himself in his career, some harder to shake than others.

Hardacre tugged at the plastic sheeting. Manx felt his blood temperature drop several degrees as he looked over the woman. She was knee bound, as if caught mid-prayer, her hands tied behind her back and her feet bound tightly at the ankles – red welts had already began to form where the ropes had gnawed into her skin. Her head was positioned between the hot and cold taps. The skin around her upper thighs and pubic area was puckered with tiny stab wounds, each one less than half an inch-long. It was as if the killer was testing his victim for doneness.

'Jesus,' Manx said.

'Splatter patterns are consistent with her being stabbed in the kitchen then dragged into the bathroom to complete the task,' Hardacre explained. 'Once in the bathroom his actions became much more intense.'

'Time of death?'

Hardacre tutted. 'Tricky one. No more than a few hours. I would take a liver temperature, but since it's been removed the reading's going to be skewed to say the least.'

Manx drew his gaze along the knotted nubs of the woman's spine towards her abdomen, which was carved open, folds of raw flesh hanging loose like curtains from her ribcage. Directly beneath lay the woman's liver: a blistered, dark tumour set against the stark white enamel of the bathtub.

'Christ. Why the liver?'

'Beyond my pay grade,' Hardacre said, 'but I can tell you the means of access. Lateral incision, probably administered post mortem then slashed, none too efficiently, to gain access to the organ in question. I don't think we're dealing with a skilled surgeon. I'll know more when I get her back to the mortuary.'

Manx crouched at the lip of the tub and looked carefully over the woman's pale flesh. It was a ritual he'd developed over the years, and one he performed not just out of respect for the victims, but as a means of committing the scene to memory. The forensic photographs would provide the cold facts, but immersing himself in the viscera of the scene would provide him the emotional connection. She had a pretty face, Manx thought. He wondered if she'd struggled, fought back against her attacker? He closed his eyes, tried to imagine her final few moments but came up short; he always would.

'Peep show's over,' Hardacre said, laying his palm on Manx's shoulder. 'I still have a couple more hours work here before we throw her in the back of the van.'

'Ever thought of a career in grief counselling, Hardy?' Manx asked, raising himself from squatting and feeling each one of his forty-nine years in his knee joints as he rose.

'I have grief aplenty of my own to manage, thanks all the same,' Hardacre said, gesturing it was time for Manx to leave his crime scene.

* * *

'Forced entry?' Manx asked, walking back to the kitchen.

'You'd have been notified,' Bevan said, without looking up.

'And the victim, I suppose you—'

'Sian Conway,' Bevan interrupted. 'She's been renting for about eight months. The landlord found her. Called round to fix some problem, expecting her to be at work, odds on he'll be taking the rest of the day off.' Bevan snorted back an inconsequential laugh.

'Where is he? The landlord?'

'Your girl, short one, looks like one of those Lego Policemen, took him. Minor, I think Nader called her. He emptied his stomach a few too many times. The girl, though, couldn't seem to get enough. Eager beaver that one.'

'You mean Morris?' Manx said, feeling the familiar swellings of agitation whenever Bevan opened his mouth.

'If that's her name, then yes,' Bevan said.

'Nader calls her Minor because she's short, and he's a tit.'

'Ah, Morris Minor,' Bevan said. 'Police humour, doesn't improve with age, does it?'

'Has that been on since you got here?' Manx asked, gesturing towards the computer.

'Connected to the mains, so I expect so,'

Manx tapped the spacebar. The screen saver floated in a whirl of shapes before revealing Sian Conway's final point of contact:

a Skype conversation. The camera screen was blank, but the duration and time of her last conversation was clear: 12.02pm seven minutes, with someone called *DonnaNightFever.*

Manx jotted down the name. As he turned towards the door, he was stopped by a loud ping of notes. He glanced at the caller ID; an avatar of John Travolta in his trademark white, flared suit, chest puffed out, right arm high and triumphant.

'Could be our killer checking in,' Bevan said, smirking.

Manx hesitated for a moment before pressing accept.

Donna's bloated face filled the screen, smiling at first then quickly turning to confusion as Manx's face stared back at her.

'Sian?' she said, rubbing her eyes.

Manx laid his palms on the table. 'No. Detective Inspector Tudor Manx, North Wales Constabulary. And you are?'

The camera cut quickly to black.

'What the fuck?' Manx said looking over at Bevan, who shrugged his usual *'not my monkeys, not my circus'* gesture and continued swabbing.

Chapter 12

Robert Balham sucked in his cheeks and pursed his thick, fleshy lips together. 'Mind if I have one?' he asked, coveting a plate of custard creams just out of his reach.

'When did you find Mrs Conway?' Manx asked, sliding the plate towards him. Balham quickly snatched a biscuit as if he were worried Manx might pull them away again if he didn't provide a swift answer.

'Told Mal already, 'bout nine this morning. I expected Sian … Mrs Conway—' he corrected himself —'would be at work, usually is that time of day.'

'Very familiar with her calendar are you, Mr Balham?'

Balham coughed, wiping a sprinkling of crumbs from his mouth. He reached for another biscuit. 'We arranged it. Told me she'd be working, so I promised to fix the toilet for her today.'

'Anyone else have keys to the house other than you?'

'Should only be me and the tenant.'

'Should?'

'I'm not running a bloody jail, am I? If they get an extra set cut for their boyfriend or the cleaner or something, I wouldn't know nothing about it.'

'And did Sian Conway have a boyfriend?'

Balham shrugged. 'Dunno. She was separated. Her husband's a bit psycho from what I heard.' He snapped the corner off another biscuit. 'You should interview him.'

'Thanks for the tip,' Manx said, flipping the cover of his notebook and pointing it at Balham, 'we might have missed that.'

Balham stiffened, unsure of how to take the remark then chewed aggressively as if he were in a hurry to swallow and say something of importance to the inspector. Finally, he leant forward, settled the remaining custard cream between his thumb and forefinger and stabbed it in Manx's direction.

'I'll tell you who you should be interrogating.'

'Enlighten me.'

'Immigrants,' Balham said, leaning back in the chair. 'It's not like we know who the hell we're letting in the bloody country any more. No records, nothing. I told the council, I won't rent to none of them without a first and last month deposit and two months' rent up front. Most of them get it too, refugee status they call it, more like a bloody Government handout. You should question a few of those, see what they got to say for themselves.'

'Steady income for you, though,' Manx said, 'Government guaranteed check every month, must be nice.'

Balham shrugged his wide shoulders, sloughing off the remark. 'Don't know how I'm going to sleep tonight, after seeing Sian like that,' he said, chomping down on the last bite of biscuit. 'Bloody horrible it was.'

'That, and all those custard creams,' Manx said, sweeping the plate out of his reach.

'Come again?'

'Never mind,' Manx said. 'And last night? I expect you're going to tell me you were in the pub or watching the telly all night?'

Balham smirked. 'Met some friends down the Ship, had a few too many so stayed over at a mate's house.'

'Outstanding,' Manx said. 'We'll need to confirm the name of that mate of yours.'

'Jones, Marty Jones, lives in Marianglas. Free to go now, am I?' Balham said, wiping his hands on the side of his trousers.

'Just don't wander too far off the island. We'll need your fingerprints and a DNA swab, check with one my PCs outside.'

'Saw that on the telly once, doesn't hurt, does it?'

Manx grinned. 'Only if you resist.'

Balham winced, running his tongue around the inside of his cheek as if he were searching for leftovers.

'One last question, Mr Balham' Manx said. 'Were you having an affair with Sian Conway?'

'Do anything for her, I would,' Balham said.

'That doesn't answer my question.'

Balham pushed back his chair. 'Immigrants,' he said. 'You're best putting your efforts there, I reckon.'

Manx watched as Balham shuffled towards the forensics team and presented himself for swabbing. Balham didn't give the impression of a cold-blooded killer, Manx thought, but then again, that was all part of the camouflage, they rarely did.

Chapter 13

Manx stood at the far end of Buckley Drive and looked over the estate across to the spine of green hills behind. Most of the houses backed onto open fields, giving the killer only two ways to enter the estate: the main road or through the fields.

'Bob Balham, give you what you need?' Nader asked, ambling towards Manx, his hands stuffed deep into his parka pockets.

Manx looked closely at his sergeant. 'You're looking pale, Mal, not coming down with something, are you?'

'Top notch boss,' Nader said, wiping his hand across his mouth, suspecting he was harbouring a tell-tale spittle of vomit in his moustache. 'You?'

Manx smiled. 'Right as rain, Sergeant.'

'So, you get what you needed from Sarnie?'

'Sarnie?' Manx said. 'If you mean the bigot with the custard cream fetish who was either sleeping with or had pretensions of sleeping with our victim, then yes. At least for now.'

'Pay no mind, he's all piss and vinegar.'

'Good friend of yours? I'll need to know of any conflict.'

Nader shrugged. 'He moved in a few doors down when his missus chucked him out. He was in a bad state. That was a few years back now mind you. Time's a healer, right boss?'

'You think that's true, Nader?' Manx said.

Nader thought for a moment, letting the question hang in the space between them. 'Aye, well that's what they say anyway.'

Manx nodded, as if keeping a note of Nader's remark for use later. 'Do we know the entry point?'

Nader flipped through his notebook. 'The doors and windows were all shut. No forced entry I could see.'

'So, Sian Conway either knew her killer and invited him in, or he had a key.'

'Maybe she likes to leave her window open?'

'Doubtful. It's eight degrees at night, no one wants that much fresh air,' Manx said. 'It would also imply the killer is an opportunist, which I doubt. Make sure Morris and Priddle get all the door-to-doors done and dusted today before everyone starts telling us the same shit they heard on the news just to keep us happy.'

'Aye, bad news travels fast,' Nader said, looking at the press pack, which had already swelled by a few more warm bodies.

'Oh, and your mate, Balham, he mentioned something about the victim's husband, bring him in as soon as.'

'He's not—' Nader began, but was interrupted by Manx.

'And by the way, why the hell do you call him Sarnie?'

It took a couple of confused squints of Mal's bloodshot eyes before the penny dropped. 'Oh! Balham. Right. They used to call him Hammy, like in ham sandwich. He got pissed off about that, said it made him sounds like a hamster or something, so we ended just up calling him Sarnie.'

Manx nodded. 'Probably the question I'll most regret asking today.'

From behind the ranks of press there was a sudden squeal of brakes and the loud slam of a car door. The crowd's attention was drawn to a man striding purposely towards the house. He cut a sharp path through the press, who, sensing a scoop, quickly took up arms and snapped at the air like hungry dogs.

The man scanned the scene as if he were sniffing out prey, and having located him, barrelled towards Bob Balham with the force of a steam train. For the second time that morning, Balham's blood drained to his boots.

He didn't anticipate the first punch, but felt its blow as it landed with a bone-on-bone crack. The second punch he saw, but was too dazed to dodge its trajectory. The third was stopped mid-flow. Manx had stepped into its path, blocking it with his hand.

The man's face tuned purple with rage. He drew back his head and thrust it forward in a short, sharp slingshot. Manx reeled from the force, his forehead throbbing – an inch lower and it would have shattered his nose. Before the man could wind up his next punch, Nader had sunk his knee into the small of his back and cuffed his wrists.

'Christ!' Manx said. 'Get him down the station, now.'

Bob Balham stumbled to his feet, rubbing at his swollen eye. 'See! Told you!' he said, pointing at the man who was being ushered, none to gently, into the back of a service car. 'Bloody psycho. No wonder she left you mate. Fucking sick bastard.'

Chapter 14

A lone bird skimmed low and fast over the Menai Strait, its chest almost touching the water. With an elegant twist of its wing it swooped upwards into the clouds and then dived back down striking the water at a near ninety-degree angle, barely fracturing the surface.

'Double-crested cormorant,' McLain said, observing the bird through the Range Rover's windscreen. 'That manoeuvre right there? The Immelmann turn. It's an old fighter pilots' trick. Retreat above your enemy's line of sight then use gravity to gain momentum and blindside them with an all-out assault.'

Glyn Lewis scrunched his pale, youthful face into a scowl. 'Who's been assaulted?' he asked, stabbing at his iPad.

McLain sighed; he should be used to Lewis by now. He was like an impatient teenager, constantly pushing back his sandy-blonde hair from his face and staring anxiously at whatever device he had to hand. Still, that's why he'd given him the job. Lewis was ambitious and dedicated, with a good nose for the next big trend thundering down the digital pipeline. The flip side of Glyn Lewis, though, he could do without. As it was, talent of Lewis's calibre was in short supply in this neck of the woods, so McLain sucked it up and tried his best to ignore it.

'Another one of your bloody motivational quotes?' McLain said.

'I prefer to call them inspirational,' Lewis said, swiping away the content. 'Didn't mean to offend.'

'What you do on your own time, Glyn, is irrelevant. This kind of work, though, takes a different kind of faith.'

Lewis flipped the cover over the device.

'Not exactly the heaving crowds you promised,' McLain said, gesturing at the thirty or so people milling around the stage.

'Early yet,' Lewis said, looking out. He recognised a few familiar faces from the Council meetings and a reporter from BBC Cymru. The remainder were curious members of the public and a handful of online followers who had been coerced into attending with a promise of a handshake with Kimble Evans-McLain, tech-entrepreneur turned philanthropist, or as the papers preferred to call him, *The Six Billion Dollar Man.* It was a gross exaggeration of his wealth, but it was the kind of moniker that sold papers and made him easy pickings for the headlines.

'Needs more colour,' Lewis observed, gesturing to the black and white banner draped across the stage. 'Warmer, cleaner font.'

'You still think the message is on point? *Connecting the Past and The Future?* Always struck me as a bit vague.'

'More latitude to change course if you need to.'

'You're the communications expert,' McLain said, zipping up his Burberry overcoat and stepping out into the dry morning.

The location for the unveiling had been carefully chosen; two acres on the Caernarvon side of the Menai Strait. The stage was positioned in the shadow of the Snowdonia mountains, ensuring any coverage would feature the snow tipped peaks in the background. To the left of the stage, Lewis's inspiration of the day growled menacingly in place: a gleaming, yellow JCB digger.

The crowd turned as McLain approached, Lewis at his side. A blustery man wearing a bright red anorak and a sloppily knotted tie adorned with miniature Welsh dragons bounded over with the enthusiasm of a puppy and extended his hand.

'Bit underplayed for you isn't it, McLain? Expected you to parachute in from that bloody helicopter of yours.'

'The Honourable Harden Jones. Never one to miss a party.'

'Aye. Well, I hope it's not another one of your long speeches, too bloody chilly for all that.'

'Cold feet? I thought you were made of sturdier stuff.'

'I'm well insulated, apparently, so the missus keeps telling me,' the councillor said, patting the round pack of his belly.

McLain gripped Harden's hand. 'I'm indebted to you and the committee for your support, I couldn't have got this far without you.'

'Aye, well it's all about the island doing what's right.'

'We should probably go,' Lewis said, ushering McLain backstage and into the hands of the young make-up girl.

'Really?' McLain said, as the girl fussed around him, padding his face with a matte brush.

'You get shiny on camera, we've talked about this, your pores sweat.' Lewis handed his boss a warm lemon tea infused with honey.

McLain took a tentative sip. 'Not exactly a full press core.'

'Mr McLain is done,' Lewis said, dismissing the girl who scuttled off with a shrug of her shoulders. He looked over at the crowd. 'It's not right, there must be something big happening.'

'Bigger than this?'

'Remember, Kimble, we are the story,' Lewis said. 'There's a well-briefed photographer in the crowd, he'll make it look like you're addressing the front rows of a Beyoncé concert. Directly after your speech we'll post it all over social media and your loyal followers will do the rest. We'll be online news before these hacks get back to the office and think up another lame headline.'

'Stage managed?'

Lewis flicked a length of lint off McLain's shoulder. 'Just smart groundwork. I lay the foundations; you preach the gospel.'

'It's not a fucking come to Jesus Kumbaya, Glyn.'

Lewis blushed. 'Sorry, just remember you're the story.'

McLain took a deep breath. 'I'll be ready in five.'

Lewis took the hint and headed to the rear of the crowd as McLain took the stage to a warm, if short, round of applause.

'Harden Jones told me to keep my speech brief, he's a little chilled apparently,' McClain said. 'Bring a hip flask next time, councillor, one big enough to hold a couple of pints maybe?'

McLain paced the stage. 'It's been said that to build anything of lasting value takes tenacity and patience, virtues that are close to my own heart, just like that beautiful island over there. I was seven years old when they added the second tier to the Britannia Bridge. My parents took me there on opening day, and it was the only time they allowed the public to walk across the span. That was over thirty years ago. Today, we have the opportunity to build again, to create something we can be proud of generations from now.'

McLain walked left of the stage and tugged on a length of cord attached to a dark drape. The crowd muttered their appreciation as the picture was revealed: a hyper-realistic rendering of the Menai Strait with two entrances on each side that looked like white, scalloped swan wings perfectly integrated into the landscape.

'The Menai Express Tunnel.'

Another ripple of applause.

'Constructed from state-of-the-art material, the Menai Express Tunnel will be the third connective tissue that unites Anglesey to the mainland. Imagine; easier commutes for workers, faster access to the natural beauty of Snowdonia National Park and, of course, easing of congestion in peak summer time. But those, they're just facts, by-products of the true meaning and impact of this project.'

Lewis beamed. He recognised the confident gait of a man who had all the money he could ever want, but still felt driven for more. Not for material wealth, but to leave his mark on the world – leave it a better place. This is why he wanted to work with Kimble McLain: men like him were in short supply, he was a visionary, a leader he could throw the full weight of his devotion behind.

'This tunnel is an opportunity to build a world-class engineering marvel here in our backyard,' McLain continued. 'What Thomas Telford did for Anglesey over two hundred years ago we can do again, today. We have the country's smartest architectural and civil engineering talent ready to put their collective genius to work. This will be a testament to what we can build today, limited only by our imagination.'

'And our bloody budgets!'

Perfect, Lewis thought, Harden was throwing out the bait, just like he'd been instructed.

'I'm glad you brought that up,' McLain said. 'This project will be entirely privately funded. All we ask of our leaders is that they share our vision and help us shred the red tape that can often stall ambitious projects like this.'

There was a communal nodding of heads. 'Today, I'm proud to announce that the Menai Express Tunnel has secured preliminary approval from Anglesey County Council and we've appointed an exploratory committee. We still have a long journey ahead of us, but today we can say we're witnessing history in the making.' McLain gestured to his left. 'Rory, start her up.'

The JCB growled, its teeth carving a shallow trench in the earth. Lewis watched and smiled. He'd created this: him and McLain. He watched his boss jump from the stage and work his way through the crowd. If he had ever doubted he was working in the shadow of greatness, today was the day to cast out all doubts.

As he watched McLain greet the BBC Cymru reporter, Lewis's mobile rang. He answered and listened, allowing the facts to slowly sink in before responding.

McLain glanced over towards Lewis, his palm placed firmly over the reporter's microphone. He might have mouthed *'What the fuck?'* but Lewis was too preoccupied to pay close attention.

The JCB growled and dug another trench. Lewis felt the earth shift beneath his feet as the shovel burrowed. He suddenly realised why McLain looked worried. The reporter knew, maybe he'd known all along. Maybe that's why he was here, this was where the real story was, after all.

God provide him strength, he muttered to himself. This was going to take some creative stage management. What had McLain said earlier? Something about an Immelmann turn? Blindsiding your opponent before they realise you're even on the offensive? He hung up, and made the call.

Chapter 15

The paperwork arrived on Manx's desk with a heavy thud. 'Easy on the noise, Mal,' he said, passing his fingers over the swelling that had sprouted like an angry, red bullseye.

'You should get that seen to,' Nader said, 'or you'll look like one of those Dalek things, big ugly lump on your forehead.'

Manx concentrated on the front page of the report. The type fell in and out of focus as he read. 'Highlights?' he said, sitting back and feeling the opening pinch of what he feared would be a long and excruciating headache.

Nader cleared his throat. 'Long list of complaints against the husband, and get this, our victim filed for divorce just last week.'

'Could have tipped him over the edge.'

'Forensics also found three hunting knives, big ones.'

'She was scared,' Manx said. 'A volatile husband with separation issues.'

'Or else he's just a bloody psycho, like Balham said.'

'Putting your friend's psychological analysis aside…'

'He's not really my—'

'It's safe to say he wasn't on board with the divorce,' Manx interrupted.

Nader thought for a moment. 'Wives are more likely to file for a divorce, but usually pull out before signing the papers, it's like they're testing the waters, or something.'

'Read that on the Internet, Nader?'

Nader looked blankly towards the far corner of the incident room. Manx noticed his eyes were like empty swimming pools, desolate and melancholy, but quickly filled back to life as Manx talked.

'Doesn't add up though, does it?' Manx said, stamping the heels of his boots on the desk. 'Fowler's running on a short fuse, if he's our killer I'd expect a messier outcome, an attempt to hide the body.'

The incident room door creaked open. 'Solicitor's arrived, sir, interview room two,' Morris said.

'About time,' Manx said, stretching out his full six-foot-three frame. 'Prints?'

'On reception, manila envelope. Digital forensics came back with the victim's phone records, too,' Morris said, 'her last outbound call was made at ten past nine last night.'

'Who to?'

Morris hesitated. 'Erm. Kimble McLain.'

Manx sat up. '*The* Kimble McLain?'

'The Six Billion Dollar Man?' Nader said. 'Wouldn't mind a bit of his dosh. They reckon he's got a bloody big helicopter in the back garden and he married some famous Japanese ballerina or something. Not that I've seen her around the island mind you.'

'Yeah, well Japanese ballerinas probably don't shop at Lidl's, Sarge,' Morris said. 'Anyway, I think she's Korean or Chinese.'

'Japanese, Chinese, Cheddar Cheese? Who the hell cares? She's a bit of all right, saw her photo in the Mail on Sunday last week.'

Manx pushed back his chair. 'Anything else, Morris?' he asked, noticing the young PC was still lingering in doorway.

'Can I observe the interview, for my training, like?'

'Transcribe the whole thing,' Manx said, 'but I want your report on the door-to-doors filed before you clock-off tonight. And, any progress from the geeks in the lab on that Skype call? We need to track her down, pronto.'

'On it, sir.'

'Okay, Nader, let's see how short Fowler's fuse really is.'

'Need a bodyguard do you, boss?' Nader said, following his DI and throwing a cocky smile at Morris as he passed.

Manx ignored the comment. He was becoming good at that these days where DS Nader was concerned.

* * *

Manx placed the photographs face down and slid them across the table. Liam Fowler stiffened and bunched his hands into fists until his knuckles turned white.

'This is not standard procedure,' Manx said, revealing the first photograph, 'but considering the severity of the crime.'

Fowler folded his arms and glared at his solicitor, a serious young woman with blonde, highlighted hair. She shuffled uncomfortably as Fowler pinned her with his narrow eyes. Manx flipped over the remaining photographs as if he were showing a winning hand of poker. 'Proud of your handy work, are you, Liam?'

'You got the wrong bloke, mate,' Fowler said, his gaze still fixed solidly on his solicitor as she smoothed down the front of her skirt.

'Just look at the bloody photos, man,' Nader said.

Fowler smiled. 'Don't think so.'

His cheekbones pulsed as if he were grinding his teeth down to the nerves. He reminded Manx of a track dog; the hollow features of a greyhound coiled with energy and set to bolt the starting gate.

'We can't force you, but we can arrest you.'

'My client insists he's innocent.'

'Oh aye? You've got GBH on a police officer for starters,' Nader said. 'And then there's you murdering your wife. You won't be attacking any women where you're going, they fight back there, nasty big bastards with tattoos.'

Fowler shrugged and glanced down at the photographs. His reaction was as immediate as it was unexpected. He jumped to his feet as if he'd been startled by a starting pistol. 'Jesus Christ!' he said, averting his gaze from the images.

'Is this really necessary, inspector? My client is already distraught by the death of his wife,' the solicitor countered.

'Brings it home doesn't it, Fowler?' Nader pressed.

Fowler flipped over the photos. 'I did nothing.'

'Doesn't make it go away,' Manx said, flipping them back. 'You've got a volatile temper. All those calls Sian made to the station. Finally got to you, did it? You killed her and then tried to make it look like something more complicated to throw us off the scent?'

'Un-fucking believable,' Fowler said, kicking the table.

'Restraining orders, calls to the station at all hours. She was sacred of you, Liam, scared of what you'd do to her.'

Fowler gritted his teeth. 'She wasn't scared of me, she loved me.'

'Sian kept three, very sharp hunting knives because she was terrified of what you might do. What kind of love is that, Liam?'

Fowler looked Manx in the eyes. 'I didn't fucking do it.'

'Help us out then, where were you between midnight and 9am?'

'Working.'

'Doing what?'

'My job.'

'Which is?'

Fowler's temper eased a percentage point or two. 'Bangor University, IT department. Systems Administrator.'

'Why were you there at midnight? Some pissed student forget the password to his porn collection?' Nader said.

'We're migrating the database to a virtual network. First migration took five hours, I was back home at six, went straight to bed.'

'Anyone who can confirm that?' Manx asked.

'I work alone.'

'Unfortunate, that,' Nader said.

'I've got to be honest, Liam, it's not looking good for you,' Manx said, stacking the photographs. 'Dead wife in the bathroom, no way to prove where you were when she was murdered and a history of violent behaviour. It's what we like to call an open and shut case.'

'Then you'll have to press charges,' the solicitor said, sharply. 'There's no evidence my client was anywhere near the victim when she died.'

'Murdered,' Manx corrected her.

The solicitor began gathering her papers. 'Are we done? My client is too distraught to answer any more questions.'

'Humour me,' Manx said, 'if you didn't kill Sian, who did?'

Fowler lent in over the desk. 'Weren't me.'

'Bob Balham, maybe? You found out he was sleeping with her, you lost your temper, killed Sian then beat the crap out of him?'

'You don't have to answer...' the solicitor began, but Fowler was already too wound up to pull back.

'She's got better taste. That creep's been sniffin' around her for months. Sian didn't want to know, so he killed her. Easy as.'

'Okay. When we speak to your boss over at the university, he'll confirm your alibi?'

Fowler offered Manx an arrogant smirk. 'I am the boss.'

'You don't report to anyone?'

'If no one hacks their research papers or fucks with their test results, they leave me alone.'

'Yeah, I'm a bit of a luddite myself,' Manx said. 'But, you have data logs, right? Digital records of when you logged in and out of the network, that kind of thing?'

Fowler shuffled uncomfortably. 'Yeah, maybe.'

'Unless you deleted them,' Manx said.

'Why would I do that?' Fowler said, sneering.

'I think we're done,' the solicitor said, buttoning her jacket.

Manx leant forward. 'One last question, Liam, why were you at Sian's this morning? You haven't been within thirty-meters of her for months. Why today, on the day she was murdered?'

Fowler shrugged. 'Coincidence.'

Manx smiled. 'We'll put it down to that for now, shall we? You can always change your statement when we formally charge you.'

Chapter 16

'Discretion is the order of the day, Manx,' Detective Chief Inspector Ellis Canton said, staring intently at Manx's forehead. 'Nasty bump, you should get that seen to.'

'So I've been told.' Manx ran his finger gingerly across the swelling. 'Competing with Kew Gardens, Chief?' he said, gesturing at several freshly potted Bonsai trees Canton was fussing around.

'Marjorie won't let them in the house, says they attract too many flies, so I tend to them in here.' He sprayed the trees with a puff of water from a miniature mister. 'You should take up a hobby, Manx, might give you some perspective on life.'

'Always felt hobbies were just for filling time in between meals, Ellis,' Manx said. 'Present company excepted, of course.'

Canton groaned and rested his considerable weight into his chair. 'The orders came in from St Asaph, they urge caution and a light touch.'

'We could just have one of his drivers bring him down to the station, save us all that faffing around,' Manx offered.

'See, Manx,' Canton said, shaking his large, solid head. 'That's why you're you and I'm me.'

'Sorry, you lost me there.'

Canton pressed his hands together and cleared his throat. 'Kimble McLain's office called DCS Troup the instant they found out about the murder. Vera then called me and I, subsequently, summoned you.'

'Nice to have friends in high places,' Manx said.

Canton huffed. 'Be that as it may, she insists we personally visit McLain. Avoid any fuss.'

'Fuss?'

'Cause undue suspicion on an influential member of the community and a generous donor to the North Wales Constabulary Widows and Orphans Fund.'

'Not sure I can spare anyone right now, Ellis.'

'You won't need to,' Canton said, rubbing his hands together. 'Vera requested that you personally make the call. She was very insistent.'

Manx nodded. 'I don't suppose…'

'Not a chance,' Canton said. 'Best be on your way, time waits for no man, not even you. In fact, especially you,' he added, tapping his wristwatch.

Chapter 17

He was a young boy then, no more than eight or nine. The night was humid and the leather from the car seat stuck to his thighs as he rested his head on his mother's lap.

The evacuation had been swift. His father, bristling with sweat, had dragged him out of bed, instructing him to pack his clothes and his Bible. *'Don't ask questions, boy, or we'll all be in for it, understand?'*

He didn't, of course, understand. How could he? The implications wouldn't be felt until decades later, like slow moving ripples cascading through time and space.

His mother was crying. He covered his ears to muffle her sobs and watched the grim figure of his father wiping furiously at his brow, glancing anxiously in the mirror for the convoy of headlights.

The radio was tuned to the only station they were permitted to listen to: The Seventh Day Adventist Devotional, a local AM station broadcasting from Lambert Beach Church. He would go there at harvest time to sing hymns and perform recitations with children from the parish.

At the port, a warm salt-wind caressed his face as his mother rushed him over the gang plank. Inside the ship's vast hold the three of them scuttled to a dark corner. Around them, other families began to settle, dragging large suitcases and bags of precious belongings behind them. Unlike his own, the other families were in a celebratory mood. A handful of the women danced to an old transistor radio playing what he'd come to understand as calypso music. When the ship finally cast off he could almost see burden slough from his mother's shoulders, as if she'd been underwater for hours and holding her breath until it was safe to resurface.

'Everything will be all right,' his mother soothed, stroking his hair. 'God has provided for us. The Lord never abandons his sheep, isn't that right, Jacob?' she said, directing her gaze to his father.

'God has provided passage, boy. Be grateful and pray for his mercy.'

He nodded, trying once again to make his father happy. A thankless task, but one that needed performing nonetheless.

'No,' his father growled. 'Now. Pray now that your sins are forgiven and salvation granted. Kneel, boy, like I taught you.'

He glanced anxiously at the other families, who were now curious about the odd, white family with too few belongings to be making the same three-week crossing. They looked even more suspiciously at the pale, blonde-haired boy. He was too sallow to be a one of them, but that kind of prejudice didn't hurt him any more; he was used to being called a *non-belonger,'* and the stigma that accompanied it. What did hurt him were the strong, thick fingers gripping the back of his neck and pushing down. He felt his father's warm, sour breath on his ear as he spoke through gritted teeth.

'God help you, boy. Pray.' He felt the vice tighten, urging him to his knees. 'Or I will bend your bones myself. Understand?'

This he did understand.

He shuffled forward, his knees scraping on the wooden floor, the splinters slicing into his skin, and prayed.

Chapter 18

A persistent drizzle lay heavy in the air as Manx drove towards the house, which was obscured from the road by a fortress of mature sessile oaks. At the entry posts, Manx stretched his arm awkwardly through the Jensen's window and announced himself.

He pulled up outside the house; a brutally modern, single-story structure with floor-to-ceiling windows that were tinted just enough to tease the onlooker as to what lay beyond the tempered glass. At the doorway, a statue of a Buddha sat atop a burbling waterfall, uttering a serene chant as Manx stepped within its purview. *Very bloody Zen*, he thought to himself. He pressed the doorbell and waited, accompanied by a soft cadence of wind chimes.

Inside, the décor was curated to perfection with several minimalist artworks hung along one side of the hall. A row of shelves ran across the opposite wall, filled with what looked to Manx like miniature wooden dolls, finely carved and their joints manipulated into varying positions. Each figure was around twelve inches high with a classically sculptured face; *Greek*, Manx thought, but he was no expert. A wide picture window at the end of the hall afforded a breath-taking view over the nature reserve at Cemlyn Bay and towards the restless roll of ocean. *Maybe the press did have him pegged*, Manx thought – this was the kind of house where you'd expect someone with the moniker of 'The Six Billion Dollar Man' to reside.

Kimble McLain emerged moments later wearing sweatpants and a loose fitting white shirt. He looked younger than his forty-eight years. A thin scar, like an unhealed animal scratch, ran along his right temple; the only flaw in an otherwise unremarkable face. There was a leanness about McLain — like his house — no detail seemed wasted. The acute jut of his nose, the narrow cut of his eyes, the urgent thrust of his chin, all gave the impression of a man who was constantly prodding at the world to see how much it could be provoked.

As Manx stepped forward to greet him, Kimble raised his palm in a 'Stop in the Name of Love' fashion. 'My apologies, we're a boots-off home. My wife's singular obsession; she's a strict student of feng shui. Shoes carry the world and all its negativity on their soles, apparently.'

'I should introduce her to my chief,' Manx said, leaning on the wall to take off his boots.

McLain winced as Manx's palm fell heavily on the glossy white paintwork.

'He's into all this Zen stuff, got an office full of bonsai trees he can't keep his hands off.'

'We can talk in the main office, it's less... restrictive.'

'Lead the way,' Manx said, rubbing his hands together and following McLain down the hall, he passed a smaller collection of the figurines. 'Not toys I'm guessing? What are they made of, wood?'

'Dark ivory,' McLain said, picking one up. 'Roman Articulated Dolls. This one was found in the sarcophagus of a seven-year old child. The grain resembles wood, but much finer and smoother. They're quite the collectors' items these days.'

'Bet the kids don't get near them,' Manx said.

McLain carefully placed the figure back on the shelf. 'Not our path in this life, I'm afraid,' he said.

Manx detected a pang of wistfulness in his voice and immediately regretted jumping to conclusions.

Turning down a narrow corridor, Manx caught wind of the familiar funk of his own feet; if he'd known this was going to be a boots-off investigation he'd have pulled on a fresh pair of socks this morning. *Best not mention that to the wife,* Manx thought as

McLain led him into a small office which overlooked a rosewood balcony and out to the Irish Sea.

The office was sparsely decorated with a spotless, white desk raised high enough to stand next to and positioned so it looked out over the ocean. On the desk was a single, silver MacBook Pro.

'No chairs?' Manx asked.

'Far better for the posture,' McLain said.

'Is that right?' Manx said. 'Who knew?'

On the opposite wall several amateur bird sketches had been framed and signed with the initials KM. *Crows*, Manx thought – the hoodlums of the bird world. He wondered if they cackled with a Cockney accent.

He directed his attention to an oil-painting of a man in a long white wig sitting in an armchair and looking out to the onlooker as if he were privy to some secret they'd never know. It was out of place with the strict Asian regiment of the house; the words *sore* and *thumb* came immediately to Manx's mind.

'One of Anglesey's forgotten geniuses,' McLain said, noticing Manx's interest. 'William Jones. Math prodigy from an early age, born near Benllech in the late seventeen-hundreds.'

'Never heard of him,' Manx admitted.

'Not surprising,' McLain said. 'In his Synopsis Palmariorum Matheseos he was the first person to express the beauty of the ideal that can only be approached but never reached.'

Manx shook his head and shrugged – he was never much good at maths; too abstract for his practical way of thinking.

'Pi,' McLain said. 'He recognised only a platonic symbol could express the inexpressible. A complex calculation beautifully condensed into three simple lines.'

'Oh, right. Three-point-one-four recurring, or something like that?' Manx said, dredging up the little maths trivia he knew.

McLain's lips flinched as if they'd just been brushed with something unsavoury. 'Somewhat close,' he said.

'Your business,' Manx said, 'navigational software?'

'In a nutshell. Our algorithms analyse data to aid international shipping routes. Weather patterns, ocean currents, tidal predictions. We collate that information, compare it to historical data so oil tankers, luxury cruise liners and the like reach port faster with less fuel. Eco-friendly and more profitable for all concerned.'

'And you sold the company for a small fortune?'

'The papers like to simplify or exaggerate; it's binary for them. The McLain Foundation spreads itself more liberally these days. Big data analytics to help feed the hungry, alleviate poverty, find water for drought-ridden areas. Data's a complex business, we like to help demystify it, make it pedestrian and accessible to anyone who needs it.'

'And was Sian part of that business?'

McLain looked down to the balcony below. 'They got on well,' he said, gesturing towards the thin Asian woman in brightly coloured workout clothes stretching across the length of a yoga mat. Her body flowed effortlessly through the air as she twisted herself into contortions that would have sent Manx directly to Accident and Emergency if he'd attempted the poses.

'Miiko, my wife, doesn't connect with many people, but her and Sian found a synergy. The news shook her equilibrium, hence the realignment practice.'

'How long have you known Sian?'

'She's worked here for five years, performing administrative tasks, scheduling my appointments, other critical functions.'

'So, she was your assistant?'

'Assigning labels to people tends to limit their potential. Sian did whatever was necessary to further the Foundation and she was integral to our Menai Express project. It'll be a struggle to replace her.'

'Did she have an office, somewhere she worked from?'

McLain pointed towards the computer on the desk.

'That's it?'

'Uncluttered spaces make for uncluttered minds.'

'I'll need to take it back to the station.'

'Of course. I've already removed the password protection, should save your IT team some time.'

Manx wondered how much else McLain might have removed. 'What was Sian's state of mind recently? Happy, worried, anxious?'

'Sian was the calmest person I've ever known. Nothing phased her, she just rolled up her sleeves and got on with it.'

'And her husband?'

McLain laughed. 'Liam Fowler? A C-grade coder with anger issues.'

'You knew him?'

'I contracted him a couple of years ago as a favour for Sian. What do they say about good deeds? Let's just say it didn't work out.'

Manx nodded. 'Last night – can you let me know where you were between the hours of midnight and 9am?'

McLain considered his response. 'I attended a function at the University of Bangor until around one in the morning.'

'Late night,' Manx said.

'Charitable commitments. Not one of those things you can duck out of, people notice.'

'And after that?'

'I came home, answered some emails, then went to bed.'

Manx flipped the cover on his notebook. 'Anything else you know about Sian that might help us?'

McLain thought for a moment as he watched his wife settling into a graceful tree pose. 'You meet people in your life, Inspector, people that you imagine will be with you for a lifetime, that you'll share the success and failures together. That was Sian. When that's taken away from you it leaves a vacuum. Myself and Miiko will miss her, so will the Foundation.' McLain handed Manx the laptop. 'I hope you'll find whoever did this.'

'No immediate travel plans?' Manx asked.

'Nothing that can't be re-scheduled.'

'Keep it that way,' Manx said. 'Murder investigations tend to throw up a lot of questions.'

'Naturally,' McLain said, smiling.

'One last thing,' Manx said. 'Sian called you last night, at around ten past nine. Any idea why she was calling?'

'Could be any number of things, like I said, she was very dedicated to the Foundation.'

'So, you didn't speak to her?'

'She didn't leave a message so I thought it wasn't important and she'd speak to me about it in the morning.'

'Good enough,' Manx said. 'I'm sure we'll speak again.'

Manx noticed a slight twitch of McLain's left eye as he shook his hand. It was probably nothing, just his instincts running on overdrive.

* * *

As Manx saw himself out, McLain watched his wife unfold herself from her savasana pose and roll up her yoga mat. She clipped her hair into a tight ponytail and glanced quickly upwards, clearly sensing someone was watching. Kimble managed a weak, resigned wave. Miiko ignored him and stepped from his view and into the sauna room below. He dug his perfectly manicured nails into his palms. It was going to be a long few weeks, he could sense it in his bones.

Chapter 19

Manx traversed the gravel slope that led to the front door, his body bent low against the wind. Above him, the swarm of grey clouds shifted quickly over the roof in a scurry of time-lapse, east toward the coast.

His sister, Sara, had requested his presence in her usual cryptic manner. *'I need a favour, Tudor, you're my last resort.'*

Sara opened the door and gestured with a lazy nod of her head that he could enter. 'Here for your monthly, then' she said, turning her back on him.

'Nice to see you, too,' Manx muttered.

He lingered for a moment in the hall, taking in the familiar smells and sights of the house he'd lived in for the first seventeen years of his life. It had remained as grey and oppressive as the heavy rain clouds now scuttling over its roof. The name, Cwm Talw — 'Peaceful Valley' — was misleading. Its posture was set on northerly slope of a hill, making it vulnerable to the elements which would pummel against its walls until it felt as if the house might be ripped from the hillside. Cwm Talw, of course, would never be shorn from its foundations. The house would stand the test of time, unlike its current inhabitants, whom Manx feared were damaged beyond repair, especially his mother, Alice, whom he now peered at through the gap in the kitchen door.

She was smiling at someone from across the table, just out of Manx's view. The action took him by surprise; he couldn't recall the last time he saw his mother express any feelings of joy, except maybe at the misfortune of others. He edged closer.

'She'll clam up if she knows you're listening,' Sara said, spotting Manx lurking outside the kitchen.

'Who…?' he began.

'Meals on Wheels, comes by three times a week. I think she's taken a shine to him. God knows what they talk about, but keeps her happy I suppose.'

'Meals on Wheels—' Manx had barely got his words out before Sara interrupted.

'Don't bloody judge me, Tudor,' she said. 'It's hard enough being a single mother without an eighty-year-old alcoholic to take care of.'

Manx took a deep breath. 'I was about to say, I'd thought they'd eliminated it, what with the council cuts.'

'They did. At least they did for someone with Mam's savings. Someone at work told me about it. Food's not bad, you just heat it up. Not cheap mind you, but she's got the money, can't take it with her, so I'm helping her spend it.'

'So,' Manx said. 'This favour I'm the last resort for?'

Sara folded her arms across her chest. 'Got this work thing at a hotel in Colwyn Bay next weekend, all right if Dewi spends the day with you on Saturday?'

'Don't … you … have?' Manx stuttered, having spent no more than five minutes with his nephew, and surmising correctly he'd be out of his depth within minutes.

'Everyone's busy and I can't leave him with Mam. It's one day, Tudor, or do you have plans?' Sara laced the word 'plans' with the requisite layer of contempt she felt it deserved.

'What would I do with him? Can't take him down the pub.'

'Jesus, it's not that hard, it's a weekend. Take him to one of those adventure parks for a few hours, he'll be happy enough,' Sara said, tapping a cigarette from a box.

'Birds of a feather,' Manx said, glancing towards his mother, who had long since given up on the concept of abstinence where Marlboro Lights were concerned.

'Forget it,' Sara snapped, throwing the cigarette packet across the hallway table. 'I'll ask someone who gives a shit.'

Manx relented. 'All right. Saturday, fine.'

'Very bloody generous,' Sara said.

'I said I'd do it,' Manx said.

'Right, so you did,' Sara said. 'I've got washing to do. Don't get her too excited with you know what. Took me hours to calm her down last time,' she added, brushing past him.

Manx loitered at the doorway for a moment, looking at his mother. She looked girlish, Manx thought, as Alice Manx-Williams patted her long, grey hair and twirled the ends in between her fingers.

'Tudor, come in,' she called.

Manx stepped through into the kitchen.

'See, I do have a son after all,' Alice said, gesturing at Manx. 'Come and meet Denny. He likes to talk to me and unlike most of my children, he also listens.'

'Oh, I expect he's very busy, Alice' the man said. He was wearing a Sospan Fawr T-shirt which was too tight for him and rode up the folds of his belly as he rose to greet Manx. He looked shifty, Manx thought. He was always wary when it came to people trying to befriend his mother. Alice was the only child from a wealthy family and, in her father's opinion, stepped several rungs below her social standing when she married Thomas 'Tommy Williams' the son of a local caravan-site owner. It would take Alice twenty-five years of marriage to reach the same conclusion; an atonement that ensured her a generous share in her father's will when he died.

Sara had given Manx the full download a few weeks ago when they had the 'big discussion' on Alice's future and what their options were when Alice needed full-time, professional care. Good Samaritans, church ministers, private detectives, even spiritual mediums had weaselled their way into Alice's affections and ultimately, her check book. Sara had calculated over tens of thousands of pounds over the years. Manx's guard was up as the man extended his hand.

'You must be Alice's son, Tudor.'

'Manx. Just Manx is fine,' he said, looking over the man for any clues as to his intentions. Other than a half-hearted handshake and face that seemed eager to please, there was scant evidence to draw any concrete conclusions.

'He's a good listener,' Alice said, patting Denny's hand. 'We talk about everything, you know, Tudor.'

'Is that right?'

'Your mother, she suffered a great loss. She's healing now, we can feel it, can't we, Alice? Sense it in your spirit?'

Manx felt a heaviness bear down on him. This was the evidence he was waiting for. He was wary of anyone playing the good samaritan role; the genuine, selfless souls of the world were thin on the ground and this one, a man with an awkward way about him and a way of looking at Alice as if she were prey, didn't strike him as the genuine type. Maybe he needed a gentle reminder that Manx was a copper to deter him from any temptation.

As he contemplated the best approach, the opening chords of Ryan Adam's 'New York' echoed through the kitchen in a bright strum of guitar chords. He should really think about changing it – the ringtone was far too optimistic for the kind of calls he received these days.

He stepped into the hallway. It was Morris. Hardacre had been calling and insisting Manx drive to the mortuary in Caernarvon, pronto. Manx hung up and was about say his goodbyes when he heard a ripple of soft laughter and caught the tail-end of a clichéd platitude or some cheesy, fortune cookie proverb. He turned away, sensing his company was no longer needed in the kitchen, at least not today.

* * *

Outside, he unwrapped a King Edward cigar and watched as the band of smoke swirled around him. He walked past the food delivery van with the cartoon of a yellow saucepan on its side; it had come to this now with his mother. She couldn't even cook for herself any more and she'd been opening up old wounds that were best left alone. It was to be expected, she was getting on, and Sara was stressed, he could see it etched in the lines on her face.

Sara didn't need the added pressure of dealing with another opportunist looking to make money off Alice. He'd sort it out. It was the least he could do.

He entered one of the outbuildings – the smell of wet dog and stale dog urine still clung to the stonework. In the far corner, Manx noticed the wheel of a bike sticking out from under a damp blanket. It was Miriam's red Raleigh, the one she'd been so proud to ride that summer she'd disappeared. Was the bike with her that day? It was one of those forgotten details, like so many others from that afternoon. It was over thirty years ago and not a day had gone by when he didn't think of his younger sister or try and recall some forgotten detail that might be the key to unlocking his past. But, the further away he was from that day, the fainter the memories had become, fading like a cloud of cigar smoke in the wind.

Chapter 20

Hardacre lined up two gurneys at the far end of the mortuary and checked the toe tags.

'Afraid you'll lose one?' Manx asked, stepping into the chilled, clinical air that never failed to send a shiver through his bones.

'Not on my watch,' Hardacre said handing Manx a pair of sanitary gloves. 'Thirty-six years. Not a body, limb, organ, or a ham sandwich leaves here without me knowing about it.'

'Impressive. They should give you a plaque or something.'

'I'd be happy with a retirement spent in abject peace and end my days like Michael Corleone in the grounds of my Italian villa.'

'Didn't he die alone?'

'We all do, after a fashion,' Hardacre said, 'I just like to have an action plan for the inevitable.'

Manx smiled. 'I never took you for the ambitious type.'

'Ah, another one of your sardonic quips, Manx. I've quite missed them. By the way, how's the injury? I've got some nuclear option grade pain killers somewhere, perks of the job.'

'I'll pass,' Manx said, rubbing his finger over his bruise.

Hardacre wheeled one of the gurneys in Manx's direction. He pulled back the sheet to reveal Sian Conway's body. 'As I expected, the victim was killed with a sharp instrument to the throat, severing the carotid artery. Mercifully, she would have bled out in minutes saving her the pain of what the killer did next.'

Hardacre passed his hand over her hairline. 'By the evidence of hair loss around the crown she was dragged by the hair into the bathroom where he bound her feet and wrists, then got to work extracting her liver and stabbing her repeatedly on the thighs and pelvic region.'

'Significance?' Manx asked.

'I wasn't sure, but then I remembered reading something similar in a medical journal pertaining to categories of serial killers—'

'Hang on,' Manx interrupted. 'One body does not a serial killer make, Hardy.'

'One body that you've found, Manx,' Hardacre insisted. 'But, point being, our killer is displaying the classic symptoms of Picquerism. Leave it to our friends across the Channel to give it a name that sounds like a romantic malady. By the way, were you aware that the first recorded serial killer was in fact French? Baron Gilles de Rais. Dabbled in the occult and rumoured to have gorged himself on the local peasant children, a real piece of *merde*, so to speak.'

'You keep saying "serial killer", Hardy, like it's a fact. We have one body, and one man who's already in custody. That's it.'

'As you wish, Manx. But this is classic Picquerism. The killer stabs the victim multiple times. He's too inhibited or too scared to rape, or he's impotent, so he stabs repeatedly until he climaxes or he's interrupted.'

'Jesus,' Manx said. 'And the liver?'

'The extraction is rudimentary. Probably isn't many 'how to' videos on the precise mechanics of the task.'

'Why remove the liver? A souvenir?'

'Mine is not to theorise, but to present evidence,' Hardacre said. 'And, to that end, take a look at this.'

He reached for a tray from the counter.

'Always a big fan of your magic shows,' Manx said as the professor tugged at a white cloth covering a dissected human liver.

'One of my techs, bright girl, wears a little too much make up for my liking, but they all seem to these days, don't they? She was practising her dissection techniques on Sian Conway's liver before we sent it to Satan's Aga.'

Manx looked quizzically at Hardacre.

'Sorry. The incinerator, in the basement. Mortuary humour. Anyway, Alison's slicing and dicing and the scalpel hits what feels like glass, inside the liver.'

Hardacre placed a small phial in his hand and pulled out a tightly rolled piece of paper. 'Here, read it.'

Manx took it between his forefinger and thumb. It was about four inches long, with clear, precise handwriting. He held it under the light and read it aloud.

'But put ye on the Lord Jesus Christ and make no provision for the flesh in all its concupiscences.'

'Biblical, of course,' Hardacre offered, 'but even a Welsh heathen like yourself would have worked that out, eventually.'

'This word, concupiscence, any thoughts?' Manx said.

'Unbridled lust or evil desire. Late Latin, if I remember correctly. Literally, the quote compels you to place your duty to the Lord above the selfish desires of the flesh. Metaphorically? It's anyone's guess. On a more practical note, I did discover plastic residue under our victim's right fingernails. I sent the sample over to the Forensic Investigators, maybe Bevan's team found something similar.'

Manx took a minute to look over Sian's body. A gradual feeling of dread overtook him as he considered the implications of what Hardacre had just proposed – *serial killer?* He couldn't contemplate that, not with just one body, it made no sense. But the ritualistic positioning, the careful planning, it was too methodical to be a spur of the moment act.

Hardacre noticed the distant look in Manx's eyes. 'You know Manx,' he said. 'People think I've got a difficult job, distasteful even, digging around inside cadavers, but at the end of the day it's relatively cut and dry. I dissect, examine, and present the evidence, you on the other hand deal with the living, infinitely more complicated and unpredictable. And now you'll have to break the news to the father. Messy business all round.'

'Her father? I think he's deceased, Hardy, some years back.'

'No, the baby's father, Manx,' Hardacre said. 'Our victim was eighteen weeks pregnant.'

Chapter 21

Kimble McLain steadied the tripod and attached the binoculars – a pair of Leica Douvoids – the best money could buy. He angled the lens to his eyeline and scouted the spread of the Cemlyn Bay Nature Reserve below.

'Any sightings?' Glyn Lewis asked, joining him on the deck.

'Sylt, in the German Frisian Islands last week and forty miles away on the coast of Pwllheli three days ago.'

'Getting closer,' Lewis said, walking towards the end of the deck to join McLain. 'You could see it yet.'

'More likely to hear it first, Lewis. The black-browed albatross cackles like a fishwife when its territory is threatened. With all the other wildlife down there I'd expect a full throated chorus.'

'Smart,' Lewis said. 'Make enough noise to protect what's yours before another scavenger steals it from you.'

McLain turned. 'So, how bad is it?'

'The online sites are all over the story, no surprises there,' Lewis said, swiping at his iPad. 'The daily rags will follow suit tomorrow, prime front page material. Woman found murdered on the island of Anglesey, police are not releasing any further details at the moment, standard journalistic waffle.'

'And are we privy to a deeper information dive?'

'Nobody's talking, yet.'

'Up the bounty.'

Lewis nodded. 'You know it's only a matter of time before the press connects you and Sian. We should control the narrative, send out a press release. She was a valued employee, she'll be sorely missed, that kind of thing.'

'Not until I know more.' McLain leant on the balcony. 'That inspector who came to see me; tall fellow, smelled of cigar smoke, looked like a funeral director. What was his name?'

'Inspector Manx, I think. At least that's what your connection in St Asaph told me.'

'See what you can dig up on him, just as a precaution, and don't use that,' McLain said, pointing at the iPad. 'Use the Linux in the den, the one with the Tor Browser. Best not set off any alarms.'

'What about Liam Fowler?'

'Let the police deal with him. Anything else?'

Lewis stammered, 'Look, this is awkward, but Thursday night, after the charity event, you didn't come back until late.' He swiped his iPad. 'Three am, according to the log.'

'Business meeting, took forever.'

'Oh, that wasn't on my schedule,' Lewis said, double-checking his online calendar.

'Not everything I do is on your schedule, Lewis,' McLain said, turning his attention back to his binoculars.

Lewis took the hint and walked towards the house.

'A man's life is not his own, for it is not for man to direct his own steps,' Lewis whispered to himself. Jeremiah, chapter ten, verse twenty-three. One of his Old Testament favourites.

Chapter 22

He wrapped his fingers around the man's fleshy ankles and dragged him towards the east of the farm. Beyond that, the fields sloped sharply to form a shallow valley which was home to a drove of Welsh blackface sheep. They'd be resting now, *sleeping the sleep of the innocent,* he thought as he wiped the sweat from his eyes. Just a few more yards, he assured himself, as he hauled the dead weight of flesh and bone towards the plunge dip.

The night was coal-black, punctuated by the infrequent flicker of a cuticle moon. The cold chewed into his bones with the sharpness of puppy teeth, but thank the Lord he had Lucy to keep him warm. What was that phrase? *A thick skin?* Yes, that's what she gave him, a thick skin.

She kept him focused and 'on task.' They always uttered that phrase, *'keep on task',* like some divine management directive. He'd always imagined the voices, when they finally spoke, would be vague declarations, but as it turned out, they were exceptionally clear: a missive from head office, simple, direct, and to be followed to the letter. Pure instruction that kept a disciple on the true path.

The thought comforted him as he prepared the body. He was harder work than the woman; twice as big and tough too, like an old ox, but Lucy provided him the strength to bear the burden. He turned the man on his back and slipped the scissors from his backpack.

It took him no more than a few minutes to shred his clothes. Next, he worked on binding the man's wrists and ankles. Lastly, he performed the incision. He did this swiftly, scoring a precise line from the sternum, to where the tuft of grey pubic hair began.

The removal was easier this time, less amateurish. He located the organ, to the lower-right of the ribs, worked swiftly at the muscle surrounding it and cradled the man's liver in his hand. It was still warm.

He was surely dead now, but the man's eyes seemed to be alive, judging him. He despised it when people looked at him that way, through the corner of their eyes, making assumptions about him that would inevitably be wide-of-the-mark. People had a failure of imagination where he was concerned – they had no idea who or what they were dealing with. He should gouge out the man's eyes, leave them to the birds, but that wasn't his mission, not tonight.

A sense of elation surged through him as he rolled the naked body into the plunge dip. It was empowering, delivering someone to their final salvation; a merciful act, one he felt privileged to perform.

The acrid smell of insecticide and fungicide from the sheep dip filled his sinuses as he positioned the body as directed: knee-bound and facing west, an affirmation of the setting sun for the deliverance of a soul into the arms of the Almighty.

There was one final ritual to perform. He made a shallow incision in the liver, retrieved the small glass phial from his pocket and slotted it into the puncture. He positioned the organ beneath the man's abdomen and poured the holy water over his forehead. It was complete. The man was now prepared and purified for the most glorious reunion any man could hope for. He smiled at the thought. Lucy smiled too, he could sense it. They were as one now, united in movement, thought, and deed.

Chapter 23

Early Saturday morning, Manx called the Major Investigation Team in for a briefing. Canton had secured two extra PCs to swell the ranks; Dick Pritchard and Rhys Williams. They were solid officers, suited to the grunt work of what Manx liked to call 'coppering,' the day-to-day shuffle of paperwork, entering evidence and routine questioning.

As the team settled, Manx directed their attention to the incident board. 'Liam Fowler and Bob Balham are our current front runners as prime suspects. Agreed?'

'Bob Balham's alibi checked out, sir' Morris confirmed. 'Stayed at the Ship until eleven and spent the night at Marty Jones's place, left about eight the following morning.'

'So, Fowler assumes the podium, lucky him. Any updates on the note Hardacre found?'

PC Rhys Williams spoke up. 'It's from Romans thirteen. Book six of the New Testament,' he said, referencing his notes. 'Erm, that's really it.'

'Find more,' Manx said. 'It's important to the killer, so it's important to us. Hardacre also confirmed that Sian Conway was eighteen weeks pregnant. Find the father. Who was Sian seeing? Boyfriends, casual relationships, anyone she was intimate with.'

From the far end of the room, Morris yelled a triumphant 'yes', and punched the air.

'What are you celebrating, Minor?' Nader asked. 'Find someone even shorter than you on Tinder?'

'Yeah, sarge,' Morris said, patting him on the shoulder as he passed. 'And she's bloody gorgeous.'

'I should get my profile up there,' Nader said, running his hands over his shirt like a pregnant woman might stroke her swollen belly. 'Who wouldn't want a share of this prime Welsh beefcake?'

'Yeah, you should,' Morris said. 'Already checked out your wife on there, sarge, good photo too.'

Nader looked at her through the corner of his eye and made a mental note to check out the site later, just in case.

Morris handed Manx a memory stick.

'CCTV?' he asked, slotting in the drive.

'Fowler's been lying to us,' Morris said, scrubbing through the footage. 'That's him arriving in the car park at twenty-two-hundred hours, and his car's still there at 6am.'

'That tallies with what he told us,' Manx said.

'Look at the time stamp at midnight. The timecode looks like it stops then starts again, it's only a few frames but I'm sure it jumps. And his car too, it looks like it shifts.'

'Could be,' Manx said, replaying the footage. 'Theory?'

Morris cleared her throat. 'I reckon Fowler left the uni around midnight, took his car, drove back a few hours later and parked it in exactly the same spot. Then he edits the CCTV footage so it looks like the car never moved.'

Manx nodded. 'He'd probably have access to the footage, whether he's authorised to or not.'

'And he's got the computer skills,' Morris said.

'And a damned good motive,' Manx said. 'Good work. So, if Fowler left the university at around midnight then returned a few hours later. What the hell was he doing for those hours?'

A flash seared through Manx's mind. 'There was a function on that night at the university, can you find it?'

'Probably on the other side of the campus,' Morris said. 'I'll need to swap feeds, that side is covered by our cameras.'

Morris clicked and played the video.

'Stop it there,' Manx said. 'That's Kimble McLain, getting out of his Range Rover at nine. His driver opens the door, then heads off. What was the function, Morris?'

Nader spoke up. 'North Wales Youth Career Opportunity. The missus volunteers there, only time I can go out for a pint without asking her bloody permission. Got them all marked on the calendar.' He tapped his mobile phone to emphasise the fact.

'Full of surprises, aren't you, Nader?' Manx said and gestured towards Morris to fast forward the video.

'There,' Manx said, 'midnight, McLain leaves the campus. Hang on, that's not the same car. Switch to the other feed.'

'Shit!' Manx stabbed the screen. 'That's Fowler's car.'

'They knew each other?' Morris asked.

'Another bloody half-truth,' Manx said. 'So, Fowler manipulates the footage to make it look like he never left, but he had no access, or was unaware, of the cameras on the other side of the campus.'

'Looks like it,' Morris confirmed.

Manx sat down and rubbed at his bruise. 'On the same night Sian Conway is murdered, McLain and Fowler, who both have a close relationship with the victim, leave together in a car then lie to us about it. What the fuck is going on?'

'Good news for us,' Nader said. 'We can keep Fowler locked up until Monday morning.'

'Or we let him go and see where he leads us,' PC Williams offered. 'If he goes straight to McLain, makes our case stronger.'

'Not a bad idea, Williams,' Manx said. 'Our victim called McLain the night she was murdered but he insists he didn't speak to her or leave him a voice mail. As we're not in possession of a warrant to search his phone, and nor are we likely to get one without divine intervention, we take him at his word, for now.'

Manx sat on the edge of the desk. 'We've got another twenty-one hours to hold Fowler. Don't waste a second. Gather the evidence, build the case. Nader, take the digital forensics team to Fowler's house and fine tooth comb the place. Retrieve every hard drive, computer or electronic device you can find. If he's hiding anything, it'll probably be buried deep in some encrypted folder.'

'Aye, boss,' Nader said, grabbing his jacket.

'Morris and Priddle, make sure you get a full account of Sian Conway's movements on Thursday night. Who she saw, who she talked to, and what they talked about.'

'Men, probably,' Nader offered as he walked towards the door. 'Running fucking commentary on our failings and fuck ups.'

'Before you go, Sergeant, you all need to hear this,' Manx said, gesturing for Nader to stop. 'Sian Conway was murdered by a brutal and cruel assailant. I know it's the weekend, but murders don't happen to a schedule. For the next few days we'll be living and breathing this case until we're sick of the sight of each other. All clear?'

'Just another day at the office, then,' Nader said, grabbing his coat and a handful of Ginger Nuts on his way out.

Chapter 24

Fowler stretched out his legs under the interview room table and yawned loudly.

'Keeping you up, are we?' Manx said. 'Because believe me, I've got better things to do than listen to more of your bullshit.'

'Yeah, we knew each other, so what? The bloke gave me some work a few years ago. Basic coding, a kid could have done it, so I quit.'

'McLain's got a different story.'

'Yeah? And because he's some fucking millionaire, you believe his story over mine?'

'Is *this* all a story, Liam? Something you both made up?'

Fowler sighed. 'It was my car, yeah, but you don't know I was driving it, could be anyone,' he said, poking the photograph.

'For the record, you're telling me that you didn't leave your office, didn't take your car from the car park and didn't meet with Kimble McLain?'

'For the record. It's bullshit.'

Manx sat back. 'Okay, so tell me about the baby, Fowler.'

'What baby?'

'You were aware Sian was eighteen weeks pregnant.'

Fowler bit his lower lip and said nothing.

'And, as you've already told us, you hadn't been near her for what, six months? So, it's very unlikely it's yours. When did you find out? Was it the last straw, your wife pregnant by another man?'

Fowler leant over to his solicitor. 'No comment.'

'My client is due to be released tomorrow morning, inspector,' the solicitor argued. 'All I see is photographs of my client's car and his digital records all point to him being at work all night. Unless you have more evidence, you're not going to get the extension you need to hold my client, who is still in a state of shock at the passing of his wife.'

'The murder of his wife,' Manx emphasised. 'I have a highly trained digital forensics team going through your home as we speak, Liam. How does that make you feel?'

Fowler shifted uncomfortably in his seat.

'Worried about what we'll find, Fowler?'

'We're finished here, my client is distressed enough,' the solicitor said, gathering her papers.

'Oh, and by the way,' Manx said, 'You should both know this is now a double murder investigator. Sian Conway and her unborn child.'

Fowler clenched his fists and looked Manx directly in the eyes. 'Well, you'd better find the fucker that did it before I do.'

Chapter 25

It was late Saturday afternoon when Manx walked into the Bull's Head. The pub had recently endured a major brewery makeover without losing an ounce of its world-weary ambience. *Maybe a place could never shake the ghost of its past*, Manx thought. For the coppers stationed at Llangefni, none of that mattered – it was their second home, where after the third pint the corporate beer formula was almost drinkable and the barmaid borderline friendly.

Ashton Bevan was sitting at the bar staring at his phone and rifling through what looked like a stack of envelopes; bills Manx guessed.

'You look like you've just lost ten rounds in a cage fight, Manx,' he said, pointing at Manx's forehead and stuffing the envelopes back into his pocket.

'You should see the other bloke.'

'I heard he's in custody.'

'Of course you did,' Manx said. 'What is it with you and these clandestine meetings, anyway? Can't you just come into the station?'

'Where's the fun in that?' Bevan said, laying his phone on the bar. 'Forensic investigations are not all swabs and samples, Manx, they're about relationships and I like to nurture mine, like children.'

'Bevan,' Manx sighed, heavily. 'I've got a murder suspect I have to release in nineteen hours so unless you've got a stack of evidence that's going to help me charge him you can buy me a half and I'll get back to work.'

'You? Ordering a half?' Bevan laughed. 'That would be worth the price of admission.' He clicked his fingers in the direction of the barmaid. 'Two pints of your best over here, sweetheart.'

The barmaid, a stout woman with badly permed hair that sat on her head like a dry mop, turned around slowly, finding little pleasure in being 'finger-clicked' and being called 'sweetheart.'

'Lager or bitter?' she asked, straddling her fisherwoman hands across the bar as if she were about to vault over and wrap them around Bevan's neck.

'Nerys,' Manx said.

'Oh, just champion, this is.' The barmaid folded her thick arms across her chest. 'No bloody getting away from you lot is there?'

'Always here when you need us, Nerys,' Manx said. 'How's your brother enjoying his detention at her Majesty's pleasure?'

Nerys scowled. 'He's all right. No thanks to you bastards.'

'Send him my regards,' Manx said.

'As fucking if,' Nerys said, wiping her sleeve under her nose and reaching under the bar for two pint glasses.

'Fan of yours?' Bevan asked.

Manx ignored the question. He'd arrested Nerys's brother, Thomas Bowen, after his involvement in the Anglesey Blue case late last year. Thomas Bowen was a petty criminal with ambitions to make it to the big leagues, but lacked the talent and intelligence to back it up. He was now serving a seven-year sentence in HMP Wrexham for his efforts.

'So, what's this about, Bevan?' Manx asked, grabbing his pint. The glass was 'fresh from the dishwasher' warm. He contemplated complaining, but watched Nerys violently fingering a bag of pork scratchings and thought better of it.

Bevan settled himself in his stool and placed a plastic bag on the bar. 'Means of entry confirmed,' he said, shaking the false rock inside the bag.

'He either knew her or he was observing her,' Manx said, taking the bag. 'I don't suppose—'

'Clean as a copper's whistle,' Bevan interrupted.

'Anything else?'

Bevan puffed out his chest like a bear staking its territory. 'We found no traces of blood other than the victim's at the location and no external DNA. The rope used to bind the victim was generic, available just about anywhere. The only other prints were the landlord's, which we expected.'

'All in your initial report.'

'Yes, initial.' Bevan took a tentative sip of his beer. 'But we ran secondary test on deposits found on the computer keyboard. We thought they were skin samples, maybe scraped from the killer, but our analysis concluded otherwise.'

Bevan began peeling the back off a beer mat. 'Skin would have been lighter and fallen less uniformly so I'd expect to see it dispersed over a wider area.' He scattered the cardboard shavings from the beer mat over the bar. 'But this substance fell directly on the keyboard, on the return key if you're interested, which means it was denser.'

Manx pushed at the shreds. 'Nice theatrics, Bevan, have you written the ending yet?'

'Patience, Manx. We determined the residue was a man-made compound, not skin, probably scraped from the killer's hands or wrists.'

'Protective gloves, not too big of a stretch.'

'Doubtful, the compound was too thick. There were no other traces in the house, but when we compared it to the samples Hardacre scraped from under the fingernails, bingo, the same substance. We just need to figure out the compound.'

'Timeline?' Manx asked,

'Couple of days, maybe less.'

'Less would be good,' Manx said, downing the remainder of his pint.

'Before you go,' Bevan said, leaning a hand on his sleeve.

Manx felt a familiar drip of anxiety. Bevan's post-briefing chats were a negotiation to be navigated with care and precision.

'My good friends over at the Met, they owe me a favour or two.' Bevan continued. 'Operation Ferryman? Wasn't that the case, Manx? The case that brought you here?'

'Jesus!' Manx said, removing Bevan's hand from his wrist. 'You're still pursuing this line of enquiry? Give it up for God's sake.'

'Just so you know, things are stirring over there, changing of the old guard and all that. Good chatting with you, Manx, as always.'

'You don't chat, Bevan, you insinuate,' Manx said, scooting this stool back. 'Just let me know when you've got something useful and leave my past out of it.'

'Like I said, just nurturing relationships.' Bevan smiled.

God, how Manx hated that fucking smile.

Chapter 26

'How's the hairdressers's, Gwen?' Manx asked, settling himself at the bar of the Pilot Arms. He'd spent the morning throwing imaginary darts at the incident board – nothing was sticking.

Gwen pulled him the usual. 'Well, I'm still working here,' she said shrugging. 'And by the way, it's a full-service hair salon, a hairdresser's is where your mother goes.'

'That's put me in my place.' Manx looked around. The pub was uncharacteristically full for a Sunday afternoon. 'What's the occasion?'

'His landlorship's got a new cook, some work experience kid. He's doing Sunday lunch, roast beef, Yorkies, the full monty.'

'Worth a try,' Manx said, flipping over the pub grub menu.

'I've seen the kitchen,' Gwen said, leaning over the bar. 'Let's just say it's not quite Gordon Ramsay ready.'

'Liquid lunch it is then,' Manx said, raising his glass.

Gwen placed the menu back in the stand. 'Haven't seen you for a few days, the landlord was getting worried, thought he might be losing his best customer. Wanted to send out a search party.'

'And what, drag me in here?'

'He's very customer focused these days,' Gwen said, tending to a well-dressed older couple who had just wandered in. They looked confused, no doubt expecting something more upscale than a rundown pub with faded fishing nets thrown over the windows and carrying a whiff of quiet desperation. Before they could make their excuses, Gwen had pounced on them, by which time they looked too embarrassed to turn on their heels and leave.

They ordered a half pint of lager shandy and a single gin and tonic, no ice, *the kind of drinks you order if you're not staying long, or you don't like the taste of alcohol,* Manx thought. He watched as Gwen coaxed the couple into glancing at the menu. She had an infectious charm, one that Manx had found himself at the receiving end of on a few occasions. He sensed Gwen never gave up her secrets easily. He knew she was separated from her husband and had a six-year-old boy, Owain; not exactly a trove of information considering he'd been talking with her at least five nights a week for the past six months. He downed the last dregs of his pint.

'Pub crawl?' Gwen asked, as Manx slipped on his jacket.

'I wish. God may have rested on Sunday, but he didn't extend that courtesy to the North Wales Constabulary.'

Gwen slid a crisp bag across the bar. 'Here, on the house.'

'Cheese and onion? Lunch of champions.'

Gwen smiled. 'Part of your five a day.'

As Manx turned to leave, he felt a hand fall across his back.

'Tudor Manx? Well, this where all the bad pennies wash up is it?'

Manx studied the man's face; flat nose, low forehead, and a wide, muscular face. He looked vaguely familiar.

'Robin. Robin Telford,' the man said, pulling up a stool. 'Moses?' he added helpfully. 'Remember? I set fire to that rhododendron bush outside my gran's house that summer? I was Benllech's most wanted for a week.'

'Moses? They don't still call you that, do they?' Manx said, the memory slowly returning to him of a skinny kid with a tuft of ginger hair and a talent for getting himself into trouble.

'You set one bush on fire and it sticks with you for life.'

Manx laughed. 'Took me a minute there, Robin. You a regular?'

'When the missus lets me out. You ever get married, Manx?'

'Once. Didn't care for it.'

Telford nodded. 'Coming up on my twenty-fifth this June. Got three teenage girls who only drag themselves off their phones to eat. It's a bloody miracle I'm not here every night drunk under the table.'

'You wouldn't be the first,' Manx said.

'You know the wife, right? Amy. Amy Harris. Her dad was that crabby old bastard who owned the Estate Agents over in Cemaes Bay.'

'I remember. Popular girl.'

Telford slapped his hand on the bar. 'To hell with this, Manx, come over for dinner, Amy would be over the moon. You can meet the coven. It's all bloody *Vampire Diaries* these days, you'd be doing me a favour, if I hear another argument about who's on whose bloody team I might drive a stake through my own heart.'

Manx hesitated. 'I'm not—'

'What? You've got a better offer?' Telford said, pointing at Manx's crisp bag. 'Write down your address, I'll pick you up.'

Manx realised resistance was futile. 'Getting bored of my own company, anyway, may as well.'

'Top man. Amy will be made up.' Telford shook his head. 'Tudor bloody Manx. I knew you'd be back one day.'

Chapter 27

PC Delyth Morris reached for a photograph from the sideboard - Donna Robinson with Sian and Liam Fowler smiling widely at the camera on a blustery day, South Stack Lighthouse in the background.

'You three were good friends?' she asked.

'Yeah. Used to do everything together,' Donna said, her eyes welling with tears.

Morris sat on the sofa next to Priddle and flipped open her notebook. 'The last time you spoke to Sian was at midnight on Thursday?'

Donna wiped her sleeve across her eyes. 'She left the club early. I wasn't happy about it, but she could be like that, once she made up her mind about something there's no persuading her.'

'So, you had an argument?' Priddle said.

'Um, I suppose…' Donna's eyes welled up again.

'And you hung up when DI Manx answered your Skype call Friday morning,' Priddle insisted.

'Erm, I'm not sure what…' Donna began, looking at Morris with worried eyes.

Morris turned to Priddle. 'You know what? I reckon Miss Robinson could do with a really strong cuppa. What do you think, Donna?'

Donna sniffed. 'Yeah, be nice.'

'Tea. Right,' Priddle said. 'Kitchen through there, yeah?'

Donna nodded, wrapping her fingers around themselves in anxious folds as Priddle's lanky form shuffled through the narrow gap between them.

'We were like sisters,' Donna said. 'We'd argue, then it was all water under the bridge, forgotten like it never happened.'

'Same with me and my sister,' Morris said. 'Families, eh? So, was Sian upset about anything recently?'

Donna thought for a moment. 'She was stressed out at work, but who isn't these days, yeah? McLain had her on call at all hours so her social life went to shit, not that she was that bothered. She loved her work. Lucky for some.'

'Any boyfriends?'

'Blokes were always asking her out, but she wasn't interested, not after everything that happened with Liam.'

'Sian wasn't seeing anyone. Nothing serious or casual?'

'She'd sworn off men for good, she said. I always told her to give it time. Fucking stupid thing to say.'

'Would she keep that kind of thing a secret from you, Donna?'

Donna looked puzzled. 'I told you, we were like sisters.' She broke down again. 'I can't take it all in,' she said in between her sobs. 'It's fucking terrible, I just can't believe it.'

'I know this is hard, Donna,' Morris said. 'But the more we know the better chance we have of catching whoever did this to Sian.'

Donna nodded. 'I'll write it down, I want to help.'

'Here, take these,' Morris said handing Donna two business cards. 'The top one has my personal number. The other one is for the grief counsellors we recommend, they're very good.'

Donna nodded, fidgeting with the cards in her palm, her gaze a million miles away. 'What about guilt counselling? Any help for that?' she asked, with a weak, sad smile that Morris sensed was hiding more than it was revealing.

'I'm not sure,' Morris said.

'Never mind, just me being stupid.' Donna brushed herself down and placed the cards on the coffee table 'Maybe I'll call them, can't do any harm, right?'

'Nothing to lose,' Morris said. 'By the way, how well do you know Liam Fowler?'

'He was a good bloke at first. Funny, a bit intense, but Sian liked that about him. He wasn't like most of the men she'd been with, just into drinking themselves into a coma every night.'

'What changed?' Morris asked.

'Kids, at least I reckon. Liam found out he couldn't have 'em, sterile he was. He took it badly, became angry at everything. He made Sian's life hell until she called it quits a year ago and started using her maiden name again. Liam was fuming, stalked her for months, kept threatening her. I never thought it would end up like this though. Never. If I'd known I would have—'

'It's not your fault, Donna, none of it, understand?

'Easy for you to say,' Donna said. 'She was my best friend, but the whole thing between him and Sian, it's like they were toxic together, but I thought it was all sorted, he was going to sign the divorce papers. But you never know what people are really thinking, do you, not really.'

Chapter 28

Telford pulled the cork on a bottle of wine. 'You a red drinker, Manx? Don't have any cider and black on hand.'

'That takes me back,' Manx said, recalling the syrupy, cloying taste of what they used to call the *poor man's rum and coke*.

Telford laughed. 'Remember that old bloke who ran the off-license in Amlwch? Mister Magoo we called him. We'd bunk off school on a Friday afternoon. I'd make sure his one good eye was facing the other way while you shoved a bottle of Strongbow up your jumper.'

'Good times,' Manx said, taking a sip. It was tart and too warm, but it might be the crutch he needed to help him navigate a stroll down memory lane. He already regretted coming; re-telling the glory days of his youth, few as they were, made him uncomfortable. He could always make his excuses and leave early if the nostalgia became as sickly sweet as he recalled cider and black tasting.

Manx followed Telford into the kitchen. A photo on the fridge door caught his attention. 'You're a fireman?'

'Ironic, yeah?' Telford handed Manx a glass. 'The kid who set alight the burning bush is now the crew manager at Bangor Fire and Rescue.'

'Making up for past transgressions?'

'Could say the same about you, Manx,' Telford said, leaning on the counter. 'After that terrible thing with your sister, you took off and became a copper. Don't tell me you weren't trying to make up for something. Hell, we probably all are in some way.'

Before Manx had a chance to answer, Telford's wife, Amy, appeared in the doorway.

'Oh, Robin, don't go boring the bloke with the good old days routine already.' She gave Manx a generous hug. 'It's good to see you, Tudor, but I'm a bit put out you didn't come and see us earlier.'

Amy looked good, Manx thought. A little wider around the waist, but he guessed three kids would do that to you. She had a harried look about her, but her smile was warm and welcoming. Manx shoved his hands in his pockets.

'Busy, you know how it goes, Amy.'

'Three teenage girls and two parents who work shifts. That's busy, Tudor. Still you're here now. Dinner's nearly ready. Come,' she said, as if she were directing a dog to heel.

As Manx drew back his chair, there was a loud rap on the door. Without waiting to be invited in, a man nearly as wide as the doorway and sporting a thick beard that looked as if it might house a family of badgers, breezed in and raised his arms heavenward.

'Tudor fucking Manx!' he said. 'And on a Sunday, praise the fucking Lord and all that.'

'Robin, you didn't?' Amy said, sighing and getting up. 'We'll set you a plate, Jack, as per usual.'

'Cheers, Amy. One in a million you are, luv.'

Jack Driscoll. The man's name came back to Manx as soon as he spoke. He had a wet lisp that was the butt of endless jokes at school. If tonight was going to be a trek down memory lane, Jack Driscoll would be leading the expedition; he had the memory of an elephant, and had acquired the lumbering gait of one it seemed, as he stomped across the room and squeezed his thick thighs under the table.

'Here they come, the belles of the ball,' Jack said as Telford's three daughters joined them, ignoring 'Uncle Jack,' their faces buried deep in their screens.

'Phones off,' Amy said.

The girls rolled their eyes and placed their devices on the table.

'Delicious, Amy,' Manx said, tucking into the roast pork dinner. It had been a while since he'd had anything other than pub grub or microwaved pies.

'She doesn't cook it herself, do you, Mam?' Angela, the older of the teenage girls offered with a snide smile.

'Yeah, she orders all the time because the bloke fancies her,' said the youngest, Jenny.

'Makes your day, eh? Thinks you're a MILF,' Angela said.

'What's a MILF, for goodness sake, Angela?'

'Really, you don't know?' Angela asked, laughing, the other two sisters joining in.

'A mam I'd like to fuck,' Driscoll said, emphatically. 'You should be proud,' he added, pointing his fork in her direction.

'It's not the kind of values I'm trying to teach the girls, Jack. Tell him, Robin.'

'Not at the dinner table, eh, Jack?' Telford said.

'Please yourselves. Reckoned it was a compliment, that's all,' Driscoll said, spearing a slice of pork and jamming it into his mouth.

'I cook when I can,' Amy said, eager to switch topics. 'I was working today and anyway I don't see any of you complaining.'

'No one would bloody listen anyway. We're the invisible generation,' Maggie, the middle child said, resting her head in her palm and picking aimlessly at her food.

'You been back a while now, aye, Manx?' Driscoll said, quaffing on a glass of wine; his third in twenty minutes, Manx had been watching. 'Didn't think to look up your old mates?'

Manx took a sip of wine. 'It's been busy, Jack, that's all.'

'Fighting crime, putting away the island's pimps and drug dealers, yeah?' Driscoll said, leaning back in his chair and waving his glass in Manx's direction. 'See, Manx, I've got this theory that the police, yeah, they're just as corrupt as the rest of us, they just protect one another with funny handshakes and all secret society stuff. What do you reckon?'

'I think it's time you eased off the wine, mate,' Telford said. 'He's a guest, let it be.'

Driscoll smiled – it was like a thin, cruel, blood-cut across his beard. 'Aye, for now,' he said, belching loudly and leaning his thick elbows on the table. 'But, remind me, Manx, why did you fuck off when you did?'

'That's enough, Jack,' Amy said.

'Fair dos, Amy,' Driscoll said, 'Just making conversation, isn't that right, Manx?'

He sat back in his chair and picked an errant piece of pork fat from his beard. 'You know, some people reckoned you were on the run. Fucking mad idea, right? I mean, she was your bloody sister, Miriam was. Mind you, we were mates, I knew my mate couldn't do anything like that.'

Manx breathed deeply. 'Then you'd be right, Jack,' he said.

'Hey, remember what we were going to do after we left school?' Driscoll asked, clutching his utensils between his fists like weapons.

'I don't know, Jack. Travel the world? Climb Everest? It's a lifetime ago.'

Driscoll laughed and shook his head. 'See, I knew you wouldn't remember. Bet Telford here a fiver.'

Telford shrugged his shoulders and slid a five pound note over to Jack. 'Sorry, Manx. He wouldn't leave it alone.'

'I'll remind you,' Driscoll said, pointing at Manx. 'You and me were going into business together. A garage. I'd fix 'em, you'd sell 'em. Had big plans, we did. Remember that?'

'That was a long time ago, Jack, kids' stuff.'

Driscoll shook his head. 'See, that's the problem with running away. The mates you leave behind, they're left wondering what the fuck happened. Heard nothing for thirty years, then here you are, back from the bloody dead. He'll get in touch, I told myself, after all this time he's got to give a fuck about his old mates, right?'

'Language, please,' Amy said, gesturing at the girls.

Driscoll laughed. 'If they're anything like mine they've heard worse, isn't that right, girls? Heard one fuck, heard 'em all.'

The girls giggled and elbowed each other as the evening plummeted into an inevitable tailspin.

Amy threw her husband a look that could have speared wildlife.

'I think it's probably time you left, Jack,' Telford said, wise enough by now to take the hint.

Manx jumped at the opening. 'No, I'll leave,' he said, grabbing his jacket. 'Early start tomorrow. Make sure Jack sleeps it off before he drives anywhere, we've got patrols all over the island this time of night.'

'Fuck you, Manx,' Driscoll said, who was at the slurring stage of drunkenness. 'I'll sleep when I'm fucking dead.'

'Right you are, Jack,' Manx said, heading towards the door. 'Thanks for dinner, Amy.'

'Hey, Manx, before you go, I've got something for you,' Driscoll said, reaching into his jeans pocket. He fumbled around for a few seconds then pulled out his middle finger and stuck high in the air. He smiled, wide and smug. The girls dissolved into a fit of laughter.

'Well played, Jack,' Manx said. 'See you in another thirty years.'

A tense silence fell over the room as Manx left, all except Driscoll who had jumped all over Manx's plate and was picking at the remains, grunting as he did so. Telford and Amy looked at him.

'What? Bloody tasty it is, shame to let it go to waste,' Jack said, shovelling another forkful into his mouth.

Chapter 29

Liam Fowler's grin was wide and cocky as he gathered his belongings from the duty officer and strode out of the station.

'Out of your hands now, Manx,' Canton said, sensing Manx's doubts as he watched Fowler drive away.

'We're keeping tabs on him, just in case,' Manx said. 'Low key, but we'll nab him if he steps out of line. Read the papers yet?'

'The ones I could stomach,' Canton said, leaning back on the reception desk.

'If they get wind of the full details, there'll be a shit storm.'

'St Asaph agrees, which is a first. No reason to panic the public any more than necessary at this point.'

Manx nodded.

'Someone's eager to get hold of you,' Canton said, gesturing at the impatient buzz of Manx's phone, which had vibrated five times in the last minute. Manx checked the number. PC Morris was texting him. *'Got to see this. Bloody urgent, sir.'*

* * *

Manx gestured for Morris to rewind the footage. 'So, how did this land in our possession?'

'Digital forensics decrypted the files,' Morris explained.

'Fowler installed Spyware on Sian's computer,' PC Priddle added, from across the room. 'Must have done it before she left him.'

'It alerted him every time Sian logged on to her computer.'

'Aye, perverted it is,' Priddle said. 'He could see everything she was doing, live. Chats, websites, email, the lot.'

'But you said, live, why do we have a recording?'

'The sneaky bastard recorded every Skype conversation she had.'

'The quality's pretty shoddy, more's the pity,' Manx said, leaning into the screen.

'Yeah, but the whole thing's recorded,' Morris said, rewinding the clip. 'Sian answers Donna's call at seven minutes past midnight. They chat for a few minutes, then this happens.'

They watched the video, none of them quite believing what they were witnessing. A figure of a woman moving slowly from the shadows behind Sian, grabbing a fistful of her hair and yanking back her head to reveal the pale slope of her neck. A flash of steel and the sudden splatter of blood over the lens. Sian's limp body being dragged by the hair across the kitchen floor and out of screen. Then, the ordinary view of a suburban kitchen, where nothing seemed out of place save the muffled screams coming from the bathroom. The three of them continued to watch as the screams faded to silence, none of them prepared to fast forward through the next few minutes of static footage, but each one of them imagining what was unfolding. They held their breaths until finally a blurred shadow passed the camera and ran from the house.

'Good God,' Manx said, running his hand through is hair. 'Any enhancement on the face?'

'Just in.' Priddle lay three photographs on the table of the figure looming over Sian's shoulder, just before the knife was drawn.

'Does that look like a woman to you?' Manx asked.

'Could be,' Morris said.

Manx stared, unnerved at the large expressionless eyes that seemed to be starting directly at him.

'Freeze it there,' Manx said, studying the moment Sian dug her nails into her killer's wrist. 'Hardacre and Bevan both mentioned finding residue at the scene. Hand me the report.'

Priddle passed over the forensics file. 'Artificial compound as yet undetermined,' Manx said.

'Probably wearing gloves,' Priddle offered.

'Light a fire under Bevan's arse. If we get the exact compound maybe we can figure out who makes it, get some traction.'

Morris spoke up, 'This definitely rules out Fowler, sir. His Spyware recorded the whole murder, he's not stupid, he'd have switched it off or deleted the video files.'

'Of course he would,' Manx said, rubbing his forehead. 'And it explains why he was there at the scene that morning. He'd seen the recording, assumed it was Balham, but it doesn't explain why Fowler was lying about his whereabouts that night, or why he met with Kimble McLain.'

Manx paced in front of the incident board. 'Women rarely commit murder,' he said, shoving his hands in his pockets. 'If they do, it's usually in self-defence or they snap one day after years of abuse, which means either we have a completely off the charts female assailant who's strong enough to drag a sixty-five kilo body and dump her in a bath or something else entirely.'

From the other side of the room, the door wedged open and the duty sergeant, Pritchard, opened the door 'Sorry to interrupt, but there's this woman in reception?'

'This woman? Do you mean a member of the public, Pritchard?' Manx said.

Pritchard blushed. 'A female member of the public, sir. She just drove up from Birmingham, she's worried about her father, Gwynfor Roberts, owns a sheep farm by Rhosnegir. Hasn't heard from him for days and the house is empty. In a right state, she is.'

Manx felt the familiar swell of dread roll through him. What if Hardacre was right, and this was just the beginning? The thought was a sharp, bone-chilling stab to his gut.

Chapter 30

Donna Robinson stood in her kitchen looking over the small garden and the new patio furniture she'd bought recently. *Summer-ready*, she'd told herself, imagining warm nights gathered around the chiminea and her and Sian listening to their favourite *Hits of the Seventies* radio show. She felt the tears rise again – another fresh bucket full drawn from what seemed like an infinite well.

She took a sip of tea tinged with just the right dosage of Toffoc: the locally made toffee flavoured vodka She always had on hand. It added a sweet hint of caramel, but mostly it just helped take the edge off the minutes of the day when she was awake, thinking about Sian and wrestling with the guilt that sat like a clenched fist in her belly.

An impatient rap at the window jolted her from her thoughts and made her jump. *Shit! Him again.* She slid open the patio door. 'Surprised to see you out,' she said, gesturing for the man to come in.

'Any chance of a cuppa?' he asked, grabbing her wrist and dragging her hand to his crotch.

Donna stiffened. 'No, it's too soon,' she said, averting her gaze. That was her only weapon against him now. Once she looked into his eyes she knew she'd do anything he asked. She hated herself for it, no, she despised herself, especially now, after everything.

'Life goes on. Got big plans. Leaving this shithole as soon as I get my money.'

'What money?' Donna asked.

'What's owed,' he said, taking her chin in his palm and compelling her to look him directly in the eyes, drawing her closer.

Her protests were half-hearted. The vodka was already blunting her reason, compromising her promises and best efforts.

'Haven't been drinking have you ?' he asked, looking at the half-empty Toffoc bottle on the counter.

'Medicinal,' she said, taking a large swig of the tea, defiantly, but still not removing her hand from his crotch, which she felt grow and stiffen as he moved closer.

'At least I won't smell it on you,' he said, sniffing around her neck like a dog.

'Leave it, please,' she said, pushing at his shoulders, but it was a futile protest. She knew it, he knew it too. It was like that between her and Liam Fowler, it always had been.

Chapter 31

He could keep it under control, at least most of the time, but on days like today, staring down at the rotting body, the waves of anxiety rolled over him like the wash of an incoming tide. He needed to sit down, breathe, ease his heartbeat back to normal.

Corpses brought it all back. Especially this one, trussed, bloodied, hacked and thrown into a sheep dip. He was the first on the scene at Sian Conway's murder too, and now felt the same pit in his stomach; the same instinct to run. The putrefying smell was making him gag. Not as pungent as the burning flesh he witnessed in the Falkland's – the stench of burning flesh as his fellow soldiers perished – but it still caught in his throat, brought him right back to that day like a bullet. He vomited behind a nearby rock, wiped his mouth and sat. The rest of the team would be here soon, he just needed to pull himself together, be a copper; do his fucking job.

* * *

Nader was still sitting, his hands resting on his thighs, when Manx and the team arrived. 'Two in less than a week, Nader,' Manx said, patting the sergeant on his back. 'Rough call.'

'You don't know the half of it,' Nader said.

Manx walked over and inspected the body. Like Sian, the man's liver had been removed and was now being carefully scraped from the bottom of the sheep dip by Hardacre.

'I'm surprised the wildlife didn't feast on this,' he said, sliding the organ into an evidence bag. 'Prime cut like this, they'd think it was Christmas Day.'

'Nice. Thanks, Hardy,' Manx said, wincing.

'No time for squeamishness, Manx, it's just a body part,' he said, handing over the bag.

Manx lifted it to the light, looking for a similar phial to the one the killer had left in Sian Conway's body.

'Christ, Manx!' Hardacre snapped, snatching back the bag. 'These kinds of autopsies are done in the damned lab, not in an open field.'

Manx walked around the rectangular sheep dip as Hardacre's team carefully extracted the body. It was like a ready-made coffin, Manx thought – the image sent a shiver down his spine. It wouldn't be his choice, cremation would be his preference; his ashes packed into an old cigar box, Cuban, if he had his choice.

'Victim is confirmed as Gwynfor Roberts. Sixty-three years old, leased the land a few years back,' DS Nader said, reading his notebook and watching as they carried the body away.

'Next of kin?'

'Mary Roberts. Thirty-three, last heard from her father four days ago. There's something else too,' Nader said. 'She mentioned her father leased the land from Kimble McLain.'

'That right?' Manx said, zipping up his jacket 'Close enough for jazz.'

'Boss?'

'McLain. His land, his tenant, my calling card,' Manx said, and headed towards the Jensen.

Chapter 32

The crackle of exhaust fire bellowed through the hills, flushing out a bouquet of pheasants from the undergrowth. Manx watched as a scream of finely engineered and perfectly tuned Italian horsepower tore past him in a fury of noise and heat.

'Can't speak to him now,' the man shouted. 'He lets it rip for a few laps, pulls in to check his times, then takes the other one out.'

'He's got two of those things?' Manx asked, watching the streak of red eat up the track like it was an afternoon snack.

'Three,' Dave London said, prodding the app on his iPad. He was a serious man with a brow that knotted intensely as he studied the lap times. 'Ferrari, Aston Martin, and a Lambo. Just sold the McLaren, handling was too twitchy and the tyres cost him a small fortune.'

'Times must be tough,' Manx said, as he watched Kimble McLain slip the Ferrari 488 GT3 through the Corkscrew then past the corner at Rocket until all he could see was the car's rear spoiler quivering like a bloodied shark fin on the horizon.

It had taken some negotiation from Manx before the young lad, Glyn Lewis, had given up McLain's location; the Anglesey Circuit at Ty Croes. Manx had seen the ads for the race track in the tourist brochures. It was carved into the west of the island with views across the sea to the Snowdonia mountain range and the Llyn Peninsula. Not that he suspected McLain was taking in the scenery as he throttled the car into the corners until it screamed for mercy.

'We get a few of your lot down here,' London said. 'Pursuit training, high-speed driving skills. They come from all over,

Chester, Wrexham, got some coming up from St Asaph next week.'

'Impressive,' Manx said.

'We don't get many like Mr McLain, mind. Most blokes come here to blow off some steam or the wife's bought them a voucher. They think they're Lewis bloody Hamilton until they get thrown around on the test lap, just about shit their trousers most of them. Best days are when we're hosting the Championships. Oh, here we go, he's pulling in now.' London gestured for Manx to step back.

McLain flicked the blood-red Ferrari through School Bus Stop Corner, and pulled up a few feet away in the pit lane, the heat rising from the V8 turbo as it idled. It had an impatient growl, as if it were already bored and ready for another thrashing.

McLain hauled himself from the driver's seat, removing his helmet and gloves. He was wearing a full racing suit, with the McLain Foundation logo embossed on the front. 'Inspector Manx. If I'd known you were a fan, I'd have taken you for a spin.'

'Classic and steady's more my style,' Manx said, looking over at his Jensen Interceptor, which stood out like a hand-cranked sewing machine in a robotics factory next to the Aston and the Lamborghini.

'Great car in its day. A true gentleman's cruiser,' Kimble said.

'Yeah, well we were all great in our day,' Manx said.

'What brings you here? Update on Sian's case?' McLain asked stripping off his gloves.

'In a way. I'm afraid one of your tenants, Gwynfor Roberts, was found dead this morning.'

McLain processed the information for a moment and leant back on the car. 'He wasn't that old, was he? Heart attack? He was a large man, statistically he was probably on the high percentile scale.'

'Murdered, I'm afraid.'

McLain steadied himself on the car bonnet. 'Are you sure?'

'It's our job to be sure.'

'The same person who killed Sian?'

'Too early to tell. When did you last speak to Mr Roberts?' Manx asked, flipping open his notebook.

'God knows. Glyn Lewis, my estate manager, he takes care of all the day-to-day matters.'

'So, you've had no contact with him?'

McLain placed his helmet on the roof of the car. 'I suppose next you'll be asking where I was last night, and who I was with?'

'I didn't mention when he was murdered.'

'Just a turn of phrase.'

'Hell of a coincidence, though. Two people you know murdered within days of each other.'

McLain grinned. 'I don't believe in coincidence, and neither, I'm guessing, do you, inspector. If the only connection you have is that I knew both victims, then there are probably another hundred people that also knew them both.'

'True,' Manx said. 'This was just a courtesy call, before the press starts spinning it all out of proportion, you know how they get, all worked up over nothing.'

McLain's left eye twitched. 'So, this is part of your community outreach? I hear Chief Superintendent Troup is very hot on that these days,' he said, reaching for his helmet and folding himself back into the car. 'I'll be sure to put in a word next time I see her, make sure you get your hours logged.'

Manx stepped back as McLain floored the throttle. He was gone in a burn of rubber and a thunderclap of engine noise. Is that what he was doing, spinning his own wheels with McLain? Manx wondered as the Ferrari's callipygian rear-end shimmied along the track. But even spinning wheels get traction at some point he thought, it was just a matter of knowing when to pull your foot off the brake.

Chapter 33

The memory of the crossing was still fresh in his mind, even now, as he sat on the edge of the bathtub examining his knees. They still bore the scars of that day when his father compelled him with the urgent force of his hand to kneel on the coarse timber planks. Some hours later, when he was granted permission to rise, his father had prohibited him from extracting the splinters that had burrowed under his skin. 'God was within him now,' he explained. Despite the pain, he felt that too; sensed God had taken root in the marrow of his bones.

A month later, they arrived on another island; this one was as cold and dour as the other was sultry and vibrant. They were home, his parents had told him, though it felt as far from home as he could imagine. He was eight years old. Had his father begun to press his interest then? Was that first cut of the sins yet to be the first of many cuts that would carve out his being?

'God's work in progress,' his father had said as he took him by the hand and led him through the remains of the church. *'A new beginning. Like Noah, tasked with the rebirth of the world.'*

The church was cold and built with thick, heavy stones. Inside its oppressive darkness scared him, the rafters rotting and the walls damp with moss. *'Your grandfather built this,'* his father explained as he led him towards the area close to the vestry. He dragged the first three rows of pews to the side, reached to the floor, and pulled on a thick iron handle.

'Do you know what's under here, boy?' his father asked. He shook his head. *'Here, pull on this with me, it's heavy.'* He helped his father tug at the thick stone, now covered in decades of dirt and dust

'This is where we'll cleanse them, wash them free of their sins,' his father explained as he pulled on an iron-bar and slid back the floor to reveal a small baptism pool. It had remained unused for decades, the walls pitted and the floor chipped and covered with moss.

'You'll work with me, boy, help me reclaim its glory. We'll prepare it for them all to be bathed in God's glory.'

He nodded, not quite understanding. That would come later, when the ripples of time finally cascaded against the shore and he understood, with God in his marrow, that he would be tasked with the same mission.

The memory startled him back to the now. He rubbed his palms hard over his knees. It felt good, the sting of it, the raw skin sloughing off as he scrubbed. She was downstairs, in the back office filling the kettle. Endless cups of tea; it was her way of dealing with the world. It wasn't his.

He stepped into the bath. The cold enamel stung his soles as he began the ritual. First the shaving: all his body hair to be removed, his skin as smooth as the day he was born into the world, free of sin.

Then, the purification: a generous slap of talcum powder applied to his skin and between his legs; especially between his legs where he was careful not to touch for too long – that kind of lingering led to dirty thoughts that then led him from the true path.

The retraction was next: he bit off a strip of duct tape, placed it on the lip of the sink and bent his knees. Carefully, he took the tape and attached it where his pubic bone began and looped it under his groin until it was wedged tight. He tore off another three strips, added them either side of the first one, and the retraction was complete. He'd learnt his lesson with the first one. No room to grow, no room for impure thoughts, he confirmed as he patted the pack of tape that now hid what made him a man; what made him like his father.

Now, and only now, could he step into her, cleansed and renewed. He felt the pure, unblemished weight of her slip over his skin. They were as one again.

Downstairs, he grabbed his backpack from the coat rack and checked its contents. He took out the knife, placed it under his nose, and ran the blade lightly across his tongue until he tasted the faint, metallic tinge of blood – the blood of those already saved – and anticipated that of those yet to be delivered.

She switched on the TV. Hearing the front door open she called out to him. 'Do you have to go out tonight? Have you eaten?'

'The Lord helps those who satisfy the thirst and fill the hunger with good things,' he called out, hauling the backpack over his shoulder.

No reply. He didn't expect one. She wouldn't pursue it – her guilt was too overwhelming to ask anything more of him. She was desperate to make up for the years of neglect and wrong doing. *Too fucking late for all that, Mother.* The thought made him smile. Lucy smiled too – he could sense it on his skin.

Chapter 34

The camera flashlights flared as Manx stood on the steps of Llangefni Station with DCI Canton. 'We can confirm there have been two murders on the island. Any more than that, we're not at liberty to reveal.'

'Are they connected?'

'Still under investigation,' Canton said.

'One of the victims worked for Kimble McLain, any comment?'

'Mr McLain employs a lot of people, you lot know that. He'd probably employ a few of you if you learned how to spell,' Canton said, receiving a rush of laughter for his efforts.

'Inspector Manx, after your work on the last case, with Blackwell, are you confident you'll make an arrest soon?'

'We're not unconfident,' Manx said.

'Okay, time's up,' Canton said, urging Manx back into the station.

* * *

'We're not unconfident? What the hell does that even mean, Manx?' Canton asked as they walked into the incident room.

'Means, we'll nail the bastard at some point, Ellis. That, I'm confident about. Joining us for the briefing?'

'Wouldn't miss it.'

'Right,' Manx said, addressing the room in front of the incident board. 'Fresh victim, Gwynfor Roberts, sixty-three years old. Method and execution matches that of Sian Conway. The hands and feet bound, the liver removed, and the same message.'

He pinned a photograph of the note to the incident board. 'There is one key difference between both murders.' Manx gestured at the close up of Sian's thighs. 'No signs of stabbing on the male victim, which means what, Morris?'

'The attacks aren't sexual in nature?'

'Exactly. So, the notes the killer leaves become critical to our case. *But put ye on the Lord Jesus Christ and make no provision for the flesh in all its concupiscences.* It could be a warning, not to put the pleasures of the flesh above your devotion to God. There's no evidence Sian Conway was promiscuous or that Gwynfor Roberts paid more attention to his sheep, or any of his other livestock, than what you'd class as healthy. Both ordinary people living their lives.'

'Sian Conway was pregnant, though, boss,' Priddle said.

'Doesn't make her promiscuous, Priddle,' Morris said. 'Donna Robinson didn't mention it when I talked to her. Maybe she didn't know or she's protecting Sian.'

'Or protecting someone else,' Manx said. 'Our killer could be religiously educated, brought up in a strict home, Bible readings, severe punishments for minor transgressions, that sort of thing.'

'That might go to motive, Manx, but are there any connections between both victims?' Canton asked from the back of the room.

'Kimble McLain,' Manx said. 'He knew both of them.'

'Hardly grounds for interrogation. He'll have a team of solicitors up my arse before I turn around to drop my trousers.'

'He's hiding something, though.'

'Everybody's hiding something, Manx,' Canton huffed.

Chapter 35

The sun had barely made its scheduled appearance over the horizon at Cable Bay. Kimble and Lewis stumbled over the stone-pitted footpath that curved uphill from the car park to the beach entrance. A sharp, bitter wind blew across the dunes, bending the backs of the marram grass into an easy submission. Liam Fowler was already there – a long shadow looming in the haze of the dawn light.

'Who's that?' Fowler asked as they joined him. 'Your boy toy?'

'Why are we here, Fowler?' McLain asked.

'Prefer to do this somewhere else? Pub maybe? Or at that mansion of yours? But then you'd have to explain to your pretty little ballerina wife what's going on. Miiko, is that her name? Fragile thing, looks like.'

'What is it you want?'

'Passage out of here, McLain.'

Lewis narrowed his eyes. 'For which you'll need money.'

'Oh, he talks,' Fowler said, looking out to the dark roll of the sea. 'Yeah, fucking money. What you owe me, McLain.'

'I told you before, if you think that patent is yours, employ the services of a lawyer.'

Fowler stepped closer to McLain and jabbed a finger in his face. 'See, that's how you rich bastards fuck people over. Courts, lawyers, that all takes time and money. My solution is much cleaner, quicker.'

Fowler pulled out a slip of paper from inside his jacket pocket.

Lewis reached for the document.

'Hey, steady on, Boy Wonder,' Fowler said, snapping it back and shoving it at McLain 'His eyes only and I've got copies, so don't get any bright ideas.'

McLain briefly scanned the document. 'Means nothing, Fowler. Nobody would care.'

'Maybe, but context is everything, yeah? To anyone else, this looks like you were paying Sian off. Paying her to keep her mouth shut while you and Tiny Dancer got what you wanted.'

'Again, it proves nothing,' Lewis said.

Fowler turned to face McLain. 'Remember when we started all this, McLain, we had big dreams; we were going to change the world.'

'He will, change the world,' Lewis said. 'Don't doubt it.'

McLain gestured for him to ease off.

'Yeah, you always had the big plans and the vision,' Fowler said. 'But the details weren't your bag. I was the record keeper, filed the patents, secured the databases, made sure we were compliant. Without me, you'd still be making apps in your bedroom and living off your parents.'

'You negotiated your own exit package,' McLain said, 'because you didn't have the appetite to sit at the grown-ups' table. You were a c-grade coder at best, a petulant child at worst. I'd have paid twice what I did to have you gone.'

Even in the dim light of dawn, Lewis could see Fowler's anger boiling; the bunching of his fists, the tensing of his neck until the veins bulged. For a moment, he thought Fowler might drop McLain with a right hook. Would he step in between them? He hadn't thought that far ahead. Thankfully, he didn't need to. Fowler relaxed his posture and handed McLain another slip of paper.

'My demands.'

Lewis tore the paper from his hand. 'Blackmail, the last resort of the sore loser.'

Fowler grinned. 'It's just business, right lads, nothing personal. Mind you, those friends of yours putting up the money for this big project might see it differently. Fickle bunch investors are, or so I've heard.'

Chapter 36

'*From garments cometh a moth, and from women, wickedness.*' *They* liked to repeat that phrase to him, lest he began to stray from the true path. He took them at their word, after all, women were as unknowable to him as God himself. What little he did know had been taught to him by his mother, and the Bible. The story of Eve had caught his imagination. God had insisted Adam sacrifice a rib for Eve and how did she thank him? By betraying Adam and her God. And for what? The promise of knowledge? What other knowledge did she need than the knowledge that God loved her? What other knowledge would anyone ever need?

She was a whore, this one, but no matter, her salvation was near. She would have the opportunity to atone for her sins soon enough.

He was wearing the high-heeled shoes he'd bought last week. They were less than two inches high, but it had still taken him a few hours of practice to walk without stumbling. He'd even watched a YouTube video instructing him on the best posture and spent the afternoon walking back and forth in front of the full length mirror until he'd perfected the walk. Graceful, poised; almost feminine.

He was confident the woman ahead of him wouldn't be suspicious. Women rarely feared other women – that much he knew. The brittle click of heels behind her told her it was just another woman, like her, walking towards the bus stop.

He knew her routine. He also knew she was a betrayer. She would come to the same pub every Wednesday night on Holyhead High Street and meet a man. By the way they kissed, intense and needy like they were devouring each other, he knew the man wasn't her husband. He was at home tending to their baby. He hoped the child had been saved, not like her, her soul already damned. But he could fix that, repair the damage.

At the bus shelter, he stood a few feet to the woman's left. She slipped a cigarette between her lips, struck a match and spoke to him. Or, more accurately, she spoke without turning as if she were addressing the night. 'Hope the bloody bus comes soon, I'm freezing my knickers off.'

He said nothing, but Lucy did. 'Yeah, you should take them off,' he said, the words having left his throat before he could stop them. It was his voice, of course, deep and masculine. The woman turned to face him. She stared at Lucy's face, took in the wide eyes, the eyelashes like the spikes of a sea urchin, the unreal texture of her skin, the puff of breath coming from between red, pouted lips that stayed motionless even as she spoke. 'Take them off,' Lucy repeated.

There was a brief moment when the woman could have saved herself, but that time had already passed. She was rooted to the ground by fear, her cigarette falling in embers as the blade whipped towards her.

Lucy was at the woman's throat before she could take her next breath. He caught the acrid tinge of something familiar: the same stench his mother's sheets had towards the end. As he held the woman tight against him he looked down to see a tell-tale stream of pee darkening the tan hue of her tights.

'No, please,' she whispered as he held the knife to her neck. 'Please, please,' she pleaded again, crying.

Jesus, he hated it when they cried. That's why he preferred to finish them before they understood what was happening. *Ignorance was bliss* – hadn't they learnt a damn thing since Eve?

He drew the knife cleanly across her throat. The crying stopped.

He dragged her body to the playground hidden behind a tall row of oak trees, laid her limp body across the rubber mulch, took out the phial of holy water and set about doing God's work.

Chapter 37

The councilman's office was thick with the fug of sweat and the sickly aroma of Harden Jones's lunch, which was still sitting in containers across his desk. Glyn Lewis's skin was prickling under the layers of his T-shirt and hoodie. He glanced over at Kimble McLain – he looked as cool as a cucumber while he listened intently to the councilman.

'Snipping at the red tape as we speak,' Harden Jones said, making an exaggerated cutting gesture with his stubby fingers.

McLain smiled. 'I knew you were our man, Harden.'

'Aye, there's a fair way to go yet,' the councilman said, loosening his garish tie decorated with cartoon leeks, and pushing his leftover lunch to the side. 'The committee in Caernarvon's on board, they just need to schedule the vote. Lazy buggers over on that side, too busy drinking their bloody craft beers and whatnot, bloody miracle they get anything done.' Harden leant his thick arms across the desk and lowered his voice. 'The Crown Land, though, that's another matter.'

'Crown Land?' Lewis asked.

'You'll be digging under the seabed between the mainland and Anglesey, that belongs to her most Excellent Majesty,' Harden said, sliding an official document, stamped with the Royal Coat of Arms, towards McLain. 'Back in 1983, the construction of the Conway Tunnel took an Act of Parliament and the Lords Spiritual and Temporal and Commons before they could raise a divot.'

'Do I need to write to the Queen personally?' McLain asked.

'No. But I'm just a council member, Kimble. You might get the investment you need, but without the political backing to get this in front of Parliament you'll be dead in the water. Make sure all those Welsh Government, EU MP's and the like are at your bash next week. I can introduce you, but that's about as far as my influence goes.'

Harden hesitated and turned over a copy of the morning's Daily Post. 'This isn't doing you any favours,' he said, pointing at the headline: *Six Billion Dollar Man's Assistant Brutally Murdered.*

McLain pushed the paper back across the desk. 'Not even a photograph of her, just me getting out of my car at the track. How the hell do they even get these?'

'We should have got out in front of it, Kimble,' Lewis said, his teeth on edge and his words coming out in staccato, angry bursts. 'We're not controlling the story. We can limit the damage, I can have something posted in less than an hour.'

'And the damage to our project, Harden, what are the costs there?' McLain asked.

Harden shrugged. 'None at all. Well, not at the moment, anyway. Like your lad here says, may not be a bad thing to address the press, plenty want to clip the wings on this project before it's even on the runway. New Labour, Plaid fucking Cymru, not to mention the eco-warrior do-gooders. Remember all the shit that hit the fan with those wind farms on the island? They'll be at your door with pitchforks and tar after the first drill hits the dirt.'

Lewis clenched his fists, his body tensing. 'You can't let that happen, Harden. This is the Foundation's legacy, you assured us all this was under control. You promised you'd manage it.'

McLain gestured for Lewis to ease off. 'I understand, Harden, circumstances are not optimal at present. I assume we still retain your support for the exploratory committee, that's not in dispute?

'Never was.' Harden assured him.

McLain smiled and extended his hand. 'Good. We've both got too much to lose for that to happen.'

* * *

'Maybe ease off on the throttle, Lewis, I've got enough unwarranted police attention.' McLain's voice was calm, controlled.

Lewis complied and brought the Range Rover to just below the speed limit. His mind, though, was racing, with a single focus on Liam Fowler's smug, arrogant face as he'd made his demands known earlier that morning. And now this with Harden Jones. It was like a conspiracy; a hewing at the sapling before the tree had the opportunity to even splay its roots.

'Pull in,' McLain said, gesturing at the lay-by overlooking the strait. 'You know, Glyn, we humans like to over complicate things, makes us feel more important I suppose.'

He pointed towards the handsome, grey bridge spanning a hundred feet above the water. 'When he finally got approval for construction, the government had one stipulation for Telford: no scaffolding. They required enough clearance for the naval ships to pass under. Telford could have fought it but instead he did what any great engineer does, he found alternative means. Chains, cables, iron bars, limestone. Necessity breeds creativity, Glyn, and with it, simplicity.'

Lewis gripped his hands around the steering wheel until his knuckles peaked white. He wasn't in the mood for a history lesson, not today. 'Fowler's toxic, Kimble, a blight that needs to be exiled.'

'You think you know him, Lewis?'

'Render the man according to his work.'

'Really?'

'If we give him what he wants, who's to say he won't come back for more?'

'And if he doesn't?'

Lewis took a slow, deep breath. 'There's only one thing more dangerous than a man with your resources, Kimble, and that's a man who has nothing left to lose.'

McLain winced. 'Lay off the blockbusters for a while, Glyn, you're beginning to sound like a bad action movie. It's not helpful. Our vector does not play out like this.'

McLain reached for the CD player and switched on his favourite Chopin track. 'That Manx character, any velocity?'

'Maybe. But he's not our irritant.'

McLain rested back on the headrest, closed his eyes and let the mollifying piano runs of Chopin's 'Nocturne in C Sharp Minor' flow through him.

Glyn Lewis, though, was seething. The meeting was the trailer to the main event, he was sure of it. Harden was painting the devil on the wall – sooner or later he'd point to it and tell them it was there all the time – if they chose to ignore it then it was their problem. He couldn't allow that to happen. Harden needed to start to earn his keep and Fowler needed to be persuaded to keep quiet. *'Your eye shall not pity,'* he thought to himself.

Chapter 38

BY late Thursday morning, the police activity around the playground had subsided. The woman's body had been discovered by one of the groundsmen. *Thank God for small mercies,* Manx thought; the notion of a young kid running into that mess on their way to school sent a shudder through his bones.

The Forensic Manager was directing the team to bag the remainder of the evidence when DCI Ellis Canton arrived. 'Three bodies in the space of a couple of weeks, Tudor,' he said, watching the body being loaded into the ambulance. 'The spotlight's growing brighter by the day.'

'Then we step out of it, Ellis,' Manx said.

Canton gestured at the clutch of press on the far side of the cordon. 'Easier said than done. The Super and the force's Press Office are pushing for a full briefing. The beast requires its nourishment.'

'Tomorrow? Buy us some time to process the evidence.'

'You've got until three this afternoon.'

Manx was about to protest, but he sensed the stress in the chief's voice – a serious tone that alerted him that this wasn't a negotiation, it was an order.

'Question, Tudor,' Canton said. 'How many bodies before we can confidently say we have a serial killer on our hands?'

'Three or more, in separate events that appear to be connected.'

'Bugger,' Canton said, wiping his palm across his face.

Manx could almost see the weight of his words settle like coal sacks across Canton's broad shoulders. 'We're about to be fed to the fucking wolves.'

Chapter 39

Manx sat in his office, picking aimlessly at a container of penne arrabiata left over from the lunch delivery – too spicy for his taste – and replayed the footage from the murders of Sian Conway and Margaret Langley side by side.

The killer was the same person; it had to be. The face, despite the poor video quality, had the same vacant stare. The eyes were large and too symmetrical and the nose too sharply drawn. It reminded Manx of Michael Jackson's nose after the countless surgeries, as if it belonged to another face entirely. The long, red hair was tied into school-girl bunches with thick, white ribbons.

Everything about what Manx watched screamed fifty shades of wrong. Her awkward walk; the gait of her step, long and wide; the swing of her arms, stiff and controlled. It reminded Manx of the collection he'd seen at McLain's house; what had he called them? Articulated dolls? That's what she reminded him of: a stiff-jointed doll. The more he replayed the footage, an idea began to take shape.

He pulled up the forensics files. The compound under Sian's fingernails was a combination of rubber and latex. The full report on Margaret Langley was pending, but she hadn't had the time to fight back; it was all she could do to pee herself.

Manx walked into the incident room. 'Nader. Find out who might use rubber and latex compounds in their products.'

'Got a hunch you want to share, boss?' the sergeant asked.

'Occam's razor, Nader,' Manx said. 'When something looks too complicated or unfathomable, go back to basics, assume the simplest explanation not the complex one.'

Chapter 40

Wash away their sins and clothe them in righteousness – his father would recite the words at the dinner table most evenings – *that dying and being raised with Christ they might share in his final victory.* After all his work, to be reunited with God, that would be his final victory.

He looked around his frugal accommodations – the same room he'd lived in as a child: first floor, last room down the hall. There was scant evidence of his childhood left now, other than the same peeling wallpaper and threadbare carpet that had been here when he arrived. Any further evidence he was ever here was now gone; drowned like a cat in a bag. Maybe it was better that way, memories were pain, but pain was also good as *they* reminded him; the reminder of pain would serve to keep him on the true path.

His memories of that time were like the fragments of a shattered mirror — disjointed and fractured. Running with his parents from the dock to a waiting car, the cold snapping at his bare legs, driving for what seemed like an endless night until they arrived here. They were home now his parents insisted. It didn't feel like home to him. Home was the lap of the warm ocean over his feet, the sweat glistening on his shoulders, the smell of Skunk Cabbage when the sun was at its highest point of the day.

He was alone much of the time as his parents busied themselves preparing the church. At least he was close to the forest and could play amongst the Corsican pines while the ravens cackled in the branches. Their calls always seemed to be taunting him, mocking him as he played.

At the end of the forest, the trees gave way to a ridge of sand dunes that skirted the ocean, though it was far too cold to venture any further than his ankles. Instead, he would stare at the restless mass, wondering if it was the same ocean he'd left behind. Maybe if he waited long enough, like the first twist of the hot water tap, the warm rush of water would finally reach the shore. It never did.

Hours went by as he lost himself in the Bible. He talked with the others who were learning the word of God, just like him. There was a young woman who took pity on him. Her face was warm and kind; *like an angel*, he thought. She played with him, read him Bible verses. *'Marsden, my little laddie,'* she'd call out to him. For the first time in his life he felt what love could be – not the harsh whip of the belt or the stiff back of a hand across his face – the kind of love his father would dispense. But this too, eventually, would be ripped from him.

Chapter 41

'Into the den of corporate bullshit,' Manx said to Canton as they walked into the briefing room later that afternoon. Inside, the air was lean and tense, like tripwire.

'Play nice, Manx,' Canton said. 'No point in poking the bear in the eye for the sheer hell of it.'

'Wait until I have a good reason?'

'That's the spirit,' Canton said, patting Manx on the back.

Manx's worst fears were confirmed. Malcolm Laird, the force's Head of Press and Media was as stiff as his online photograph implied: late forties, a padded down comb-over and cheeks puffed and blushed with decades of four-pint lunches. His tone was monotonous and rehearsed; a nap-inducing drawl of corporate-speak wrapped in a neat bow of meaningless waffle. Mercifully, his speech to the Major Investigation Team on the three P's of Policing, *'Public Trust, Perception, and Purpose,'* was cut short by the entrance of a tall, spectre-like presence that seemed to suck the air from the room as she entered.

Manx had first met Detective Chief Superintendent Vera Troup on the steps of St Asaph's Police Headquarters a few months ago when she'd publicly commended his 'heroic and beyond the call of duty actions' in solving the Anglesey Blue case. *She didn't look much in the mood for showering praise today,* Manx thought, as she directed her stern gaze towards Malcolm Laird and stabbed impatiently at her wrist watch.

The local coppers had taken to calling Vera, 'ElVera' on account of her jet-black hair, which she wore long and straight, and the translucent pallor of her skin; as if sunshine was something she avoided at all costs, like carbohydrates and refined sugar. Her one concession to her femininity was her bright red lipstick, which she applied on her lips like blood across snow.

Laird quickly wrapped up, conceding the spotlight to DCS Troup who took a few seconds to size up the room before speaking.

'You probably think I'm here to give you a pep talk, one of those motivational speeches that gets you all fired up, lights a fire under your arses?' she said, making sure she made eye contact with each of the officers. 'Well, tough shit, I don't do those.'

A low murmur of hesitant laughter filled the room.

'Here's a fact: if you're not already on fire, you don't belong here. And by the virtue that you are all here I'll take it as a given that you'd each sell your own grandmothers to solve this case.'

'How about the mother-in-law?' DS Nader offered. 'I'd sell her at the drop of a hat.'

'If I were your mother-in-law, Sergeant,' Troup said, 'I'd probably write the advert myself.'

This time the laughter was unrestrained. Nader shrugged his thick shoulders and accepted the ribbing with a nod of his head.

'Right, settle,' Troup said, pacing the room. 'By tomorrow morning the phrase *serial killer* will be headline news. The press will coat this with a sheen of glamour, start quoting half-truths, pocket book psychology, bring in so-called experts. But they're wrong. Murder is not glamorous. We're police officers, we're aware of the lives it destroys and the families it tears apart, which is why whatever nonsense the papers choose to print, none of it will distract you from your duties to lawfully and diligently solve this case.'

Troup leant on PC Priddle's desk, addressing him directly. 'Three people murdered, on our watch, it's a fucking sobering thought, right?'

The young PC blushed and nodded. 'Yes, ma'am.'

'Yes ma'am, indeed.' Troup stood up and addressed the room. 'Three murders and we don't have a scrap of positive news to share with the families of these victims. Nothing. I won't be the first to say this, or the last. The press will not let up, the public won't hold back in their criticism, even your nearest and fucking dearest won't let you off the hook. And you know what, they shouldn't, and that's going to hurt like a knife in the gut. So, what do you do? You channel all that bile and anger into this investigation, every last ounce of it, because it's not just your job to solve these murders…'

Troup let her words settle in the air for a few moments for dramatic impact '… It's your job to prevent the next one.'

This time the room fell silent, each officer processing his own thoughts on the Chief Superintendent's words.

'This case is now a Category A investigation. For those of you unsure what that means, a Category A is a case of grave public concern, where vulnerable members of the public are at risk, the identity of the offender is not apparent and significant resource allocation is required to secure evidence. In other words, no freeze on overtime, you'll be working your arses off, and you can kiss goodbye to any holiday plans until our suspect is apprehended. Clear?'

There was a shuffling of chairs and a mumbling of agreement.

'I'll be sending a support team from St Asaph. Canton, I expect you'll find them a room with decent internet access and working phone lines. They'll be here to help, not hinder your investigation. Use them.'

Troup stuffed her hands in her trouser pockets and gestured at Manx. 'The floor is yours, Inspector. Now, weave me an irresistible story about how you're going to catch this offender before he strikes again. And in case you've heard rumours to the contrary, I'm a big fan of happy endings.'

Manx walked to the centre of the room. 'Sian Conway, Gwynfor Evans, Margaret Langley, were all murdered in a similar manner. Video footage of the first murder shows a woman's face as she kills Sian Conway. We also have CCTV footage from the bus stop where Margaret Langley was attacked, also by the same woman.'

'Goes against all conventional wisdom and criminal profiles, Inspector,' Troup said. 'Women serial killers are a rare species, almost mythical, like unicorns.'

'I have another theory,' Manx said.

The room turned its full attention to the inspector. 'The video footage shows what looks like a woman, but if you look closer, something's not right. The issue is more pronounced in the CCTV from the bus stop. Her movements don't match those of a female. The gait is clunky, the walking too stilted.'

'A man dressed as a woman?' Troup said. 'We're looking for a transvestite serial killer?'

'More sophisticated,' Manx said. 'The plastic residue we analysed from the crime scenes, specifically from Sian Conway's murder, is a combination of latex and rubber that's used in the film industry for prosthetics and make-up for special effects.'

'A mask?' Troup asked.

'A full body suit,' Manx countered. 'I think our killer is wearing a full, latex body suit, maybe custom made for him, which he wears when he murders the victims.'

Troup swallowed hard. 'Consider my full attention gained, Inspector,' she said.

'Living Dolls,' Manx said, loading a Google search page of images. 'A subculture of men who like to dress like dolls. They wear body suits, masks, anything that makes them more feminine. We believe the residue found under the first victim's fingernails is the same compound of latex and rubber used in the manufacture of these body suits.'

'You find the company, find who they shipped to and bingo you nail the killer,' Troup said.

'It's a soft lead,' Manx said.

'But a lead nonetheless,' Troup offered. 'Do we think the murders are sexual in nature, acting out some twisted fantasy?'

'The female victims had evidence of picquerism, multiple stab wounds around the thighs and lower torso, that implies some sexual motive, but the male was clean. So, difficult to tell at this point.'

Troup looked directly at Laird. 'Details to be withheld, Malcolm.'

'We'll have to give them something, ma'am,' Laird said. 'We ask for the public's help, usual protocol.'

'And how would that play out? We alert the public to be on the lookout for a serial killer dressed in a bloody doll suit a few weeks before Easter bank holiday? No, contain it. The murders are unconnected, the force is deploying all its resources to solving the cases, members of the public are asked to be diligent and report anything they think is suspicious. That, Malcolm, is our usual protocol at this stage.'

Troup turned her attention to Manx. 'Inspector, I want you to talk to a friend of mine.' She scribbled on a scrap of paper. 'Daniel Alvarez at Bangor University. He profiled serial killers in the past before taking a cosy tenure over at the university. He's a bit full of himself, but most Americans are. Call him, make an appointment. That's an order.'

Manx took the paper.

'Anything else that connects any of these murders? Anything that would suggest a motive?' Troup asked.

Manx hesitated. 'Kimble McLain,' he said. 'Sian Conway was his assistant, Evans was his tenant, and our latest victim, Margaret Langley was one of his house cleaners.'

'Statistically, it's not that relevant. People in McLain's position know a lot of people, goes with the territory.'

'So he mentioned,' Manx said.

'You already approached him?' Troup said. 'That explains all the missed fucking calls. Anything concerning Kimble McLain goes through me, understand.'

'He's already lied to us…' Manx began.

Troup held her finger in the air in a hush manner. 'I know you see yourself as bit of a maverick, Inspector, but we tread with caution where Kimble McLain is concerned. No skirting the law, bending the rules to suit your investigation. By the book, all the way. Got it?'

Manx nodded. You were only ever as good as your last solved case, that was true of every copper, proving yourself never stopped. There was always the next case and what had gone before was the past. It was part of the job, he understood that, but it smarted just the same.

Chapter 42

He hated the other one on sight: a serious looking boy, his hair blonder than his, he was thinner too, all skin and bones. He'd put on weight since he'd come to the island, his father had taken to calling him chubby, or if he was feeling kindly, the fatted calf. The other boy always had his head stuck in a book, the kinds of books that questioned God's creation, tried to explain it away with science; books his parents had long since banned from the house.

The other one had arrived at the beginning of the summer holiday, a hot July day. From the moment he arrived, his 'angel' had turned her attention towards him. He was now thirteen, the other boy maybe a couple of years younger – he never spoke to him long enough to ask.

Was there anything crueller than that? To give love then to take it away? The way she showered the boy with affection, held his hand, read the books with him just like she'd read the Bible with him the summer before.

She'd always beckon him to join them, but he wanted no part of sharing. He was no longer her 'little laddie.'

Late that summer, he saw the boy wander into the forest. He followed him and watched as he sat under one of the pine trees, sketching the ravens perched on their branches. They were conspiring to hurt him, the boy and the ravens, he was sure of it.

He watched for a while. It was at that moment he first heard *their* voices. He was unworthy of her love, *they* said. This Raven Boy was a Godless urchin sent to taunt and tempt him like the devil had tempted Jesus for forty days and forty nights in the wilderness. He needed to be taught a lesson, this Raven Boy, a lesson he'd carry for life.

Empowered, he ran towards him, pushing the boy to the ground, ripped his sketches and scattered them on the forest floor.

'Raven Boy,' he spat at him and picked up a stone that was the perfect fit for his hand. He bought it down on the crouching boy's head.

A sting of satisfaction rang through him. He dropped the stone and ran, the cackles of the ravens echoing through the high branches as he headed back to the church where he would kneel and beg for forgiveness.

He fell back onto his mattress, his mind now a million miles away from that summer. He laid his head on the thin pillow with the feathers that prickled at his cheeks. But the feathers were like the splinters from the ship's hold; a pain to be endured as a reminder of his sins and the redemption still to come. He opened the trinket box and looked at the photograph of the young woman; her hair long, her eyes bright blue and filled with the innocence of youth. He had found her again, but she too had betrayed him. After all the hopes he had harboured, it turned out his angel was a whore too, just like the others.

Chapter 43

Thick ropes ran across the woman's chest and thighs, biting deep into her canary-yellow dress. Another woman, Amazon in stature with a mink pelt drawn across her chest, stood over the cowering body of a man, her gold-barrelled pistol aimed at his face and her steely smile punctuated with the tip of her cigarette holder. A ripped bodice hung with a seductive wink from the shoulder of the next woman, revealing a milky temptation of cleavage as a man with a wolf-like grin watched her scream in terror.

'Wouldn't get away with this sort of overt sexuality back in Berkeley,' Doctor Daniel Alvarez said, striding into his office. 'The head of feminist studies would be shitting in her pant suit before storming to the Dean's office with her Birkenstocks in a twist complaining about male oppression and female objectification. As if it hadn't been so since our ancestors dragged their womenfolk back to the cave.'

He closed the door and shook Manx's hand. 'I guess I'm a sucker for the laid back vibes in your green and pleasant lands. I could do without the weather though, probably why you have so many pubs, shelter from all the rain.'

'Hadn't thought of it that way,' Manx said, looking over the neatly framed rows of book covers with titles like *Kill Me A Little*, *Naked When We Die*, and *My Lover Wears Black*.

'First edition pulp fiction,' Alvarez explained. 'They captured the zeitgeist of the time. Serial killers were just emerging as a phenomenon. People were crammed into cities, it bred frustration and violence, living so close to our human brethren. These books weren't so much escapism as they were means of projection; read all about it in the pages of some pulp novel and maybe it won't happen to you. We humans are very adept at finding coping mechanisms to fit the age we live in. Take terrorism. We stick our heads in the sand box of those devices we're so attached to because the alternative's too goddamned petrifying to contemplate; and, if we look up for a second, we might be faced with what's really scaring the bloody hell out of us...'

The doctor looked Manx directly in the eyes. 'That we're powerless to stop any of it.'

Manx nodded, not quite sure of the correct response and noticing Alvarez's use of the phrase '*bloody hell*' – it always sounded peculiar when said with an American accent, as if it were being tried on for size and was rarely the correct fit.

'Vera Troup—' Manx began.

'Whip smart, that one,' Alvarez said, sitting behind his desk. 'So, I'm guessing you're one of her front line troops?'

'Detective Inspector,' Manx said.

'I'll never get used to the police rankings in this country. Constable this, sergeant that. Still, if Vera sent you, I'm guessing there's a clusterfuck brewing.'

Alvarez was in his late sixties, Manx guessed, with a permanent tan that spoke of days spent under a cloudless Californian sky. He had close-cropped grey hair and bright, inquisitive eyes. He wore what Manx understood as a 'soul-patch' beard, peppered with grey, under his bottom lip.

Alvarez gestured Manx to sit. 'So, give me the download.'

Manx hesitated. There was something unnerving about the man. His directness was probably an American trait, but there was something more, a charismatic intellect that Manx guessed made his lectures amongst the most well-attended on campus.

'Anything we discuss in here is confidential. By your body language, I'm guessing you're only here at Vera's request, so let's cut to the chase.'

Manx respected the man's honesty and took a deep breath before briefing Alvarez on the highlights of the case.

'So,' Alvarez said a few minutes later, passing his fingertip over his postage-stamp of a beard. 'A killer who kills while wearing a doll suit, performs picquerism on his female victims, but not the male, and extracts the liver. Quite the laundry list.'

'Any immediate thoughts?'

'Why he removes the liver? The liver purifies the blood. The Egyptians called it the seat of the soul, the Babylonians thought it had the power to predict the future and often used it in sacrificial rituals. It's a powerful metaphor, however you slice it.'

Manx blanched at the doctor's humour. 'And there's this,' he said, handing Alvarez a copy of the note. 'He left one in the liver of each of the victims.'

Alvarez studied the note. 'Unusual. It's taken from the Catholic Douay Rheims translation. Later translations simplified it, but it's the same message; put God before all lustful desires. I have an PhD in theology, in case you're wondering, but like REM, I lost my religion a long time ago. Turned to more secular pursuits, the pay's better and the students better looking.'

'So, he could be a Catholic?' Manx said, unimpressed. 'That narrows it down to a few million.'

'Methodists, Baptists, Seventh Day Adventist, take your pick. This version of the Bible was widely used by missionaries to spread the good word. Cheap prints were lighter to ship to whatever Godless corner of the world they wanted to infect. Not that there's much in it, after all, every translation says pretty much the same thing, it's the interpretations that fucked up the world.'

'Religion aside, any other conclusions?'

Alvarez rose and walked towards the window. 'The FBI recognises several categories of serial killers. This one, I'd venture to say falls into the mission-driven category. If he's leaving biblical quotations at the scene, he's on a mission. The picquerism shows signs of sexual latency, but it's not his sole motive.'

'What sort of mission?' Manx asked.

'Why do any of us do what we do, Manx? We're all driven by something: selfish needs, desires or maybe he's directed by outside forces, like Joan of Arc for instance.'

'Visions?' Manx said. 'Pretty far-fetched, Alvarez. In my experience criminals make a choice and inevitably they end up making the wrong one.'

Alvarez smiled. 'Have you ever read *The Dawn of Consciousness in the Bicameral Mind*, Inspector Manx?'

'Unless it was written by Lee Child, no.'

Alvarez walked back to his desk. 'Julian Jaynes believed that, for hundreds of thousands of years, we humans were automatons acting on orders from God. It made things very simple, no internal life, no existential dilemmas to wrestle with. You did as you were instructed, no questions. Then, around three-thousand-years ago, that all changed. The great Greek dawn of human consciousness took root, maybe precipitated by a natural disaster or war, but with it came the burden of consciousness, self-doubt, ambition, envy; all that messy stuff that makes us human.'

'I'm not quite—' Manx said, wondering where the hell this lecture was heading and if his time wouldn't be best spent in the pub throwing more imaginary darts at the investigation.

'Stay with me, Manx,' Alvarez urged. 'Humanity eventually lost the ability to hear His voice. God had, in effect, shut the fuck up, and we, his children, were lost. Three thousand years later, we're still trying to get him to answer.'

'How does this help my case, Alvarez?' Manx asked, the pangs of impatience gnawing.

'Getting there, Manx. As humanity became the sheep lost in the wilderness, a rare few still heard the voice of God: prophets, soothsayers, call them what you will, but these people were treated with reverence and respect; they were the conduits to the lost word of God. These days we casually label them schizophrenic and shovel drugs down their throats.'

'So, you think our killer is schizophrenic, hearing voices?'

'As I said, we all need a reason to do something. The notes, the removal of the liver and the trussing of the bodies, it's ritualistic, as if he's being directed.'

'This might all sound great in a lecture, but do you have anything actually practical? Troup mentioned you profiled these kinds of cases,' Manx said, checking his watch.

'Sure, I can give you the textbook download. He's no more than forty years old, if psychopaths haven't surrendered to their baser instincts by then, they probably never will. He'll be local, most predators don't tend to stray too far from home. He recently faced a traumatic event that triggered this behaviour; the death of a parent, a loved one, his dog. He's a functioning member of society, blends in wherever he goes. But, you could have read this yourself, Manx, you're here because you think that if you understand his motive the better chance you have of finding him before he kills again. That's your biggest worry, am I right? Another victim?'

Manx stiffened. 'Right. So, we're looking for a male, no more than forty years old who suffered a loss recently and is hearing voices that are telling him to murder innocent people. Outstanding. Glad I came.'

'Innocent to you and I, Inspector, not to him.'

'I've never been convinced about this kind of criminal profiling, Alvarez,' Manx said. 'It's too narrow at the start of an investigation and too broad once we're in the middle of it. I find most cases are solved by good old fashioned coppering.'

Alvarez smiled. 'Coppering? I'll have to add that to the lexicon,' he said. 'Here's my advice, take it or leave it. You're dealing with someone who's religiously motivated, probably deluding himself he's doing the work of God. He's a zealot, and zealots aren't born, they're made.'

'Made? How?'

'Parents. Most likely a father figure who didn't spare the rod and a submissive mother, a very strict religious upbringing.'

'You mentioned something about missionaries earlier?' Manx said, catching sight of a faint glimpse of clarity amid the confusion.

'The most zealous of the zealots. I can't imagine this part of the world had a shortage of recruits.'

Manx made a note. 'What about the doll suit, any thoughts? Practical ones.'

Alvarez sat back. 'Not having personally studied him, I'd guess it's classic deflection. When he's wearing the suit he's someone else, it makes it easier to deflect the guilt. He'd be a fascinating case study. Once he's apprehended, I'd appreciate an opportunity to interview him, I'm guessing he's harbouring some pretty interesting demons.'

'He's a murderer, not a test case, Alvarez,' Manx said, getting up to leave. 'If you do get to interview him, it'll be in prison.'

'Who cares where it is? I'm damned sure he won't,' Alvarez said, guiding Manx towards the door. 'Remember, he's not too different to millions of other lost souls out there, Inspector, waiting on God in a godless world.'

*   *   *

The doctor's words still resonated with Manx an hour later as he stood on the pier at Beaumaris and lit his first King Edward of the day. The Strait was calm with the mere traces of whitecaps where it met the Irish Sea. The tide was out, revealing a wide torso of mud flats with the stick-figure peaks of boats abandoned like children's beach toys awaiting the incoming tide. Around him the 'oggy, oggy, oggy' bark of seagulls cut through the silence.

'Waiting for God in a godless world' – Alvarez's parting shot had taken Manx down a deep rabbit hole he was just now emerging from. Not one to adhere to fanciful theories, Alvarez's words had nonetheless struck a chord with Manx. He'd never believed in God, at least not an omniscient being who looked over everyone. If that were true, where was he looking the day his sister disappeared?

But the doctor's theory, as outrageous at it was, appealed to Manx's investigative nature. Alvarez had pegged religion, that was for sure, people searching for divine guidance, or purpose, and desperate to put their faith in some higher power. Maybe Alvarez was right and the killer was acting under some divine instruction. How this helped him, he had no idea, and was running on fumes with the mere whiff of evidence guiding his senses. Alvarez's offhand comment on church missionaries, though, had sparked an idea. He was about to call the station and direct the team to contact the Archdioceses of Bangor for some preliminary research, when his mobile buzzed. A text from his sister, Sara, reminding him he was looking after his nephew Dewi tomorrow.

He hadn't forgotten to book the adventure park? Or that he was picking him up early, eight o'clock?

Shit. It was the last thing he needed.

Didn't forget. He replied, having of course, completely forgotten. *And yes, I'm looking forward to it.* He tapped send before launching his web browser and searching for nearby adventure parks.

Chapter 44

It should frighten him, being here after everything that had happened, instead it brought him a sense of peace. He couldn't remain here for long, the ceiling was low and the light from the old kerosene lamp was barely enough to read. If he pored too long over the names, his back would cramp, but it was a small price to pay.

A few years after settling into the church, his father had received a van full of paintings, each one the same, printed on thin paper and framed with cheap wood. At the top of the picture was the all-seeing eye of God bearing down through the clouds. Below were two winding pathways, one leading to the heavens and signposted with charitable deeds and sacrifice, and the other, leading to the depths of a burning hell fire littered with the temptations of the flesh and sinful appropriations. He would stand in front of the painting, losing himself in the images and their meaning while his father, moist from sweat and anticipation, knelt at his waist.

'You're a good boy, Marsden. God loves good boys,' his father would mutter as he went about his business. It was wrong, he knew that in the deepest pit of his soul, but it felt good to be loved, even for those brief minutes when his father would fall, knee bound, muttering incantations with dewy lips to his son. He felt powerless at the will of his father, at least until afterwards, when the tables would turn and he would become the powerful one as his father scrambled at his feet begging for forgiveness. His forgiveness.

He was Beniah now, *they* had told him. The soldier that defeated the Lion in Snow, the warrior that led David's Guard.

Like David, Beniah had slain giants and commanded great forces. He would be a General with an army of one, *they* had instructed him, and would be tasked with the cleansing of souls and delivering them at the feet of God – he would be the Lord's anointed Beniah.

The charge filled him with power; the kind of power he felt when Father had begged for his forgiveness. If there was one thing the painting had taught him, it was this: only God could forgive, Beniah would provide the soul, ready to accept divine justice.

He opened the old ledger and ran his finger down the list of names. It had taken him months to trace them all. Some had moved away, others had already died; damned for eternity and probably roasting on the devil's spit. But the ones that were still here on the island would be the first. Later, he could find the others. It would take time, but he had plenty of that. He wrote their addresses in the margins of the ledger and studied them with the patience of Job and the tenacity of Noah. He was Beniah made flesh. Him and Lucy.

He would need to leave soon or else she'd ask too many questions. Best to adhere to her whims, at least for now. Her sins would be paid for later, when she had outlived her usefulness. She provided him with shelter, that was all, but *there was always shelter under the roof of God for the true believer* – she had told him. What was that saying? One saved soul is worth an eternity in heaven? Eternity, it was a comforting thought as he underlined the next name in the ledger.

He guided the faint glow of the lamp towards the newspaper clipping and studied the face. The snow-tipped peaks of Snowdonia Mountain Range loomed in the background. In the foreground a bright yellow JCB digger gleamed in the sunlight, and to its side two men shaking hands, smiling.

He took a deep breath and tensed his muscles. He'd need to be strong for this one. The men were always more trouble than the women.

Chapter 45

Manx didn't consider himself an impatient man, in fact, he valued patience as one of the cornerstones of being a good copper, but the last few hours with his nephew, Dewi, had stretched that consideration to its breaking point.

The omen for the day had been planted early in the morning. Dewi had clung like a limpet to his mother's legs as Manx waited at the doorway. Dewi was adamant he was going nowhere and wanted to stay with nan Alice. It required the exceptional bribe of the promise of fish and chips for dinner followed by ice cream and another encore viewing of *Finding Nemo* before he finally relented and threw himself, belly-down, on the back of the Jensen complaining that it 'smelled funny.' Manx quickly slid into the driver's seat and locked the doors.

'It's old, that's how old things smell,' Manx explained, spinning the back wheels on the loose gravel.

'Don't like old things,' Dewi said, struggling to clip his seatbelt.

'No one does,' Manx said, plugging his iPhone into the unsightly hole in the dashboard where he'd had a local mechanic, Lloyd Lugnut, dig around and jerry-rig an auxiliary port. It was an affront to purists, Manx imagined, and probably made the Jensen look like some old duchess trying to make herself look young and trendy with a nose-ring and shoulder tattoo. Not that he cared – the car was a means to an end, that was all. Any sentimental value had been stripped long ago.

He selected a playlist to see him through the thirty-minute journey from the island to Greenwood Forest Park – the only

123

attraction that was open this time of year and with enough distractions to keep a six-year-old occupied for the day.

Being Saturday, the park was swarming with harried parents scurrying after over-excited children jacked up on an early-morning sugar rush. Dewi had insisted Manx join him on the Green Dragon Coaster – a ride, that to Manx, resembled several green coal shuttles strung together on shaky metal tracks. After a while, a creeping nausea began to fill his stomach and he wondered if the boy was deliberately torturing him with an infinite loop of some parallel world that went nowhere and back again – it was uncomfortably close to his own life. On what Manx guessed was his seventh tour of duty, he persuaded Dewi it was lunchtime and he'd buy him a burger and a coke on the condition he didn't tell his mother.

The collusion appealed to the boy, and he followed Manx towards the Green Oak Cafe. As Manx queued, his mobile buzzed. Probably Sara checking up on him; he'd keep it short, tell her the boy was an angel and having a great time. He didn't need the white lie, it was PC Priddle.

'We got a lead on the company that makes the costumes, over near Bootle,' Priddle said. 'I described the face, they said it could be one of theirs, but they need to see it. I didn't think we should send it over via email, so I'm not sure—'

'We can't have that picture leaking all over the Internet.' Manx saved him the effort of an explanation. 'I'll call round, in person.'

Manx hung up; it was the first concrete lead they'd had. Alvarez's left field theories notwithstanding, this was the practical evidence he was looking for.

He leant down to ask Dewi what he wanted to eat, but this was another boy, younger and chubbier and appeared as if he might too burst into tears as the tall man loomed over him like a fairy-tale giant come to life.

'Shit!' Manx said to himself, frantically scouring the tables for any sign of Dewi. He was already gone.

He ran out into the courtyard and scanned the immediate area – no sign of the boy. The screams of children at the Solar

Splash water slide made him turn. He watched the kids skim down the long stretch of orange peel set against the canopy of green. He wasn't there. Where would he go? Maybe back to the coaster? Manx checked the queue and the ride. Dewi was nowhere in sight.

Manx was sweating, his initial twinge of concern turning into a mild panic. But he couldn't go there, not yet. He jogged around the perimeter, looking over the lines of kids queuing – they all had responsible parents in tow.

He was tempted to ask the other adults, but that could wait – he wasn't that desperate; at least not yet, and anyway what would he say? A six-year-old boy with blonde hair. He couldn't even remember what colour jacket he was wearing, or if he was even wearing one. And anyway, it would have been the same as admitting Dewi had gone missing on his watch, and what kind of copper loses a six-year-old in an adventure park? *A fucking stupid one,* he confirmed.

After about ten minutes of fruitless searching, he stopped to catch his breath. The worst of thoughts came to mind. Children were snatched all the time from under their parents' noses, most of them probably far more diligent than Manx. To the right of the main entrance he noticed the gift shop. He ran across the courtyard.

'So where did you arrange the meeting point if you were separated from your child?' the woman behind the counter asked, picking absentmindedly at the plaster over the back of her hand. Her name tag said Shelly in bright, primary colours.

Manx looked at her blankly.

'I see,' Shelly said, reaching for her radio. 'We always recommend parents make sure they have an agreed meeting point if they get separated. Common sense, like.'

'I'm not the parent,' Manx said, as if to absolve himself of all blame.

Shelly wasn't buying it and held her head at a slightly ironic angle as if to say, *'obviously.'* She turned her chin to her radio.

'Anyone seen a boy, six years old, goes by the name of Dewi? What was he wearing?' she asked, looking at Manx.

Manx shrugged. 'A jacket?'

Shelly let out a disappointed sigh. 'Hair colour?'

'Blonde, definitely blonde.'

Manx waited as Shelly relayed the information to the security patrol. 'Happens all the time,' she said to Manx, reaching over to ring up a customer buying a bright green plush-toy dragon. 'Kids, they get excited, can't control themselves.'

It didn't make him feel any better. He felt the judgemental stares of the other parents sear into him like hot pokers as he stepped aside and waited.

'Ten four,' Shelly said a few minutes later. 'There's been some sort of situation down by the Bunny Village. Sounds like it might be your lad,' she said.

'A situation at the Bunny Village?' Manx said, the words sounding even more ridiculous as he said them out loud.

Shelly pulled out a map, but Manx was already out of the door.

Dewi was sulking against the fence, a member of staff crouched in front of him. Next to him stood another boy, around Dewi's age. He was crying, holding a bloodied tissue to his nose, his parents fussing around him like a pair of humming birds.

'Christ, Dewi,' Manx said, jogging towards him. 'Don't ever do that to me again.'

Dewi looked up briefly then directed his gaze back to the floor.

'Oi! You this lad's dad then?' the man said, flapping nosily towards Manx, his fleshy cheeks purple with rage.

'No, I'm—'

'You're raising a bloody hooligan. Hit my son for no reason. The little bugger won't apologise either,' the man said, poking his index finger in Manx's face.

Manx gently pushed away the man's finger. He knew little about kids, but he understood human nature enough to know that people rarely lash out without a reason, however irrational it might be.

'Dewi, why did you hit this boy?'

Dewi scuffed his shoes in the dirt and kept his chin to his chest.

Manx crouched next to him. 'Listen, do you want your mam to find out about this? She might not let you come again, and you can kiss goodbye to that fish and chips and the film she promised you, probably send you straight to bed.'

Still nothing. Manx thought, then reverted to the behaviour he'd seen garner the most effective results earlier that morning.

'You know what, Dewi? I saw a Welsh dragon, like the one on the roller coaster, at the gift shop. You'd like one of those, right? I bet your friends don't have one.'

Dewi looked up and slumped his shoulders, realising he'd been outmanoeuvred. 'He said he was better than me because he had a dad to bring him here and I only had my uncle to bring me, so I hit him,' Dewi said flatly.

His words landed like a punch to Manx's gut.

'Still, no excuse is it? We should call the police, teach the boy a lesson,' the man said, slowly backing away.

Manx pulled out his badge. 'I am the police. Detective Inspector Manx. I can take your statement down at the station, should only take up a few hours of what's left of your Saturday.'

The man's wings seemed clipped as he stumbled over his words. 'Well, a policeman's son, he should know better.'

'As I tried to tell you, he's not my son,' Manx said, his patience now so gossamer thin he could feel it fraying at the edges.

'Well, whoever's son he is, he shouldn't be acting like that. At the least he needs to apologise to Bryn.'

Manx nodded. 'Fair enough. Dewi?'

'Sorry,' Dewi said turning to the boy, who had stopped crying and was already reaching to pet a large white rabbit that had hopped over to crinkle its nose at the commotion.

'Outstanding,' Manx said. 'Job done.'

* * *

The fifteen-mile drive back was mostly silent. Manx couldn't even find it in him to select a suitable playlist to listen to – there wasn't one for the collision of emotions he was feeling right now.

By the time twilight descended, like a slow dimming of the day over the Snowdonia mountains, Dewi was asleep on the back seat. As they crossed over to the island, he awoke, as if some instinct told him he was back home. Safe.

'Did my dad go away because of the bad men, Uncle Tudor?' Dewi asked, his words slurred with sleep as if he were dreaming the conversation.

Manx swallowed hard and searched for the right response, of which there was only one. Honesty.

'Very bad,' he confirmed.

'Was my dad a bad man too?'

Manx took a deep breath. This question was one that Manx himself had wrestled with. Whatever Shanni Morgan was, it wasn't his place to pass judgment on him, not in front of his son. 'Your dad loved you and did everything he could to make your and your mam happy, Dewi,' Manx said.

Dewi seemed satisfied with the response, and placed the green dragon Manx had bought him against his head and drifted off again.

Manx looked back at the boy, his tiny chest rising and falling like the steady swell of a calm sea. Did the guilt ever stop, he wondered? Would the mistakes he made, and still blamed himself for, set the rot in this boy's life too? Dewi's father had died because of a cascade of fuck ups that were even now hard for Manx to accept. *At least there was time,* he thought. Dewi would recover, but a niggling thought was beginning to take shape. Maybe he should make more of an effort to be part of his nephew's life, not that he needed another tether to the island, but he felt he owed something to the boy, however meagre it might be.

Chapter 46

Night dropped like a brick over the island; heavy and fast. Seven minutes past nine. Glyn Lewis was running late. He should have been there at nine. Not that it mattered; he imagined Fowler wasn't a stickler for punctuality.

A short text message was all he offered: *Information on the murders. Bring money. Newborough Beach Car Park, 9pm Saturday.* No sender ID. But he knew it was Fowler, it had the same curt efficiency he'd come to expect from him.

Money, the same old beef; the thought irritated him as he eased the Range Rover into a lay-by and began the mile-long walk to the car park. Greed – it would be Fowler's ultimate undoing, he was certain of that.

Lewis clicked his torch and shone it across the thick trunks of pine trees lining the track that twisted down towards the beach. It was closed to traffic this time of year. *Probably why Fowler wanted to meet here, the fewer witnesses the better*, Lewis thought.

He tipped the beam skywards and across the finger spread of branches flickering nervously in the breeze. Under his boots, the undergrowth cracked and shattered like dry bird bones. The tale of *Little Red Riding Hood* came to mind:

'My, what big teeth you have Grandma!'

'All the better to chew you and spit you out, Glyn.'

He shook the thought from his head and followed the spill of light towards the sea which was folding itself in a steady slap and slosh against the shoreline.

Twelve thousand pounds. It was more than McLain had agreed to. He could have probably bartered with Fowler, beaten him down on the price, but that would have entailed more human contact than he was prepared to deal with. He wasn't well equipped for those kinds of negotiations; the subtle diplomacies that required a careful reading of the opposition's facial expressions or body language.

As he entered the car park, the steely clouds fractured to reveal a full-bellied moon low on the horizon. Fowler was waiting for him, the outline of his frame like a paper cut-out against the moonlight. He noticed a pinpoint of red and a swirl of smoke; he didn't know Fowler was a smoker. *Another vice, along with avarice to add to the list*, he thought.

'That's far enough.' A terse bark, followed by a harsh cackle – a smoker's cough if ever he heard one.

Fowler was dressed in black, a wide-brimmed hat — *a trilby*, Lewis guessed — pulled low and tight over his brow.

'Bit dramatic isn't it?'

'Put the money on the table.'

Lewis slid an envelope from inside his jacket and edged towards the picnic table.

'In the middle, then walk away.'

Lewis followed only half of the direction.

'Not without what we're paying for. Lay it on the table, I take it, we both walk away.'

Another bleak cough, followed by a drag on the cigarette to ease the pain. A flick of red light fell over his face. Lewis studied it. It didn't immediately resemble Fowler. The face seemed fleshier, the lips thin, a miserly kind of mouth, he thought; the kind of mouth used to uttering blasphemies. It was probably just the light.

'Where's the rest? We agreed twelve, there's less than three here.'

There was a nervousness in the voice, a trait he wouldn't have usually applied to Fowler; he was normally cock-sure of himself. Another vice: pride.

'You'll get the rest if we decide your information is worth the payment. Think of it as a deposit.'

'That wasn't the agreement.'

'Take it or leave it,' Lewis said.

Another pull on his cigarette. 'I could fuck you over, too. I know who it's for. If word got out he'd paid for this then he'd be in the shit.'

He couldn't argue. It made perfect sense to Lewis; logical, simple, no room for negotiation. 'Then we've both got something to lose,' he said, slipping the package into his jacket.

'I swear, if he fucks me over, I'll go to the police. I've got connections, people who respect me. Understand?'

Another fracture in the cloud cover and the sliver of moon light fell over the man's face. Lewis was now sure this wasn't Fowler.

His stomach flipped. Fowler, he knew how to handle, had some history with, but this stranger? He had no clue how to interact with. All bets were off.

'It's good to be respected,' Lewis said thoughtfully before turning on his heels to leave.

'That would be a terrible thing to lose, your reputation.'

Chapter 47

The woman had called it a factory, but the assortment of amateur-looking mechanical apparatus spread haphazardly across the floor reminded Manx of a hobbyist workshop that had, much to its own surprise, become a successful commercial enterprise.

'Just like the real thing, eh, flower?' the woman said, leading Manx past the assembly line. ' We churn out a few a week these days.'

He looked over the latex body suits hanging like human skins off tattered, cloth mannequins. 'Business must be booming,' he said.

'Can't complain, luv,' the woman said, ushering him through the head mould department where several overly painted faces with empty eyes and blushed lips stared out at him with a blankness Manx found as unnerving as the video footage that had led him here.

'We look after our customers. Repeat business, it's our bread and butter. They always want the latest models, upgrade their wardrobe. Everyone loves a change, eh? A pinch of spice in the casserole.'

The woman, Lydia Atherton, co-owner and matriarch of Second Skin Productions, was in her mid-sixties with an accent Manx placed somewhere between Scouse and Mancunian: she would glide effortlessly across them as if relishing in the idiosyncrasies they both offered. Her white hair was pulled back to a bun and she wore purple glasses with a matching, beaded chain that clinked on the buttons of her cardigan as she walked.

'So, what's so urgent on a Sunday afternoon?' Lydia asked, unlocking the door to her office. 'On the lookout for one yourself? Private showing?'

'Um, no. Thanks all the same,' Manx said.

'Never know 'till you try it luv,' she said, winking.

'This,' he said, placing the photo taken from Margaret Langley's murder, carefully cropped to just show the face. 'Is it one of yours?'

'Quality's shite,' she said, sitting at her desk and examining the picture from all angles. 'Can't tell.'

'Did you ship any orders to Anglesey recently?'

Lydia removed her glasses. 'They faxed your warrant over last night, can't say I was too happy about it.' She slid an envelope across the desk. 'We value discretion, so do our customers.'

'Understood,' Manx said.

'Tyler, my eldest, he's the artistic one, does all the sketches and custom orders, he'd know.'

'Can I talk to him?'

'Not unless you've got a ticket to Lanzarote. He's on holiday, won't be back 'till a week Sunday night.'

'No chance of contacting him—'

'Sorry, luv,' Lydia said, grabbing a mobile phone from the desk. 'Off-the-grid,' he calls it. Time to recharge his creative batteries, you know how these artistic types are.'

No. Manx didn't. Art or not, this was another delay in his investigation; one that could cost someone else their life.

'What are those?' Manx asked, looking at the gallery of Polaroids pinned to the wall behind Lydia. Doll faces of every kind, some close-up, others on a wide angle displaying the full outfits. Under each photograph was a single name.

'Our Dollies,' Lydia said. 'That's what they call themselves. They like to share, and Tyler loves to see his work out in the world. Living art he calls it.'

Manx studied the board carefully, checking the blurry screen grab against the gallery.

'Do they all send in a picture?'

'Nearly every one of them, flower. They like the attention.'

Manx looked closer at a portrait to the top left. The face was pale, overly drawn, and had striking red hair separated into bunches tied with thick white ribbon.

'Lucy,' he said, reading the scribbled name.

'The customers give them the names,' Lydia said, 'Tyler doesn't agree with it, he thinks it's like giving a name to a piglet you know is headed for the slaughterhouse, best not get too attached.'

'Can I take it?'

Lydia reached back and unpinned the photograph. 'Bring it back in good condition, eh?'

'Will do,' Manx said, handing Lydia his card. 'And make sure Tyler calls me the second he gets home.'

'Top of my list, flower,' Lydia said, pinning Manx's card to the wall under the photograph of Delilah from Darlington.

* * *

It was late Sunday evening when Manx pulled into the station car park. The sun had already tucked itself in behind the spine of the mountains and the street lamps buzzed to life along Llangefni High Street.

In the reception area, the air was thick with the smell of food; it reminded him he hadn't eaten since breakfast, and he couldn't be sure if he'd eaten or just rushed from the house with a palm full of cornflakes.

As he walked past the man stacking pizza boxes on the front desk, he recognised the logo on the T-shirt. *Shit*! He didn't need this now. Denny needed a damn good dressing down, but now wasn't the place or time. Before he could brush past, the man spun around, catching Manx as he buzzed himself in.

'I saw your mother today, she's improving I think.'

Manx felt a familiar weariness settle over him. Far from comforting him, the lad's remarks just confirmed what he already suspected. Alice was easy pickings.

'Might see you at the house soon?' Denny asked as he walked out. 'Alice talks about you a lot.'

'Yeah, I'm sure she does,' Manx said.

Denny smiled; a patient, knowing smile. Manx couldn't figure out if it was out of pity or just his own, personal amusement. Manx bet it was probably both. Either way, he needed to put him straight and soon.

The incident room was buzzing with activity. It felt good to watch the wheels of an investigation churning. It was that steady, machine-like hum that Manx knew would always get results.

'Names and addresses, boss?' Nader asked, pointing at the envelope in the inspector's hand.

Manx handed him the envelope and pinned the photograph on the incident board. 'Another one for the rogues' gallery.'

'Ugh, give me the creeps that does,' Priddle said, looking at the badly lit Polaroid, a ghostly shadow falling across the doll mask.

'Didn't you date her in school, Priddle?' Nader said, walking to the incident board. 'Lucy, yeah that was her name, aye?'

Manx gestured for Nader to sit. It was late and he was in no mood for the class-clown act. 'It's a face and a name. Just about all we've got to go on. No idea if the name is real or made up. Priddle, anything from the Archdiocese over in Bangor?'

'Weren't much help, but me and Morris did some research on the web. There was this religious group out by Newborough back in the nineteen forties called the Points of Light Ministry They had a lodge where they trained the missionaries. Either closed down or some kind of dosshouse now. It was ages ago, so not much on the Internet about it.'

'We got the address though,' Morris said, handing Manx a slip of paper.

'Pin it to the board, Morris,' Manx said. 'This one can wait until tomorrow.'

Chapter 48

If Glyn Lewis could have raised the capital without so much as a handshake of human interaction, he would have gladly done so. He'd come to realise that McLain was old-school when it came to raising money, or maybe McLain just understood, far better than he ever would, how to manoeuvre close to people and persuade them to open their wallets with a smile on his face. Lewis, on the other hand, had never had much luck at making friends – the true kind or the political kind. The social cues that came naturally for people like McLain, Lewis found baffling and inefficient. Smiles, frowns, eye contact: it was all the same to him, blank faces that contained no pertinent information.

'You were right not to cancel,' Glyn Lewis said. 'Who knows when you'd get all these people together in the same room again.'

'It was a close call, so soon after Sian,' McLain said, as they walked through the reception of Henllys Hall and into the billiards room which had been decked out with strings of tastefully glowing lights, tall vases stuffed with freshly cut lilies and a semi-famous harpists who plucked bravely over the constant hum of chatter.

'Wouldn't have brought her back,' Lewis said. 'If you falter in trouble, how small is your strength.'

'It's a party, Lewis,' McLain said, reaching for a glass of champagne and thrusting it in his hand. 'Loosen the fuck up.'

McLain had chosen the venue, a converted Victorian mansion, for its close proximity to the Menai Bridge and the luxury accommodations his guests would expect. He was also a shareholder of the hotel, along with the accompanying restaurant and golf course.

'The beast never strays far from its prey,' McLain said, joining Harden Jones at the bar, who was already dewy-eyed and ruddy faced.

'Used to be a monastery back in the day. Now they come to worship at the temple of the nineteenth hole,' Harden said, raising his fourth Scotch of the evening and gesturing towards the windows and the expansive view towards the Irish Sea. The sun had begun its graceful exit behind the silhouette of the Great Orme, shading a highlighter-pen of orange over the low clouds, which would soon dissipate into darkness.

'Mind you, they should have kept brewing the mead,' Harden said. 'I'd have dressed them all in monks robes, could have marketed the hell out of it, what with all these gastro pubs and new restaurants around here. Progress, they call it.'

'The only constant is change,' McLain said. 'That, and your godawful ties,' he added, pointing at Harden's neck ensemble. 'What is that? A dancing sheep?'

Harden dipped his chin and shrugged. 'The missus reckoned it was waltzing. Waltzing Matilda, the sheep. A present from Australia when she visited her sister,' he said, inspecting the tie with a more critical eye than he had when knotting it earlier this evening.

McLain slowly guided Harden towards a fireplace large enough, and hot enough, to roast a suckling pig over. 'Lots of eager investors keen to hear good news, Harden. Your introductions have been duly recognised and rewarded.'

'Aye, power and influence, you pay for what you get,' Harden said, looking around at the hundred or so guests dressed in perfectly tailored suits or expensive dresses that swished elegantly at their ankles. Elaborate canapés were being passed around on silver plates, offered by wide-eyed wait-staff, nervous and awkward as they scurried through the sparkling jewellery and cut-glass accents.

McLain lay his hand on Harden's shoulder. 'Are you familiar with the origin of The Buddha, Harden?'

The councilman shook out his handkerchief and mopped at his perspiring brow. 'Chubby bloke, sits with his legs crossed?'

McLain nodded. 'When he was a young man, a prince in his father's castle, he had never seen the outside world. Then, one day, he steals out of the gates to observe the world for himself, empirically. What he witnessed there affected him to such a degree he vowed to spend the remainder of his life seeking enlightenment, which he was finally granted under the shade of the Bodhi Tree. That, Harden, is how I feel about this project.'

'Come again?' Harden said, taking a mouthful of Scotch and feeling the heat from the fire prickle at his skin.

'I've experienced both sides of the coin and I know which I prefer, after all, no one ever complained they had too much money. Unhealthy attachment to worldly belongings, though, is the core foundation of human misery and suffering. But cut the cord to that attachment and the path to enlightenment opens up before us.'

'I still don't get it, Kimble?' Harden said, running his finger under his shirt collar. 'You a Buddhist now or something?'

'You're missing the point. The Buddha wasn't remembered for being his father's son, he was remembered for being the Buddha. That's how I want to be remembered, Harden, for this.' McLain ushered Harden over to the perfectly rendered model of the Menai Express Tunnel positioned in the centre of the room.

'Everything else, my foundation, my investments, are just attachments, transient. This, however, is my Bodhi Tree, Harden. My stake on permanence in the world.'

'Aye, well, we all want this project to succeed, Kimble.'

'Glad we're on the same page,' McLain said, walking off.

Harden grabbed another Scotch from a passing waiter. *On the same page as Kimble McLain? That would be a first*, he thought. He wondered sometimes if he was even on the same bloody planet.

* * *

The night had a nervous chill around its edges when Harden Jones stepped outside. The party had wound down with just a few die-hards now taking up space in the lounge bar. By this point, Harden had correctly guessed his company was surplus to requirements. Welsh Government officials, European Union Parliament Members, Westminster Civil Servants; the players buzzing like flies around McLain were out of his league. Heated debates on the value of PFI schemes, complex leasing deals, shared maintenance costs and EU grants and special Acts of Parliament to kick-start the project beyond his exploratory committee were way over his head. At least he'd steered the project this far, and McLain had kept his promise – a stash of money secured in a bank in Dubai; the kind of bank that didn't ask questions. He'd take the wife there after he retired, she liked the heat, and it was closer to her sister.

He shuffled, still woozy from the Scotch, towards the stone wall marking the boundary to the eighteenth hole. The sky was star-filled and cloudless, a half-slice of moon set high over the mountains.

He reached for a cigar; one of several he'd procured from one of the 'cigarette girls' hired for the evening. He'd taken a fancy to one of them: Melanie, according to her name tag. She was just his type: long red hair, tall and with a wide generous smile which he imagined was directed solely at him. He deserved some fun, he rationalised, as he stalked Melanie around the room. The wife wouldn't need to know. He was staying the night and anyway, *'what happens in Henllys Hall, stays in Henllys Hall.'* Maybe it was that clunky, clichéd pick-up line he whispered into Melanie's ear that had sealed the deal. He didn't see her again for the remainder of the night.

Harden undid his tie and examined the sheep waltzing across its kipper-finned tail. His wife wasn't stupid. Her insistence he wore it was clear. Melanie and the rest of the staff were probably having a good giggle at the sad fucker with the sheep-shagger tie and potbelly who tried to pick-up on her. Still, he was too drunk to care at this point. Or too old; it was hard to tell these days.

As he mused over his conundrum, drawing deeply on the cigar, he noticed a woman walk from around the corner. She made her way slowly towards the large chessboard painted on the west patio of the hotel. The over-sized pieces were already perfectly aligned, waiting for battle to commence. The woman leant against the wall and glanced his way.

It was Melanie. The long, red hair and the way she held herself. He felt a flutter of optimism. Maybe the game was still on after all.

'Lovely night,' he called out, stuffing his tie deep into his jacket pocket.

She said nothing, looked at him blankly. He'd seen that look before: the brush-off. 'Got a smoke if you want one,' he said reaching for a pack of cigarettes in his jacket pocket.

She stepped back, as if sizing him up before accepting.

'Aye, don't worry, luv, I don't bite,' he said. 'Unless you want me to, like,' he said with a wink, then instantly regretted the remark as She cocked her head as if she were trying to figure him out.

As she stepped towards him, her heels clicking loudly on the concrete, Harden Jones felt the first flutter of uncertainty – a slow motion drop of the penny which was exaggerated by the alcohol blurring his sense. It took several moments before his initial optimism turned to confusion and finally to outright fear. It could have been the awkward gait of her walk or the face that betrayed no emotion or trace of humanity, but something was off, something that he was too muddied to figure out. The flash of steel she drew from inside her jacket glinted in the moonlight. It was the cold-shower of sobriety he needed.

He twisted awkwardly on his heel and ran towards the chessboard, tripping over the child-sized pieces as he scrambled towards the opposite side. Behind him, the woman was barely breaking a sweat, gaining on him square by square.

Pawn to G2 – it was Harden's first misstep. The queen was already two moves ahead, blocking him at F3. He stumbled, his cheap shoes slipping across the damp surface. He lunged to H4, tripping over one of the black pawns as he ran. Queen to G5. She was looming over him now, her expression blank and emotionless.

His hands slipped across the board, struggling to lift himself and run, but it was a futile attempt.

E7 would be her checkmate move. The queen was now in control, commanding E6, bearing down on him so close he could see the wisp of breath seep from her perfectly painted lips. She lifted the knife.

The last thing Harden Jones felt in his world was the cold sting of steel slice through his neck. The last thing he saw, was his own blood spurting in torrents from his neck and onto the expressionless face of the woman.

His head fell back. D8, black, the furthest edge of the table: the queen's dominion.

Chapter 49

I

t's called the cold light of day for a good reason, Glyn Lewis thought as he watched the police activity unfold. There was no place for the day to hide under the harsh scowl of the morning sun.

The loud and harrowing scream of one of the maids had alerted the staff to the body splayed across the chessboard. The guests were now gathered in the car park, wandering aimlessly like discarded pawns in their complimentary white spa gowns, none of them happy at being woken before having the chance to sleep off their hangovers.

The police had arrived an hour ago. Lewis recognised the tall one directing the activities, Inspector Manx, from the photographs and information he'd been given by the man he thought was Fowler.

The details on Manx were sketchy. Some incident in London followed by a swift posting to the island was about it. But Manx was secondary news. The press would be more interested in the minutia of the murders than some middle-aged copper with a ropey back story.

He watched the uniformed officers take the witness statements and try to put last night's events into some kind of narrative that made sense. Harden Jones was their conduit to stewarding primary approvals from the councillors in Llangefni and Caernarvon – without them the project would have a hard passage reaching the national stage. And, there was the other issue, the one McLain had directed him to take care of. Another payoff. He was sick of them, those people who always had their palms extended and expecting McLain to grease them.

As he watched, McLain walked over to join him. 'What you said, last night, Lewis, about faltering?'

'No,' Lewis said, cutting him off. 'It's a setback, that's all. Fortitude, Kimble, that's what's required, fortitude and resolve. Harden was out of his league for the next stage, he knew it.'

'I think I saw it yesterday, or at least heard it.'

'The albatross?'

McLain nodded.

'A good omen.'

'Or an extremely bad one,' McLain said. 'It made me realise I'm focusing on the wrong vector. That business with Fowler, I'm going to settle it once and for all, it's time.'

'An eye for an eye?' Lewis said.

'Purging the system. Scouring the code for bugs before going live, standard protocol,' Kimble said.

'I can make the delivery, keep you out of it.'

'No, this is my responsibility,' McLain said, turning to leave.

Lewis stood for a moment, watching McLain walk away. The confident strut he admired so much the day McLain made his speech was gone, replaced by a resigned, slump-shouldered shuffle. He hated to see Kimble this way; this was not how things were meant to play out. Was he going to pay off Fowler, or something more permanent? He'd never been good at second-guessing what people were thinking, especially Kimble McLain.

Chapter 50

She could sense her whole being slowly ripping apart like a rag doll being pulled at the seams. She'd let him spend the night again. Another mistake she couldn't avoid making. It was like her default setting these days.

Liam Fowler snapped the buckle on his belt and grabbed the GoPro camera he'd set on the bedroom dresser last night.

'So, you ever going to share that, like?' Donna asked.

'With you?' Fowler said.

'Yeah, of course bloody well with me. You're not going to put 'em up on that YouTube or something, are you?'

'Not with that lighting,' Fowler said, pointing at the faint glow of the bedside lamp.

'Well, I might want to see it someday.'

Fowler laughed. 'Yeah? Didn't peg you for a porno freak.'

'Fuck you, Liam,' Donna said, tossing his Metallica T-shirt at him.

Fowler smirked. 'Yeah, all right, set the night,' he said. 'We'll hook it up to the TV, see yourself in high definition. Dirty bitch.'

He leant down as he walked from the room. Donna turned her head towards him, offering her lips. Fowler refused the offer and tapped her lightly on the cheeks with his palm. He may as well have slapped her, slapped her hard, Donna thought as she heard the door slam close, the hurt would have been about the same.

She hated herself for Liam. Wished she could just break it off for good, but she knew she was powerless when it came to him. She wasn't strong enough, never had been. Another trait her mother had berated her for; one in a long list of many.

It wasn't just her selfish need for Liam that clouded her judgement it was something else. It was as if being with him brought her closer to Sian, however twisted that sounded.

A loud rap on her front door shook her from her thoughts. Maybe Liam had decided to come back, spend the day with her. She threw on her dressing gown, patted her face with an optimistic dab of make-up and answered the door with the widest smile she could muster.

'Morning, Miss Robinson. DS Nader, North Wales Constabulary. Just wondering why Liam Fowler was seen leaving your house in the early hours? You must make a killer cup of tea. Either that or you've got a load of computer viruses that need fixing, eh?'

Chapter 51

'Who the fuck leaked this?' Manx bellowed, storming into the incident room and throwing the *North Wales Daily Post* onto the desk. The headline screamed at him: *Doll-Faced Killer Terrorises Isle Of Anglesey.'*

'How he ties them up. The fucking doll mask. Only we knew about this so if anyone has anything to tell me start talking now.'

'I think I speak for all of us, boss,' DS Nader said, his shackles on high alert. 'We're not fucking stupid.'

The rest of the team nodded, all looking expectantly at their detective inspector. 'You're right, Mal, sorry,' Manx said, softening his tone. 'But someone did, and if it wasn't from this station then it was someone who had access to the files.'

'With this kind of coverage, it'll go national,' DCI Canton said, walking into the room, a grave look carved into his face. 'We'll need to contain it. I'll call St Asaph, pronto.'

'Four murders, four, and we're no closer than we were a week ago to solving them. We were meant to prevent this last one, what the fuck happened?' Manx said.

The team shuffled uncomfortably, each avoiding Manx's steely gaze.

'I finished going through all the names from that Second Skin company,' Priddle offered. 'They're mostly post box numbers. There were a few addresses, down south, but nothing around here.'

'Makes sense,' Nader said. 'Bunch of fucking shandy drinkers down there.'

'Brilliant observation, Nader,' Manx said, throwing down his notebook. 'Do me a favour and keep it shut unless some semblance of an intelligent thought takes shape somewhere between your

146

brain and your mouth. Morris, any new leads? Connections with Harden Jones and the other victims?'

'I googled his name, and this came up,' Morris said, showing Manx the photo of Harden Jones and Kimble McLain at the unveiling of the Menai Express Tunnel. She turned to answer her phone as Manx leant over her screen.

'Forest fucking Gump,' Manx said. 'He keeps turning up. McLain needs to start sharing, there's too many coincidences here for my liking. Bring him in.'

'Um, don't think you'll need to sir,' Morris said hanging up the call. 'Kimble McLain is in reception. Got three solicitors with him and they don't look too happy by the sounds of it.'

* * *

'And that's your story?' Manx said, exasperated.

'Our client has been more than co-operative, Inspector. Mr McLain came here out of his own volition and he's answered every question to the best of his ability.'

'He hasn't said a word,' Manx said.

'That's what he pays us for,' the other solicitor offered.

'What about your meeting with Liam Fowler the night Sian was murdered?'

McLain ignored Manx and whispered in his solicitor's ear who slid an envelope across the table. 'Signed affidavits from Mr McLain's wife stating he was at home, with her, when these murders took place. All except for the one at Henllys Hall. You'll find the key card records for that night show Mr McLain never left the room until the commotion that morning.'

'The commotion?' Manx said, shaking his head and addressing McLain. 'Harden Jones, another close associate of yours, murdered, it's quite the pattern.'

The third solicitor spoke up. 'The loss of Councillor Harden Jones is a tragedy, we will be reaching out to his family to extend our condolences. He was a devoted leader and a champion for our project, there's no reason for my client to have killed Mr Jones.'

'Other than maybe he knew too much?' Manx said.

'You're clutching at straws, Inspector Manx,' McLain said, pushing back his chair. 'No one can ever know too much. Good luck with your enquiries.'

* * *

A flank of press ambushed McLain as he left the station. He stood on the steps and gestured for them to calm down.

'I came here voluntarily to help our dedicated police officers and offer my services as a citizen. What happened is a tragedy beyond words. Today we are all mourning the loss of loved ones and colleagues, they are all in our thoughts. As a proud native of this island, I'm still in a state of shock that these atrocities could happen on our doorstep, but I'm confident the police are putting the whole weight of their resources towards solving the case. Thank you.'

Manx watched from his office window. He was addressing the press like a preacher at a revivalist meeting, he thought, as McLain finished up and jogged casually towards his Range Rover. Manx felt a surge of anger; McLain had stage managed the whole farce. The bastard was smart, he had to give him that. But McLain was hiding more than he was giving away; it was a classic deflection. But what was he deflecting? His part in the murders, or something else he was equally desperate to hide?

Chapter 52

Cats were inherently devious, Manx mused as he stood in the reception of The Points of Light Ministry Lodge, staring into the eyes of a fat, ginger tom. The cat was hunched on the edge of the desk, glaring at Manx as if it might spring on its hind legs at any moment and make fast work of his face with its claws. *You always knew what dogs were thinking,* Manx thought, cats, on the other hand, seemed to make it their life's work to figure out what you were thinking. He stepped back as the cat arched its spine and took one last unimpressed gaze at the inspector before lifting its thick boa tail and showing Manx the equivalent of the feline middle finger.

Outstanding start to the day, he thought as the cat scurried to the back room. Manx looked around. The Lodge had seen better days. The walls and ceiling were smudged black with burn marks. Finger-wide cracks, like white lightening blots, struck out along the walls from ceiling to skirting board. A large religiously themed painting, a cheap print by the state of the faded colours, hung above the sofa – the all seeing eye of God looking down in judgement on his creation. In the backroom, the soundtrack from an old film crackled through a small TV.

Manx tapped the greasy dome of the brass bell for the second time and wiped his finger down his jeans. A pack of business cards was stacked against the computer screen: Sospan Fawr. *'Good Food, Delivered.'* the tag line proclaimed. Jesus! He had enough on his mind without having to worry about Alice. The next time he met the man, he would throw him subtlety under the bus, scare him off, make sure he didn't come around with his outstretched hands and empty pockets.

He heard the soft pad of footsteps as Isla Logan shuffled through the doorway, the cat purring at her ankles and a mug of tea in hand. She was in her sixties, Manx guessed, but held herself like a much older woman. There was a weariness about her that reminded him of Alice: the look of someone who found no joy in life and had long ago resigned herself to the fact. The resemblance became more exaggerated as she stepped into the harsh glare of the fluorescents, which also highlighted the stark blueness of her eyes.

'Thirty quid a night for a room,' Isla said without looking up. 'If you can't afford that, there's space in the barn. No drugs, no alcohol, and I don't tolerate any hanky panky.' She had a soft, Scottish accent that was in contrast to her curtness.

'Bet you say that to all the boys,' Manx said, smiling and showing his badge.

Isla gripped Manx's hand and drew it closer. 'You look like a bloody copper,' she said, pushing it back. 'We run a clean establishment. That why you're here? Some kind of police raid?'

Manx looked around. 'Not much of a raiding party.'

'Why you here then? We don't want any trouble.'

'I've got a few questions about the missionaries.'

Isla removed her glasses and squinted. 'Why do you want to know about them?'

'Routine enquiries.'

'Ancient history. Been no missionaries here for years. You wasted your time,' she said, ushering the cat to heel like she would a dog.

'Goronwy Bedortha-Owens,' Manx said, reading the name from a slip of paper given to him by Priddle. 'He was the founder?'

Isla hardened her gaze. 'Best not go digging around the past, doesn't ever do anyone any good.'

'Nineteen forties, just after the war?'

'Why are you asking me if you already know?'

'Added colour?' Manx said

Isla sighed. 'If it'll make you leave sooner, yes, him and his wife, Margaret. They looked after evacuee kids from London during the Blitz, godless little urchins he called them. Found his calling and set up the Lodge to train the missionaries.'

'What happened?' Manx asked, looking around the shabby reception.

'People stopped believing, what do you think?'

'Where were they posted?'

'All over. Africa, Asia, South America. They called him a fire and brimstone Baptist, but he never took it as an insult. He lived by the Old Testament teachings, not like that happy-clappy rubbish they sell these days, all bloody tambourines and teacakes.'

Manx pointed at an old photograph on the wall. 'That him?' he asked, examining the tall, serious-looking man in a wide brimmed hat and what Manx assumed was his family either side of him, equally stiff.

Isla nodded. 'His wife Margaret and son, Jacob. Sent him off to the Caribbean I think, or was it Canada, not that it matters, all water under the bridge now.'

Manx looked carefully over the rows of photographs on the wall. One in particular caught his attention, a black and white print with the date 1976 written in the margin. The remainder of the writing had faded. It was of another family of three, this one younger and less formally posed. They were standing outside a makeshift hut, a hastily scribbled sign hanging in its entrance. Manx looked closer: *The International Points of Light Ministry, BVI.* To the right of the man was a woman holding a baby while a group of young black children crowded around her, peering at the child. The woman's body was angled away from the man, suggesting she was distancing herself from him. Her left arm cradled the baby while her other hand was adjusting her hair: it was as if she'd been caught mid-action with no opportunity for a retake. The man was tall and stood with his chest puffed out, offering the same serious look as Goronwy.

'Is that the son, Jacob?'

'No idea,' Isla said. 'Could be anyone. He sent out hundreds over the years.'

'Mind if I take it?'

Isla ran her left index finger along the top of her right hand and shrugged. 'Suppose I can't stop you.'

'Much appreciated,' Manx said, unhooking the frame from the wall. A flurry of plaster accompanied it, scattering to the floor. He leant down to gather up some of the pieces.

'Leave it,' Isla said. 'They'll be bulldozing the whole place in a few weeks. Sold it to make holiday flats or something.'

Manx placed some of the debris on the reception desk. 'What happened to Goronwy?'

'Died, like expected. None of us outlive death.'

'And his son, Jacob? Wasn't there some scandal?'

Isla stiffened, rubbed her finger along her hand again as if soothing herself. 'Told you already, does no good digging around what's passed. He's being judged by a far higher power now.'

'Don't suppose you have any records of the missionaries that were sent out?'

'All our records were destroyed years ago in a fire,' Isla said, gesturing at the black blemishes across the ceiling and walls. 'The church sends a few lost souls over here every year; the true believers know they can find shelter. They stay a while then move on. If that's all, then I've got to get back to work.'

'Good film, is it?' Manx asked, noticing how Isla kept glancing behind her towards the backroom.

'*Whistle Down the Wind*,' she said. 'Another bloody repeat.'

Manx nodded. 'Thanks for this, I'll bring it back.'

Isla huffed and pulled her cardigan tight across her chest. 'Don't bother. I'm not the sentimental type.'

Outside, Manx leant on the Jensen's bonnet, lit up a King Edward and looked over the dilapidated lodge and the neglected grounds, which were rife with overgrown pathways that seemed to lead nowhere. The roof of the old Victorian mansion had several slates missing and the windows were peeling and cracked, untended for decades he imagined. The barn Isla had mentioned was to the right of the building. Manx walked over and peered inside. It smelt of hay and damp: obviously no one had taken Isla up on the offer of free accommodation.

The whole place made him feel uneasy. Above him, a flock of ravens circled and cackled before settling on the branches. Manx could feel their inquisitive eyes on him as he watched them. He looked again at the photograph. Isla Logan was a cagey old bird herself and he doubted he'd get much more out of her without a warrant.

It was time to call on a higher power, he thought, as he spun the Jensen's wheels, the crackle of the exhaust scattering the ravens from their perches.

Chapter 53

Donna's eyes were red and sore, the tears falling freely as if she were flushing herself of all the guilt and remorse. But there always seemed to be more; always a fresh reserve to draw on.

'So, you're admitting Liam Fowler was at your house the night Sian Conway was murdered?' Manx said.

Donna nodded and wiped her nose.

'And you didn't think to mention this before now?'

'I'm not proud of it, not proud at all,' Donna said, sniffing loudly.

'How long have you been seeing Liam Fowler?'

'Since they split up about a year ago.'

'Did Sian know?'

'No way, I couldn't do that to her, not Sian.'

'But you could sleep with her husband?'

'Like I said, I'm not proud of myself,' Donna said, a steelier edge to her voice.

'Was Liam Fowler with you all night?'

'He picked me up around eleven, we went back to my place.'

'That's when you Skyped Sian?'

'I wanted to make sure she was okay.'

'When did Liam leave?'

'I was asleep, he was gone when I woke up in the morning.'

Manx took in the information and leant back. 'Tell me, when did Sian tell you she was pregnant?'

Donna's eyes grew wider. 'No. She'd have told me.'

'Even friends have secrets, Donna.'

Donna smarted at the remark. 'Maybe it was a mistake, she was going to get rid of it, didn't want to tell me. I don't know.'

'Who was she seeing, Donna? There must have been someone, casual or serious.'

Donna shook her head. 'No one. Like I told the other girl, Sian was off men for good. Worked all hours she did. I reckoned it was just her way of keeping herself busy.'

'For Kimble McLain.'

Donna shrugged. 'Likes his pound of flesh that one. Suppose that's how people like him make all their money, on the backs of people like us.'

The germ of an idea began to form as Manx listened. Was McLain covering something up? Like Doctor Alvarez had said, *we all need a reason to do what we do.*

He walked into the incident room, gesturing for Nader to join him in his office. 'Fowler and McLain met the night Sian was murdered. They're hiding something, both of them, and it might be connected with Sian's murder. Might not, but it's a loose end, and loose ends make me nervous.'

'Want me to bring him in for questioning?' Nader asked.

'No, that ship's sailed, he's under no obligation to comply. Arrest him.'

Nader sat up straight. 'Aye, happy to. On what charge?'

Manx rubbed his finger along the bruise on his forehead. 'Assaulting a police officer. Maybe we can scare him into confessing whatever the fuck is going on between those two.'

Manx could have sworn Nader had a skip in his step as he left the office.

Chapter 54

He was fifteen years old when his father withdrew what meagre rations of love he had deigned to pass out to his son. The boy was fleshing out his bones too quickly. His body was changing, growing wide and stocky, like a farmhand. He never saw his bulk as an advantage but as a handicap, making him awkward and lumbering compared to the other boys in school. Maybe that's why he never thought to use his size and strength against them. That would change.

They mocked his accent, an unfamiliar mix of English and Dutch Creole. He'd attempt to make himself invisible, but they'd always find him, grab at the leather satchel strapped across his shoulders – an affront to the cool Adidas bags the other kids carried – and throw it amongst them in a cruel game of catch. No matter where he was it seemed he would always be a *'non-belonger.'*

It was early June, the air thick with the anticipation of summer, when he found the courage to fight back. Three boys had cornered him behind the gym where the older kids smoked. They pinned him down, ripped open his satchel and tossed his lunch to the birds. When they found his Bible they laughed and tore out the pages, scattering them like confetti. Minutes later, their initial amusement now turned to boredom, they left him.

He was on his knees, wiping the tears from his eyes and gathering up the ripped pages when a faint voice from within spoke to him. *Justice will be served,* it whispered. Like Job, he would just need to be patient.

He spied on the boys, listened to them talking and found out what it was they loved the most, what would hurt them to lose; hurt them bad.

The dog was his first victim. A border collie. He swung the wooden head of a golf club he'd found in the church basement at it, with no mercy, until it stopped its whimpering.

The other boy was a runner, proud of the medals he had won in the cross-country championships. *Pride comes before a fall,* he thought as he waited for the boy at the edge of the woods one early evening. He struck him from behind, slammed him with the same golf club, then set about his knees until they were both shattered.

The third boy was a singer and competed in Eisteddfod competitions. He followed him from choir practice one evening. When the boy was on the footpath he grabbed him from behind, looped a length of old electrical wiring around his neck and pulled until his face turned purple. His competition days were over.

It felt good, the violence of it. The surge of power thrilled him to the marrow. It was like when his father begged for his forgiveness or when he'd struck the Raven Boy – the same, quivering anticipation that made him whole, defined him.

The police visited the school. Hysteria ran rife for a few weeks, but by the end of term they were none the wiser. Not that he ever felt the cool glare of suspicion: he was the quiet, preacher's boy with little to say for himself. His invisibility, he soon realised, was as much of an advantage as it was a curse.

Chapter 55

The bishop slid a folder across the table towards Manx. 'The sins of the father are to be laid upon the children,' he said leaning back in his chair. He had a round, blushed face, like a kind uncle a little too fond of the communion wine. Below them, the faint echo of music rose up through the thick stone walls of Bangor Cathedral.

'Another bloody Bible quote, seems this case is stiff with them,' Max said, flipping open the folder.

'Shakespeare, actually, *Merchant of Venice*. Inspired by the Book of Exodus, but the bard saw fit to make it palatable to the masses.'

Manx nodded, glancing over the print outs. 'Pretty thin.'

'It was my predecessor's cross to bear,' Bishop Alun James explained. 'Our diocese extends to Anglesey so we were aware of the incidents. Not that we were implicated, you understand, the Independent Church in Wales was cleared of any involvement. As far as I can tell, it was one of those ultra-conservative splinter religions.'

'The Points of Light Ministry,' Manx said. 'Baptists?'

'Fire and brimstone,' the bishop confirmed. 'We were all tarred with the same brush for a while. I'd venture to say we're still struggling to corral some of the lost sheep back to the flock.'

'No doubt. I bet there's a bunch of Catholic priests feeling a bit hot under the dog collar these days,' Manx said.

The bishop offered a thin smile. 'Ours is not to judge,' he said. 'Jacob Owens was suspected of historic child abuse but took his own life before he was tried.'

'Straight to the big man, then,' Manx said. 'Bypass the jury of your peers and hope divine justice has a softer touch.'

The bishop shuffled uncomfortably. 'Our church condemns the act of suicide in the strongest possible terms.'

Manx nodded. 'Of course. What about Owens's wife and child? What happened to them?'

'No idea. The shame would have been a heavy burden for any family, I imagine. If there's nothing else I can help you with, secular or otherwise, I really need to get back to work, we're very behind on rehearsals for our Easter service as it is.'

Manx followed the bishop down the narrow stone steps that led to the chapter house then on to the nave. On the stage, behind the pipe organ, the cathedral 'house band' was in full rehearsal. Two men, one on electric guitar, the other on a sharp-looking ovation acoustic number, nodded their heads to the beat of the drummer who pounded at the bass drum in the hope that he might rock the Lord from the heavens and kick start the second coming. At the microphone, a young woman in a knee-length dress and open toed sandals tapped a tambourine against her thigh, while belting out a sentimental Christian Rock dirge sung in the sickly sweet key of Jesus.

'Happy clappy?' Manx said, turning to the bishop, who was tapping his foot to the beat.

'Sorry?'

'Never mind,' Manx said. He was about to walk out when he noticed a young man in one of the pews. He was rocking back and forth to whatever rhythm was pounding inside his head. As the man shifted from seated to kneeling, he lifted his face heavenward towards the statue of Jesus on the cross. Manx thought he recognised him – the arrogant young lad he'd first met at Kimble McLain's house, Glyn Lewis. *He didn't look so arrogant now*, Manx thought as Lewis gripped his hands in prayer and rested his forehead on his clenched fists muttering to himself.

'One last question,' Manx said, turning to the bishop. 'The sins of the father, what exactly does it mean as it's written in the Bible?'

The bishop thought for a moment. 'I like to tell my congregation it's like *The Lion King*.'

'*The Lion King*?' Manx asked, resisting the urge to smile. "Hakuna Matata"?'

'The other one,' the bishop said. "Circle of Life'. We're all God's children, part of his divine plan. What we do, what our parents did, it's all connected, a circle. It's the kind of cultural reference we're forced to adopt these days to fill the pews. But to answer you from a strictly theological perspective, if the father misleads or brings evil upon the family the descendants will pay for those transgressions. Multi-generational karmic payback, if you will.'

'Any wiggle room for redemption?' Manx asked, looking again at Glyn Lewis, who was now muttering louder and sweating profusely across his brow as he repeatedly tapped it against his fists.

'Oh, there's always wiggle room, Inspector,' the bishop explained. 'Religion is like a fluid body of water, it charts new courses as it finds its way to God. Like justice, I imagine, it shifts with the demands of the time.'

Chapter 56

Donna hummed along to 'White Rabbit', the Jefferson Airplane classic, as she cradled the Toffoc bottle in her arm and walked to her patio.

The afternoon was chilly but held the faint anticipation of spring around its margins. She sat on the sun-lounger and wrapped a blanket around her legs. It felt as if she hadn't slept for weeks. The pills did what they promised, at least for a few hours, until she woke and for a few seconds her life was like it was before Sian died. Moments later, the cold reality of her life would kick her squarely in the teeth and the inevitable cycle would begin again.

She struck a match and lit the kindling in the clay chiminea. As the fire slowly crackled to life it reminded her of better days. Her and Sian, huddled around the fire, laughing and listening to the hits of the sixties and seventies until one of the guests renting out the holiday home next door shouted at them to keep it down. '*Fuck you, fucking tourist,*' Sian shouted back. '*Go back home if you don't like it, give the house to someone who fucking needs it.*' They both giggled like schoolgirls before running back into the house and watching three episodes of *The Walking Dead* until they both fell asleep.

Those days were over now, for good. Donna felt the endless well of sadness fill her from the feet up.

'One pill?' she said to herself and chugged back one of her zopiclones with a shot of the vodka. *No*, she thought, laying back on the lounger, *one pill would never be enough*. She filled her tumbler with the remainder of the Toffoc, shook the rest of the pills into her palm and swallowed.

As the afternoon sun dipped slowly behind the fence, Donna felt a lightness she hadn't felt for weeks. Numb to everything around her, she didn't notice a spark of kindling fall from the chiminea onto the lounger, burning through the blanket around her knees.

Chapter 57

L iam Fowler slugged a mouthful of beer and swallowed a wrap of amphetamine paste. He looked through the window at the lights from Beaumaris and Bangor reflecting on the calm surface of the Menai Strait. *Goodbye to all this shit,* he thought as he sat at his backup computer, the one he always kept hidden in the server room, and entered his password.

He preferred the graveyard shifts. No spotty-faced students poking their noses in his business, no flustered professors nervously handing him their laptops and begging him to repair some virus they'd downloaded from whatever dubious website they'd recently trawled through. Their browsing history was the breadcrumb trail that led to the gingerbread house and the secrets that lay under the floorboards – secrets that even their own wives were clueless about – desires and perversions they couldn't begin to imagine. At the end of the day, it was all currency, money in the bank that he could draw on come a rainy day. He kept records of everything – meticulous and blind encrypted. But tonight, that was all trivial: the fetishes and transgressions of a handful of kinky college professors was child's play compared to the story he had to tell about Kimble McLain.

He set his headphones across his ears and launched his music app. Harsh, intense electronic beats – *music to code by,* he liked to call it. The distorted pulses lulled him into a hypnotic state until the real world faded into the background and the only world that mattered was contained in the boundaries of a fifteen-inch screen.

The newspapers were already champing at the bit. He'd sell to the highest bidder, after all, they were all the same to him. They printed anything that would make them money, and the uncensored story about how the Six Billion Dollar Man had made his money, who he'd screwed along the way, the dirty secrets Fowler kept encrypted, deep in the bowels of his hard-drive, had proved to be as irresistible as he imagined. If McLain wouldn't pay up, he had three national newspapers that would.

They were already talking big numbers – plenty for him to get out of this shithole and move to California; Silicon Valley. But first he'd make the pilgrimage across the country, hire one of those American convertibles and drive the whole continent in six weeks before getting serious about work, and secure funding from one of those venture capitalist companies; they were throwing money at kids with half his talent. He'd rent a room in one of those tech incubators he'd read about where they sit around their swimming pools coding all day and changing the fucking world. That last part he could take or leave: changing the world was secondary, making a shit-ton of money, that was life fucking changing.

But, before he got down to work, there was one final task. He'd seen her, the slack-mouthed bitch, walking into the police station yesterday. He'd teach her to go gabbing like that, she'd be telling them everything. He slotted a memory stick into the slot and dragged over a folder full of videos. He slid the drive into a small manila envelope addressed to Donna Robinson and placed it in the outgoing mail.

He turned back to his screen and began to type, his neurons sparking like firecrackers. He was in full flow, fuelled by the beer and the amphetamine rush. Behind him, the office door swung open, as if caught by a stiff breeze. He didn't notice – his senses were elsewhere.

He didn't hear the footsteps either, or the heavy, nervous breathing at his right shoulder. What finally caught his attention was the reflection in the screen – a woman's face staring blankly at him. There was no time to register the image. A strong, gloved hand had already gripped its fingers around his chin and yanked his head backwards until he felt his shoulders brace against the chair, his neck exposed and vulnerable.

The first cut was brutal but not fatal. A hesitant slicing over the ridges of his Adam's apple, like a razor nick, sharp and bloody. The second cut found its target, carving deep into his flesh and puncturing his carotid artery. Instinct compelled him to clasp his hand to his neck. The thick flow of blood seeped between his fingers like warm honey.

Fowler slipped from the chair and felt the inevitable fade into darkness. His blood swarmed across the carpet in a tidal rush of crimson towards the man's shoes.

He stepped around the body, and got to work binding Fowler's ankles and knees. After all, God was in the details.

* * *

Back inside the Range Rover, he took off the mask and wiped the sweat from his brow. The cheap plastic face, speckled with blood, looked up at him accusingly. He flipped it over and pressed play on the CD player. Chopin's 'Nocturne in C Sharp Minor' filled the cabin. He stayed there for a few minutes, letting his heart rate simmer to a steady thud. There had been enough pay outs, enough greasing of palms, at least now the code was free of bugs, the system purged.

PART TWO
AND DEATH SHALL
HAVE DOMINION

Chapter 1

By his third summer on the island, the congregation in the Points of Light Ministry had grown to over two hundred loyal members. The flock would come and listen to his father preach his fiery sermons. The baptisms, though, were always his favourite. His father would pull back the heavy floor of the baptism pool, balance the sinner's head in the palm of his hand, lean them back so their eyes were directed heavenwards before gently urging them under the water.

He always held his breath as they went under, as if he himself were being cleansed. When they resurfaced a few moments later, their faces beaming and wet with the grace of God, he would smile. He saw the change in his father's face too; filled with glory as he lifted them up and delivered them into eternal salvation. One day he would feel the same rush of power and righteousness – it was just a matter of time.

It was clear to him that his father had lost interest. He was becoming a man now and his transformation repulsed his father, who could barely stand to look at him. He should have felt grateful, but instead, he felt empty, as if his father had carved out his soul.

That summer, his father had organised a religious day camp of sorts for the younger boys. A morning of Bible readings followed by physical activity and church maintenance. One hot afternoon, he snuck down to the basement where it was always cooler. As he walked down the steps he heard his father talking to a young boy – a skinny one with thick blonde hair. He recognised him immediately – the Raven Boy – the one who always had his head stuck in a book. The boy his 'angel' had taken into her light while casting him out into the darkness.

He crouched on the steps and watched as his father knelt at the boy's waist, sweat dripping from his brow. He was dizzy, felt the rush of blood to his head as he watched. To calm himself, he focused on the picture on the opposite wall of the all seeing eye of God. But God wasn't judging the sinners today, God was questioning. *What was he going to do about it? What was he going to do?*

He turned away, but could still hear his father spit out the same incantations that he had once blessed him with. He had no words for the cascade of feelings rising within him. Was he grateful he no longer had to endure his father's attention, or angry that he was now parsing out his love to this boy? He was rejected, again. The sting hurt like God's disapproving eye which bore into him from the painting.

The confusion overwhelmed him, filled his mind with impure thoughts that compelled him to kneel down and slap the palms of his hands against his temple in the vain hope he could rattle them free and be rid of them. God, it seemed, would not grant him that release. At least not yet, there was much work to be done before that final victory.

Chapter 2

'When were you going to tell me about the fight?' Manx's sister asked as he walked into the hallway of Cwm Talw.

'Dewi spill the beans under interrogation?'

'Told me it happened, never told me why.'

'Kids, eh?' Manx said. 'Bloody mystery.'

Sara looked at him warily. 'Something you're not telling me?'

'Dewi here?' Manx asked, ignoring the question.

'Of course not, he's still at school,' Sara said.

'Shit, I forgot. Anyway, I got him this,' Manx said, handing her a scruffily wrapped package. 'It's a red lorry. I remember he used to have one, before Shanni…'

'Yeah, he lost it, ta,' Sara said, eager to shift gears on the conversation. 'Mam's in the kitchen. Even heard her laugh a few minutes ago, thought she'd forgotten how to do that.'

Manx began to make his way down the hallway. Sara placed her hand on his cuff. 'Don't go causing a big fuss, Tudor. It's probably nothing.'

'She asked for her will, and her solicitor?' Manx said.

'Yes, but it might not be what you think. He's good for her, Tudor.'

'Good for you too?' he said, then instantly regretted the remark as Sara threw the package on the sofa and walked off.

Alice and Denny were deep in conversation. Alice was pouring over the old family Bible that hadn't seen the light of day since Manx was a boy.

'Haven't seen that for a while,' Manx said.

'Your mother has found great comfort in it, haven't you, Alice?'

'Better that than the bottom of a gin bottle, I suppose,' Manx said.

Denny flinched at the remark before composing himself and opening his hands. 'Open your heart, and he will be revealed.'

'See, Tudor, he understands,' Alice said, clasping his hands in hers.

'All this,' Manx said, pointing at the Bible, 'how exactly is it helping?'

'By sharing her grief, Alice will find her path.'

Manx felt the familiar bite of impatience. 'Dredging up old memories. Thought you were an atheist, mam, thrown that old Bible out years ago?'

Alice shrugged.

'She who is lost, shall be found,' Denny said.

'And you're an expert because you deliver food in a van? Not exactly a calling, is it?'

Denny flinched again. 'My work has its own rewards.'

Manx sighed and leant in close. 'I know what you're up to,' he said. 'Let's walk into the other room, slowly, and talk, eh?'

Denny smiled. 'I'll be back in a minute, Alice.'

In the living room, Manx gestured for him to sit. 'I don't know you from Adam, but I know your type, a good samaritan with empty pockets and a way with the old ladies.'

'I'm not—'

'You might have my mother fooled, but not me. If she offers you money, wants to write you into her will, if she as much as offers you a fucking chocolate digestive, you refuse it, understand?'

'I'm not sure I do understand, Inspector, I would never—'

'I'm sure you wouldn't, but just in case temptation gets the better of your good nature, resist. Understand?'

'And if she doesn't want to accept my refusal?'

'Persuade her otherwise,' Manx said.

As Manx left the house a slow drizzle was settling in the late afternoon air. He leant on the wall, looked out to the faint outline of the mountains to the south-east and lit up a King Edward.

He didn't expect coming home would be a picnic, but he didn't expect to be pulled into some elder-abuse drama with his mother either. His phone vibrated in his jacket pocket. He answered and listened as Nader relayed the emergency call they'd just received. He snuffed out the cigar on the wall; it felt as if he'd just stabbed his own gut with the embers as he walked to the Jensen.

Chapter 3

His face was rough with a three-day stubble that itched at his skin. He couldn't remember the last time he'd left it so long before shaving. His wife, Miiko, preferred him that way, clean shaved, but she'd been so distant the past few weeks she barely acknowledged his presence, except for reluctantly signing the affidavit stating he was home with her the night Sian died. Of course she'd agreed. After all, what choice did she have? Her hands were as dirty as his were.

He was on the deck, looking over the flat, wide plains of the nature reserve when Glyn Lewis slid open the patio doors.

'Any luck?' he asked.

'I had it in the palms of my hands, Lewis, and now it's slipping through my fingers,' McLain said, a heaviness in his voice. 'I was this close.'

'There's always tomorrow, Kimble, and the next day.'

'I'm beginning to think Fowler was right after all.'

'Are we talking about the same thing here, Kimble? The black brow?'

'Fuck the damned albatross,' McLain said, slapping his hand on the deck railings. 'The project. No one's returning my calls, I'm like a bloody pariah. It's a grade one disaster.'

Lewis walked towards McLain and opened his backpack.

'Takes me back,' McLain said, glancing at the battered old PC laptop Lewis had just placed on the table. 'Recycling or repairing?'

'He who turns the sinner from the error of his ways will save the soul from death.'

'Spare me. I'm in no mood for your religious bullshit today, Lewis. In fact, not any day.'

Lewis smiled. 'Fowler saw the error of his ways and agreed the past should remain buried.'

'Just like that?' McLain said, a wary tone in his voice. 'Unlikely.'

'He had a change of heart, decided to move on. Good news for us and the project, Kimble.'

Instead of relief, McLain felt the immediate tidal wave of anxiety. From somewhere deep in the marshes of the nature reserve, he was sure he heard the strident call of the black-browed albatross, but it was merely background noise. There was a far more commanding sound grabbing his attention; it rung out clear and precise, like the toll of a bell.

'What have you done, Lewis?' he said, grabbing the lad by the shirt collar. 'What the fuck have you done?'

Chapter 4

PC Delyth Morris sat in the waiting area of Gwynedd Hospital's Accident and Emergency department playing Candy Crush. She'd been waiting two hours already and wasn't even in line for treatment. She felt a pang of sympathy for the twenty or so people sprawled across the chairs half-asleep, a resigned look in their eyes as they waited. She'd heard the NHS was straining at the seams, but witnessing it first-hand was an eye-opener. Half an hour later, the doctor finally appeared.

'Are you the next of kin?' she asked, checking her clipboard.

'No. Don't even know why I'm here to be honest.'

The doctor handed Morris her own business card. 'Insisted we call you.'

Morris nodded. 'What the hell happened?'

The doctor adjusted her glasses. 'Attempted suicide. We pumped a bottle full of zopiclone from her stomach, but she has severe burns on her upper highs and hands.'

'She set fire to herself?' Morris asked 'Bloody hell.'

'Nothing quite so dramatic,' the doctor said. 'A spark from an outside fire caught on her blanket, she was already unconscious. If the family renting the house next door hadn't seen the flames and called the fire service, we'd be having a very different conversation.'

Morris felt a deep pit open in her stomach. 'Can I see her?'

'We're keeping her in ICU, she's not out of the woods yet. She wasn't a suspect or anything was she?' the doctor asked. 'Or a witness?'

Morris shook her head. 'No. I just think she was sad,' she said, sighing. 'Just really sad.'

Chapter 5

Manx stabbed the spacebar on his keyboard. 'There's something off about this, but I can't put my bloody finger on it.'

'It's our man, no doubt, boss,' Nader said. 'Cut his neck and tied him up like the others. I should have arrested Fowler sooner, the bugger would still be alive.'

'Where have you been, Morris?' Manx snapped, as the PC walked into the incident room. 'Briefing started half an hour ago.'

'Sorry, sir. Bangor A & E, took bloody hours.'

'Forgot the stabilisers on your bike again, Minor?' Nader said.

'Donna Robinson, attempted suicide.'

'Jesus,' Manx said.

'Always thought there was something off with her,' Priddle said.

'Well, despite your expert opinion, Priddle, the doctor reckons she'll pull through,' Morris said, irritated. 'What's that?' she asked pointing at the CCTV footage.

'Victim number five,' Nader said.

'Bloody hell.' Morris put her jacket on the back of the chair and stared at the screen. 'Bangor Uni?'

'Liam Fowler,' Manx said. 'Murdered at his desk last night.'

Morris watched the figure walk down the hallway, disappearing before emerging some fifteen minutes later carrying a laptop.

'Any angles that show the face?' Morris asked.

'Back and side views only. He knew the cameras were there, did a good job of hiding himself this time.'

'He's getting smarter,' Priddle said.

Manx looked over the incident board. 'There's something about the press coverage that's not making sense,' he said, pointing to the newspaper clippings 'Why didn't they print anything about the removal of the liver or the notes we found?'

'Saving it for an exclusive?' Nader said.

'Doubtful,' Manx said. 'What if that's all they had? Maybe whoever leaked this only had the information of the doll face and that he bound his victims. As far as we know, Fowler's liver was left intact, no removal, no note.'

'Maybe he was interrupted, had to scarper before finishing the job,' Morris said.

'Maybe,' Manx said, sitting on the table edge. 'Let's go back to what we do know. Five murders, each one with the same MO, except the female victims who he stabbed in the thighs and torso. We have two photographs; one we think could be a selfie of our killer in his party frock, the other a family portrait from outside some church, somewhere, sometime in the seventies.'

'British Virgin Islands, sir,' Morris said. 'BVI. I looked it up when I was in the waiting room. Bugger all else to do there.'

'Good, Morris. We also have two elements that connect the crimes,' Manx continued. 'Number one, religion. Biblical quotes left at the scene. Our killer could have spent some time on the British Virgin Islands, maybe as part of a missionary expedition. Morris, dig into this Points of Light outfit; historical documents, press clippings, whatever we can find. It's like a creep-show over there, put the hairs on the back of my neck on notice.'

'What's the second connection?' Priddle said.

'Kimble McLain.'

'Thought we were warned off him by the ElVera,' Nader said.

'Doesn't mean we can't dig around what's public knowledge. If there's any connection to McLain and the Points of Light Ministry, we have probable cause to formally interview him.

Either way, Troup's going to be all over this investigation like a fly circling shit. We've already got her band of merry fucking men in the other room, won't be long until she sends in some senior officer on permanent secondment if we don't make some progress.'

Manx walked over to the incident board. It looked how the inside of his head felt – a jumble of ideas, unresolved connections and tangents. His mobile rang. He looked at the incoming number: Head Office, St Asaph. The day didn't look like it was improving.

Chapter 6

Praying gave him a sense of calm at times like this: times when his whole being vibrated as such a frequency it felt as if his skin was on fire.

He was huddled on one of the pews in St Deniol's Cathedral, Bangor, feeling the weight of sin urging itself on his shoulders. He'd dropped McLain off earlier for a meeting with his solicitors. Lewis had taken the opportunity to consult with his own counsel, one that required more faith than it did an hourly rate.

Easter weekend was only a couple of weeks away – a celebration of resurrection and rebirth. His spirit lifted at the thought. Maybe that's what he'd given McLain, the possibility of rebirth; that from the ashes he could resurrect his vision, stake his permanence on the world.

He'd never been on board with McLain's pseudo-Buddhist philosophy, it was too vague for him, too esoteric. At the same time, he'd never understood McLain's atheism. In fact, not just atheism, it felt more like hatred, a deep intractable hatred. But maybe he too would see now how the power of faith could move mountains, and would understand what he did was for the greater good, how he had acquired the mantle of sin for him.

As he prayed, he watched one of the cathedral elders fill the vases with fresh daffodils – bursts of bright yellow, pinpoints of optimism and life. It filled him with a sense of hope. All was not lost. Not yet.

The cathedral organist shuffled herself onto the stool and ran the scales. She made a show of placing her hands in just the right position above the keys, brought them down with gusto and played the opening chords of 'All Things Bright and Beautiful.'

His breath caught in his throat as he listened. Seven, soul-stabbing notes that bore deep into him. As she played, the notes appeared to him like long nimble fingers wrapping their tendrils around his heart until he could barely breathe.

Chapter 7

Manx was led to a table overlooking the Menai Strait by a fresh-faced young waiter who was overly keen on the chit-chat. As he walked through the restaurant, he noticed how full it was for a Wednesday afternoon. It was noisy too, conversations echoing off the high ceilings and tall windows. The brightness from the light spilling in from all corners hurt his eyes – Manx preferred his restaurants like his pubs: dark, quiet, and cheap.

'Any significance to meeting here?' Manx asked as he sat and took the menu from the waiter.

'Kimble's you mean?' Malcolm Laird said, flipping over a beer mat with *Kimble's* written across it in a swirling font. 'He's got three, all over North Wales. Tourists love the food, the locals love having a trendy gastro-pub on their doorstep. Win-win all round.'

'Nice ego boost, not that he needs one,' Manx said.

'You should see the toilets. Pictures of him everywhere, when he was a kid, family snap shots and the like. Not the sort of thing I want to look at when I'm taking a piss.'

Malcolm Laird smiled – it was the kind of smile that put Manx on guard. He looked sleazy, like he could be running a seedy strip club. Still, he shouldn't hold that against the man, some of his most valuable informants back in London owned seedy strip clubs.

Manx looked at the menu, zeroing in on the beer list. 'Food any good?'

'Rave reviews,' Laird said. 'I've ordered the fresh fish platter, plenty for two.'

'You on the frequent diner program or something?'

Laird laughed. 'Perks of the job. Sorry, more like perk of the job. I get wined and dined a lot, comes with the territory.'

'Is that what this is? You're wining and dining me?'

Laird leant his elbows on the table and spoke softly. 'Listen, if Troup knew I was meeting with you, she'd be spinning in whatever coffin she chooses to sleep in at night.'

Manx laughed. Maybe he'd misjudged Laird after all. He might look like a sleaze-ball, but at least the man had a sense of humour.

'I figured this place would be safe. Not too many coppers.'

'Beats the lounge bar at the Bull.'

Laird took a sip of water and cleared his throat. 'When I heard about Fowler's murder, I called some contacts at the daily rags. Seems Fowler was shopping around for a buyer.'

'A buyer. For what?'

'Kimble McLain, This Is Your Fucking Life,' Laird said, badly imitating the Dublin brogue of the show's presenter, Eamonn Andrews.

'Showing your age there, Laird.'

The Press Officer ignored the remark. 'You do know they started in business together, right? There was a falling out. Fowler leaves and basically becomes a computer repairman. Kimble McLain? Well, he becomes this,' he said, extending his arms wide.

'How did I not know about this?'

'McLain employs a team of people to keep his image clean, Manx. They scrub whatever he doesn't want seen out there, especially his past. Dig long enough and you'd find it.'

'Christ, that puts a fresh spin on things.'

'There's more,' Laird said, slipping an envelope across the table. 'A list of McLain's business interests and investments. I'm not sure if it means anything but it's worth a look.'

'Why are you doing this, Laird?'

'I was a journalist myself, before I signed on for this. I saw the writing on the wall for newspapers a while ago, but I still believe in a free and democratic press, so long as it doesn't damage an ongoing investigation or put public safety at risk. Bottom line, I think Troup's wrong on this one.'

'Wrong. How?'

'You don't get to Kimble McLain's level of wealth without making enemies along the way. The public have a right to know certain things. We can't be censors, Manx, that's not our job.'

Manx thought for a moment. 'The leak to the press, on the serial killer. Was that—'

Before he could finish the question, Laird had slammed his palm on the table and hardened his face as if he'd just been smacked with the smoked mackerel now being delivered by the waiter.

'Look, I know I'm not a very likeable person, Manx, hell I doubt my wife likes me that much. But I've got a job to do. The press hate me because they're in a news cycle that demands more, the force hates me because they always want to release less, it's a fucking untenable situation. But leaking something like that? Fuck you, Manx!'

Laird pushed his chair back and flung his napkin on the table. 'Enjoy your fucking fish.'

Chapter 8

He took a final glance at the church from the back seat of the taxi. As the memories of his time on the island dissolved into the window he knew he'd be back someday; just like his own father had returned to his father. *It was a perfect symmetry,* he thought as his mind flashed back to that day and the events that completed the circle.

It was never clear who had reported his father to the police, but he remembered clearly that knock on the door. It was a hot August afternoon. He was sixteen, failing at most of his O Levels, except religious education. Not that his parents cared much. He would be shipped someplace to preach the word of God soon enough. School was merely a legal obligation to be endured until he was free to leave its secular confines.

It had been two summers since he'd seen his father in the basement with the Raven Boy. How many more had there been since then? He would never know. Sometimes he would think of the other boys, wondered if they felt like him: dirty, unworthy of love from anyone, not even God.

His father was led from the Lodge in handcuffs, his neck bent, as if anticipating the swing of the executioner's blade. His mother was on her knees, her chest heaving with the weight of grief and sobbing like she had done the night they left the other island. But this time there would be no midnight dash to the port, no ocean crossing, no divine resurrection.

Days later his father was released on bail. There was insufficient evidence to charge him – or at least that's what he'd read in the papers. As the weeks passed, his father became more withdrawn, locking himself in his bedroom for days on end.

They hid the newspapers from the boy, but he would always find them. Headlines screaming for blood, terrible accusations; admonishments by church elders vowing punishment and the purging of such evil from their ranks. More boys had come forward, each one with a similar tale at the hands of his father.

A few days later it became clear those hands would do no more damage to his own son, or any other boy. As he walked into the church to perform his prayers, he saw his father silhouetted in the stained glass window, the afternoon sunlight pouring through in broken shards of blue and red. The thick rope around his neck was chaffing against the rafters, which creaked like the slow beats of a clock, as his father's still warm body swung in time to the tick-tock rhythm.

He felt eerily calm as he fetched a ladder, loosened the rope from around his father's neck, and carried him across the aisle. He slid open the wood flooring, stepped in and dragged the body into the baptism pool, cradling his head in his palm as he stood, waist deep, in the water.

He pushed his father's head under the surface. He repeated the ritual until his arms grew tired. This was how he could make his father happy now. It wasn't his place to pass judgement, that was God's divine work, all he could do was cleanse his soul in preparation.

Several months later, his father laid to rest, they left the island. His mother had secured a safe home far away from all that had happened. Another fresh start. He would be the new boy again, but he wasn't afraid any more. He belonged with God now, and God was everywhere.

Chapter 9

Priddle ran into the incident room, crashing into one of the chairs as he entered. 'Buggering hell!' he said, rubbing his knee.

'Nap time over already, Priddle?' Nader said as the young PC hobbled past him towards Manx.

'CCTV footage from the uni, sir,' Priddle said, breathlessly. 'The car park on the other side of the campus. We've nabbed the bastard.'

Manx slipped the memory stick into the port. 'Our man?' he said, clicking play.

'Yeah, he's still got the laptop,' Priddle said, reaching over and fast-forwarding the timeline. 'He runs off to the west of the car park. We lose him for a few minutes then he drives right past, bold as brass.'

'Dumb fucking criminal or what?' Nader said.

'In a bloody Range Rover,' Manx said. 'Don't tell me...'

'Digital forensics already confirmed that it's Kimble McLain's.'

'Christ,' Manx said, wiping his palm across his face. 'He can't be that bloody stupid, surely.'

'As I said, dumb fucking criminals, we always get the stupid bastards in the end,' Nader said.

Chapter 10

I t didn't take Cain and Abel software long to crack the password. Fowler had become lazy over the years. An overnight pass through the program was all it took. By ten that morning, McLain had full access to the laptop.

Fowler was right: he had been a file hoarder. Thousands of documents spanning decades. McLain felt tired just looking at the desktop as it filled with folders and sub-folders tagged with cryptic names and extensions. He leant back in his chair. Did he really want to go digging around in there? It would take days, and anyway, there'd be nothing new for him to see. It was ancient history that didn't need excavating. He flipped the lid shut and headed out onto the deck.

The chorus from the nature reserve below did little to calm his mind. Lewis hadn't admitted to what he'd done, but he knew, and the question was, what was he going to do about it?

His wife, Miiko, slid open the doors and handed him an envelope.

'This just arrive for you,' she said.

'Who?'

She shrugged her shoulders and turned away.

'I'm sorry,' McLain said, quickly. 'About everything. Really sorry.'

Miiko stopped and turned to him. 'Easy to be sorry afterwards, anyone can say sorry, Kimble. Sorry needs action attached or else it's just words.'

'I'll make it up to you, promise.'

'You find another one, then you can talk to me.'

McLain grabbed her hands. 'I've made an appointment, we can try the other way again, we didn't give it a chance last time, we were too impatient. It will work, Miiko, I won't accept that it won't.'

Miiko shook her head. 'What are you going to do, Kimble? Will a child into the world? Create one, like magic?'

She pulled her hands from his.

'But you'll come to the appointment?'

'I'll think about it,' Miiko said and disappeared back into the house.

At least it was something – she'd *think about it.'*

He checked the scribble on the envelope:

FAO Kimble McLain, Raven Boy.

A knot formed in his throat. A mistake? It must be.

His fingers trembled as he slid out the single sheet of paper. The sketch of a solitary raven, perched atop the branches of a Corsican pine, its head turned towards him, its eye accusing him.

Under the tree was a quote:

'For all have sinned and fallen short of the glory of God.'

His blood rushed to the soles of his Louis Vuitton loafers. He steadied himself on the railing. It couldn't be? Not after all these years, surely?

Chapter 11

Manx sat in his office replaying the CCTV footage as if it were a favourite movie scene. By the time the white Range Rover had sped past the camera for what seemed like the hundredth time, he had decided on a firm course of action.

Despite Troup's orders to keep McLain at arm's length, the evidence was too persuasive to ignore. How could he have been so stupid? It didn't add up. The information from Laird had thrown a new light on the investigation. If Fowler was out to sell an exposé on McLain, there was good reason for McLain to have the man silenced, for good.

The envelope Laird had given him was still unopened. He reached across and extracted the printout.

Kimble McLain's life history: born on the island and adopted when he was a few weeks old by a family on Anglesey, both doctors, who had died some years back. Stellar student, double honours at Cambridge in computer science.

Another list contained his investments and business holdings, all in alphabetic order. The names were unfamiliar, mostly high-tech companies Manx had never heard of, and a property development company located here on the island – so far, so legal. As he expected, he had some offshore holdings, mostly in Dubai, but nothing that stood out as suspicious. It wasn't until he got to the letter 'S' that something triggered his memory. He called out from his office.

'Hey, Morris.'

'Be right there,' she said.

'Sospan Fawr. Does it mean anything to you?'

Morris scrunched her brow, confused. 'Um. Berwi ar y llawr?'

'What?' Manx said, before quickly realising her reference point; an old nonsense rhyme that was a staple of every Welsh kid's upbringing – *big saucepan, boiling on the floor.*

'No, Morris, Sospan Fawr, that food delivery app thing. Some new outfit on the island.'

'Oh aye, read something about them in the papers last week.'

'Did you know Kimble McLain was an investor?'

'Yeah, I think they mentioned it in the story, it's probably still online,' she said, tapping out the web address for the *Holyhead and Anglesey Chronicle.*

Manx read the story and checked out the photograph of Kimble McLain outside a grey industrial building shaking hands with Councillor Harden Jones.

'Thick as thieves,' he said.

'Yeah, says here that Jones helped secure the planning permission.'

'What are the odds that if we dig around Harden Jones's accounts we'd find some irregularities?'

Manx looked again at the photograph on website. There was a woman standing to McLain's left; tall, pretty, with a thin smile.

'And she's the key,' Manx said. 'Sian Conway. Did Hardacre get back with the DNA from the foetus?'

'Nothing yet,' Morris confirmed.

Manx walked to the incident board. 'If what Donna Robinson tells us is true, and Sian didn't have a social life, no men, there was one man that she was very close to,' he said, stabbing at Kimble McLain's photograph.

'Sian Conway and McLain?' Morris asked.

'Why not,' Manx said. 'Liam Fowler's got eyes all over Sian. He intercepts some communication between her and McLain and makes a connection. He's furious, but he's not stupid. He sees an opportunity to push McLain for more cash.'

'We'd need McLain's DNA,' Morris said, 'to prove he was the father.'

'Or a confession,' Manx said, 'both as unlikely as each other.'

He looked over the board. 'McLain's not our killer, but he's hiding something.'

'Okay, so where next then, sir?'

Manx pointed at McLain's photograph. 'We go back to the beginning. Find everything we can on McLain before he became headline fodder. A wise man once told me, everyone has something to hide, I'm guessing Kimble McLain is no exception.'

Chapter 12

Cadwalader Walden-Powell almost choked on his afternoon scone when he caught sight of Manx's shit-eating grin from behind the evidence room reception desk.

'No bloody way, Manx,' Cadwalader said, spitting the crumbs from the scone onto his shirt. 'I did you a solid last time, damn well nearly cost me my job.'

'But we nailed him, thanks, in part, to your sterling work.'

'Forget it, Manx. My scones buttered up enough without you laying it on thick,' Cadwalader said, taking a large gulp of tea. 'You promised, no more of these under the table shenanigans, my heart's in no condition to handle this kind of stress.' He patted his chest as if to prove his point. 'Surveillance is like GCHQ these days. Cameras, fingerprint access to all the evidence rooms, biometrics they call it. Bloody liberty if you ask me, a man's life isn't his own any more. They'll be monitoring the bloody toilets next, HD cameras, the lot.'

'Yeah, that doesn't bear imagining,' Manx said, pointing at the pair of nipples staring up at him from a well-thumbed copy of *Escort* magazine.

Cadwalader's walrus-like face beamed bright red. He dragged a copy of last week's *Daily Post* over the magazine. 'I expect this is to do with all that?' he said, stabbing the newspaper headline; the same one Manx had seen last week. 'Whole place is talking about it.'

'Your opportunity to contribute to the greater good.'

Manx handed him a slip of paper. 'Signed and approved by the DCI.'

Cadwalader examined the paper. 'I think you just like fucking with me, don't you Manx?'

'Has its moments,' Manx said.

'You could have just given me this when you walked in.'

'And spoil what little fun I have in my day?'

Cadwalader huffed and read over the evidence request.

'Child abuse case back in the late nineties,' Manx explained. 'Some nut-job religious outfit out on Anglesey, missionaries apparently. Jacob Owens was accused but took the easy way out and hung himself before he could be charged or stand trail.'

Cadwalader stroked his thick, drooping moustache. 'I think I was here when that all happened.'

'Where else would you be?'

'One of your officers on the island, Mickey Thomas, I think. He was the SIO until they shuffled the case to someone more senior.'

Manx nodded. 'Good information, Wally, I'll talk to him. Poor bastard's probably bored to death at home all day now he's retired.'

'Jesus, Manx, the whole Wally thing!' Cadwalader said, looking around and lowering his voice. 'I told you before, took me years to get over that whole 'Where's Wally' bullshit. The memories still grate on me, you know, psychological. I'm probably scarred for life.'

'Sorry,' Manx said. 'Now, how about fetching me those case files, Wally?'

Chapter 13

Ashton Bevan's face contorted into a serious grimace as he navigated the more complex steps of the paso doble.

'Relax, for Christ's sake, Ashton, you look like you're trying to pass a stool. Let the beat lead you.'

Bevan took a deep breath and fixed his best 'dancehall' smile as he led his wife, Sherri, across the living room floor. He wasn't feeling it, not today. He tried putting his best foot forward but succeeded in stamping heavily on Sherri's toe in the next measure.

'Jesus, Ashton, what is the matter with you? It's like amateur hour. You'd better shape up before next month's regionals,' she said, kicking off her shoes. 'If we get a tap on the shoulder before that snooty couple from Rhyl, I swear to God I'll be tapping somewhere else with my stilettos, and it won't be your bloody shoulder.'

Bevan slumped onto the sofa.

'A little help?' Sherri said, turning her back on her husband.

He lifted himself up, unhooked the top of her sequin dress and unzipped it. Sherri unravelled her carefully constructed bun, held in place by several hair pins. Bevan glanced down at the small scorpion tattoo on the small of his wife's back, barely visible under her dress and only ever revealed in the bedroom. As her perfectly highlighted blonde hair fell to her shoulders, he traced his finger down her spine, as if stroking an exotic bird he never imagined having the good fortune to touch.

'For God's sake,' Sherri said, shaking her husband's fingers away. 'Your timing's as clumsy as your footwork,' she added, grabbing the straps of her dancing shoes and stomping up the stairs.

Bevan sighed and turned down the volume of 'Matador Paso', wiping the film of sweat from his brow. As he ran a mental check-up on his choreography his phone pinged with another email, this one confirming the tickets were booked for late July: an all-inclusive resort in the Dominican Republic. Peak season, peak prices.

He sighed. *My credit cards do runneth over,* he thought to himself as he threw the phone onto the sofa. That lad had better pay him the rest of the money and soon, or else Sherri would be taking more than her stiletto heel to his balls.

Chapter 14

The low hum of the incident room was interrupted by the loud whir of the fax machine spinning to life.

'Bloody hell, 1984 is calling,' Nader said, looking behind him.

Morris dropped what she was doing, ripped the document from the machine and studied it carefully. 'Marsden. Marsden Owens.'

'Forensics were taking too long, so I called the local police on the British Virgin Islands and sent them a scan of the photo. They gave me the number for the editor of a local newspaper, the *Lambert Beach Recorder*.'

She checked her notes. 'Masie Devlin, nice woman, been there for years, she said. Told me she took the photo for the paper, it was just after the boy's christening. They gave him a local name, apparently, wanted him to fit in.'

Manx read the article. It was the same photo but taken a few seconds later than the one he took from the lodge. The woman's hand was now settled on the boy's brow, her pose a little more considered. He read the by-line:

'The Points of Light Ministry brings hope to Lambert Beach with a new mission to spread the word of the Lord. The Reverend Jacob Bedortha-Owens, his wife Elsie and baby son Marsden.'

'And get this, sir,' Morris said, barely able to contain her excitement. 'She told me they were there for around eight years, then one night they just vanished.'

'Don't tell me,' Manx said waking to the incident board. 'Another scandal?'

'Huge, sir. There were rumours that Jacob Owens was abusing young boys at the church. She told me the parents went over to confront him, but he'd already gone, just disappeared in the middle of the night. The locals ended up setting the church on fire, burnt the place to the ground.'

'Jesus,' Manx said.

'So, you think this Marsden Owens is our killer?' Priddle asked as Manx wrote the name under the photograph.

'Number one suspect, Priddle. Marsden is Lucy, Lucy is Marsden. If any of you has a contrary opinion, speak now or forever hold your peace.'

There was no rumble of complaint from the team.

'Right. Let's put that team Vera Troup sent over to work. We need everything we can get on Marsden Owens. Address, movements, medical records, the lot. Priddle, you can give them the good news.'

'Sir,' Priddle said, racing to the other room.

'If this Marsden Owens is on a mission, what is it?' Manx asked.

'Revenge?' Nader said.

'On who?' Manx said.

'The world?' Nader replied. 'There's no connection between the murders, so it could just be random, he's taking it out on the world, he picks out easy targets. Women alone, older men who can't fight back.'

'There's a connection, Nader, we just haven't made it yet,' Manx said.

'If it is revenge, he might have a list of names he's going through,' Morris added. 'He's crossing them off his list, one by one.'

'If that's the case, then the answer is somewhere in here,' he said, slapping one of the eight evidence boxes Cadwalader had given him yesterday.

'We search these files like they're the Rosetta bloody Stone. Cross reference any names that tie back to the Jacob Owens case and back to our case. Tomorrow is Friday, three weeks from the first murder. Marsden Owens is planning to kill again. He probably has no address, no real footprint we can trace, online or otherwise, and we don't have a recent photo.'

'That's another weekend gone to the dogs, then,' Nader said, peering warily into the reams of paperwork spilling over the rim of the evidence box. Morris, on the other hand, already had her sleeves rolled up and was elbow deep in the first evidence box.

Chapter 15

Loud music bled through the walls of the neatly appointed dormer bungalow as Manx strode up the pathway. Ukuleles and steel guitars, he guessed. He pressed the doorbell several times before Mickey Thomas appeared, cocktail in hand and sporting a red floral shirt that did his sunburnt complexion no favours.

'Bad time?' Manx asked, pointing at the slice of pineapple and cocktail umbrella poking out from the glass.

Mickey Thomas smiled. 'Bad time? I'm bloody retired, Manx, it's never a bad time. Just got back from Hawaii. Jenny and I thought we'd invite a few friends over for a luau.'

'Come again?'

'Luau, Hawaiian feast. The whole village slaughters a big pig then they bury it and cook it for three days underground. Never tasted pork like it.'

Manx looked over to the throng of people gathered in the small patio area. 'In your garden?'

Mickey laughed. 'You must be joking, too much hard bloody work. Just threw a few pork chops and some pineapple slices on the barbecue. Got a spare one if you want it?'

'I'll pass. Got a few minutes in between your cocktails?'

'Front room,' Mickey said, slurping at the last dregs of his Mai Tai.

'Jesus, that takes me back,' Mickey said, after Manx finished speaking. 'I led the case for the first few days, arrested the bastard myself, but then they brought in a DCI from Colwyn Bay to take over. Shunted me out, but life goes on, didn't need the headache to be honest with you.'

'When you arrested Owens, were his wife and child there?'

'I'd say so. Yes, the wife was wailing like a Banshee. Can't blame her I suppose, hell of a shock finding out your husband's a bloody kiddy fiddler.'

'Anything else you can remember? Anything unusual?'

'Jesus, that's over twenty years ago, Manx, I can barely remember what I had for breakfast.'

'It's important, Mickey.'

'Connected to this whole serial killer thing? Nasty business.'

'Maybe, not sure yet.'

Mickey furrowed his brow. 'I remember the body was odd. When we got there he'd already been cut down, but the body was wet, like he'd drowned or something.'

'Any follow up on that?'

'Not that I knew of. All the evidence pointed to suicide, and as I said, they shunted me back out to desk duty after a few days.'

'Thanks anyway, Mickey,' Manx said, getting up to leave.

Mickey took a large gulp of his cocktail. 'The past never leaves us alone does it, Manx? The dead ones, the unsolved cases.'

'Not unsolved yet, Mickey,' Manx said.

'Aye, keep on it. It's all one big puzzle. You'll put the pieces together eventually, figure it all out.'

He wished he could share Mickey's optimism, but there was something in his tone that caught Manx off-guard.

'You're talking about this case, right, Mickey?'

'What else would I be talking about, Manx?'

Chapter 16

'You're one hundred percent sure?' Manx said, looking Aston Bevan directly in the eyes.

'Better men than you have doubted me, Manx,' Bevan said. 'Don't make the same mistake.'

'Jesus, who pissed all over your shoes?'

Bevan took a long swig of beer and ordered another.

'Drowning your sorrows or something?' Manx asked.

'Just keeping up with the Manx's,' he said, smiling and taking the pint from Nerys, who looked at both of them with her usual snap disdain before turning on her heels.

'Liam Fowler's blood in McLain's Range Rover pushes the case in a whole new direction. If we fuck this up he'll hang us all out to dry.'

Bevan sighed. 'Here's the report,' he said, slamming the folder on the bar. 'Believe what you want, but it's evidence not conjecture. Science, Manx.'

Bevan took another gulp of beer. 'Any new developments on the case I should be aware of? New information? Doesn't seem like you're making much progress from where I'm standing.'

'We're making progress, Bevan,' Manx said, a steely tone in his voice. 'Listen, were you here when that nasty business with the child abuse case came up? Some missionary outfit by Newborough beach in the late nineties?'

'Before my time,' Bevan said. 'I've been on the island less than fifteen years, barely qualifies me for a tourist visa.'

'Learn the language, might win you some points.'

'Who's got the fucking time, Manx? Too busy making a living to pay the bloody bills. Anyway, not enough vowels. It's like a bad letter draw on *Countdown*.'

'Just a suggestion,' Manx said, gathering the folder.

Bevan looked ahead and ignored him.

'What, no parting shot across my bows, Bevan?' Manx said. 'No vague allusion to my past you want to leave hanging?'

Bevan turned to Manx. 'Executed all the due diligence I need to, Manx. I'm just a spectator now. Take care, eh?'

He turned back and looked directly ahead as if he was taking full stock of himself in the bar mirror as Manx left.

Chapter 17

'Shit on a stick, Manx. You'll get one shot at this, at best.'

'His Range Rover, Ellis, no doubt about it. It's enough to get a warrant to seize the vehicle.'

'Maybe,' Canton said. 'Supporting evidence?'

'I was informed by a reliable source that Fowler was shopping a story on McLain to the newspapers. With Fowler dead, the story stays buried.'

'Troup's not going to like this, not one bit, she's already requesting your balls on a silver plate over McLain,' Canton said, snipping a pair of miniature clippers at a dwarf pomegranate.

Manx winced as Canton pruned. 'With all due respect, Ellis, DCS Troup isn't the SIO, I am.'

Canton picked a dry bonsai leaf from his desk and crunched it between his thick fingers. 'Don't fucking remind me.'

'You'll put in the request?'

Canton sighed. 'I'll call the magistrate, then I'll call Troup. Christ, I'm getting too old for this.'

Chapter 18

'I'm sure DCS Troup did not approve this,' Kimble McLain said over the shrill beeps of the tow truck as it backed up to the front end of the Range Rover.

'We have a warrant to seize your vehicle in connection to the murder of Liam Fowler,' Manx said gesturing for the driver to back up a few more feet.

'I'm calling my solicitors.'

'We'll be gone by the time they arrive, Mr McLain, and I bet those blokes don't come cheap, save yourself a few quid.'

The driver jumped from the cab and attached a hook under the front bumper.

'Looks like new,' Manx said, looking over the car. 'Have it cleaned recently?'

'I have a man who comes round every week, cleans all my cars.'

'Of course you do,' Manx said. 'Mind telling me where you were two nights ago, Mr McLain?'

'You mean the night Liam Fowler was killed?'

'Bingo.'

'At a memorial service for Harden Jones. Some of us went to the pub afterwards, I left at around eleven and came home. My wife—'

'Will confirm you were home,' Manx interrupted.

As the mechanic fired up the towing mechanism, Manx heard the familiar cadence of soothing chimes carrying from the porch to the driveway. McLain's wife had come out to check on the commotion. She didn't looked particularly soothed.

'Kimble, I need the car. Why are they taking it? Did it break down again? I told you, should have bought a Lexus, more reliable.'

'Use the Mini,' he said. 'It's in the garage.'

'I have to pick up the new plants for the Japanese garden today. Mini's too small, I need the Range Rover,' she said, folding her arms in defiance.

McLain breathed deeply. Manx could almost see the Zen evaporating from his body as he dug deep for the best response and came up empty handed.

Manx jumped in. 'Sorry about the inconvenience, Mrs McLain, we'll have it back in a couple of days.'

Miiko looked Manx up and down, taking careful consideration of his boots, which were caked in a thick wedge of mud.

'If they come in house, you make sure they take off boots,' she barked at McLain. 'Outside world stay outside. You understand?'

McLain sighed deeply and slumped – he looked like a man with the weight of several worlds resting across his shoulders. *Six Billion Dollar Man or not,* Manx thought, *he had the same problems as everyone else.* The kind of problems that money couldn't begin to solve.

Chapter 19

'Did Manx deliberately ignore my orders, Canton, or did you?'

Vera Troup was in no mood for pleasantries as she entered the viewing room and squinted through the one way mirror. McLain and his three solicitors hung their jackets on the back of the chairs and made themselves comfortable.

'All by the book, Vera,' Canton said. 'You were informed about the warrant when it was approved by the magistrate. I's dotted, t's crossed.'

Troup turned and looked Canton directly in the eyes, a disconcerting, accusing glare he was all too familiar with.

'For future reference, Ellis, voicemails are not sufficient notification for something of this magnitude. Face to face. Do I make myself clear?'

'As a bell, ma'am,' Canton said, gesturing they should both sit.

'Right, tell Manx to get this circus over with quickly,' she said, sitting down.

Manx dragged his chair close to the table. 'Thursday thirteenth, the night Sian Conway was murdered, you met with Liam Fowler, why?'

'Unfinished business.'

'And did that business get finished that night, or a couple of nights ago, when Liam Fowler was murdered.'

'My client has an alibi for the night in question, his wife—'

'Will sign another affidavit, yes I know,' Manx said. 'Back to the night of the thirteenth. What was this unfinished business with Fowler.'

'Stuff from years ago, when we started the company together, he felt he was owed more money.'

'Was he?'

'He took the package we offered, signed a contract, he should have abided by that. He was blackmailing me, some information he said he had. I never saw it, but I couldn't take the chance, not with the Menai Express project at a critical stage.'

'So you paid him off?'

'Didn't come to that.'

'Convenient,' Manx said.

'Is that a question or a statement of fact?' McLain's solicitor asked.

'You tell me,' Manx said.

'I'm not the kind of person to have people killed, Inspector.'

'You'd be surprised what people are capable of when pushed into a corner. But let's put that aside for now. A successful man like you, I'm sure you must get this all the time, though, another chancer on the make? I'd imagine those expensive solicitors of yours take care of most of those, so why did you handle this yourself?'

'He was a friend once.'

'And Sian Conway's estranged husband.'

McLain's eye twitched at the sound of her name.

Manx leant back. 'Here's what I think, Mr McLain, and feel free to jump in at any time. You were having an affair with Sian Conway. She was pregnant with your child, Fowler found out, and that's why he was blackmailing you. Not some story from your past, this was personal, wasn't it, McLain?'

'You don't have to answer that,' his solicitor advised.

'No you don't. But, let's look at all the connections. Sian Conway is murdered, three other people connected to you are murdered and now, Liam Fowler, who you just admitted was blackmailing you is also murdered.'

Manx pulled out a photograph. 'This is the blood we found on the seat of your Range Rover. It's Liam Fowlers. How did it get there, Mr McLain?'

'No comment.'

Manx placed his iPad on the table and pressed play. 'This might help jog your memory.'

McLain watched the CCTV footage of the man running past the camera then driving past a few minutes later.

'It was too dark to get a decent close up, so we don't know the identity, not yet, but we're working on it. Thing is, Mr McLain, we have sufficient evidence to charge you with the obstruction of justice for not disclosing this information earlier. I don't think you're a cold-blooded killer, but you're not telling us the whole story.'

Manx clicked off the video and leant in close. 'Here's what's going to happen. I'm going to arrest you for obstruction and within a few hours you'll be out on bail. When the press get wind that Kimble McLain's been arrested, it doesn't matter what for, they'll make it look like it's connected to the murders. I can't stop that, they'll print what it takes to sell papers. But, start talking and I'll rethink that obstruction charge. Simple choice, Mr McLain.'

McLain's solicitor was about to protest when McLain gestured for him to stop.

'It's not what you think,' McLain said, taking a deep breath. 'Myself and my wife, Miiko, we both loved Sian, but not in the way you're insinuating.'

'I'm listening.'

'It was all above board, legal, we had a contract drawn up with Sian. She would have been well compensated, set for life.'

'Your wife knew of the affair?'

McLain sighed. 'There was no affair, Inspector, haven't you got that yet?'

'Not until you spell it out to me, McLain.'

'Miiko and I have everything we could ever want, all except a family. Sian was our saviour. She agreed to carry the child to full-term.'

The answer drew itself in crayon for Manx.

'A surrogate? Sian was your surrogate?'

'Miiko adored Sian, she jumped at the opportunity, we both did.'

'And Fowler found out?'

'He wanted money. I was happy to pay it, get him out of my hair for good. He'd have gone to the press, we didn't need that kind of publicity, especially Miiko, she didn't deserve that.'

Manx sat back and took in the information.

'So, both you and your wife stand to benefit from Liam Fowler's death.'

'I don't have people killed, Inspector, it's ridiculous.'

'But someone did kill him. The night Liam Fowler was killed, who else had the keys to your vehicles?'

McLain looked over at his solicitor. They made eye contact and nodded. He knew the answer, discussed it with the solicitors beforehand. If it came to this, there was no other choice.

'Who else, Mr McLain?'

McLain took a deep breath. 'Glyn Lewis, my communications director.'

'You think that's him,' Manx said, pointing at the footage.

McLain nodded.

'Can you speak the words, Mr McLain, for the tape.'

'Yes, I believe that's Glyn Lewis.'

'And where is he now?'

'I haven't heard from him for days.'

'Before leaving, you'll supply us with all the places you think he might be. Home address, work, favourite beauty spots or if you do know where he is, compel him to turn himself in, or this might reflect badly on both of you. Understand?'

McLain took a deep breath. 'Hand me a pen.'

PART THREE
THE LAST ENEMY

Chapter 1

Gwen Schofield had the anxious demeanour of a woman harbouring a secret she was itching to share with the world. When Manx walked into the Pilot Arms, her words were out before he'd ordered his usual. 'Some woman's been looking for you,' she said, pulling hard on the pump. 'Thought you'd like to know.'

'Some woman?' Manx said. 'You'll have to give me a starter for ten, Gwen. Did she look happy, angry, indifferent?'

'Oh, narrow it down for you, would it, if she was happy or angry?

Happy or angry, Manx thought, it would be a short list of women on the island tracking him down. 'Simple deduction,' Manx explained, 'so I'm prepared for either scenario.'

Gwen smiled. It always seemed to catch Manx off guard, as if he would forget from one day to the next how such a simple act could light up her face and fill her large, bright eyes with a momentary burst of sunshine. 'She was about my age, black woman, nice hair, very pretty,' she said, winking

'Well, that should narrow it down in this place,' Manx said.

'Oh, great compliment that is,' Gwen said, wiping down the bar in a determined fashion. 'Remind me why you're not in a relationship again?'

Manx realised how big a boot he'd just wedged into his mouth. 'I meant her being black, not, you… the other stuff… about being pretty…' He stopped himself, unsure of what other drivel might spill from his mouth if he continued.

'I think you can stop there,' Gwen said. 'Wouldn't want you saying anything that might get you arrested.'

Manx nodded. 'Quiz sheet?'

Gwen reached under the bar and handed him the paper. 'Usual rules: no Google, no shouting, no copying.'

'Got it. By the way, did she leave a name?'

'The pretty woman who's looking for you? No. Said she'd come back this evening. I told her you're here most nights by yourself taking up space at the bar. She said that sounded like the man she was looking for then left.'

'Outstanding.' Whoever she was knew him far too well.

Manx grabbed his pint and joined a table of two young lads, both wearing a similar style of plaid shirt, and a young girl, with heavy, black eyeliner and jet-black lipstick.

'What's this week's name?' he said, sliding a chair between them.

'The Young Farmers and Old Macdonald,' Clai said, and nudged the other lad, Bryn, with his elbow.

'Fuck you too,' Manx said. 'I was thinking something like 'Police and Thieves', like in the Clash song.'

He received a blank look from the table, all except Amanda, who scowled through her lipstick. 'And what are we? The thieves?'

'Just an idea,' Manx said.

'Too late, already approved,' Clai said. 'It's on the board.'

Manx turned around. 'Bastards,' he muttered under his breath, then lay his paper flat on the table 'Right, I hope you're a lot smarter than you are funny.'

Friday night was pub quiz night. It was the closest Manx had to a routine outside his work. Being here cleared his mind, gave space for his subconscious to trundle away in the background. Marsden Owens was the best lead they'd had in days, though, as he expected, the extended team had found little evidence other than an old cell phone account opened in the Queen's Park area in London. There were no credit cards and no medical records. Manx suspected he and his mother would have changed their names after leaving the island. He still had one lead to follow up on. The lad from Second Skin Productions was due back tomorrow and, if he hadn't called by first thing Monday morning, Manx would personally drive up there and drag it out of him.

The team tracking down Glyn Lewis were equally frustrated. All the places McLain had provided turned up nothing. He'd probably gone to ground, maybe even left the island by now. Either way, his gut told him the slow grind was paying off; the pieces gradually falling into place.

As the Pilot Arms gradually filled, he scanned the room for the woman who seemed far too familiar with his habits. The landlord cut the jukebox and hammed it up on the mic. The first round was a picture round, a montage of B and C level celebrities that Manx had never heard of, but which Amanda possessed an almost gleeful knowledge about. He fared little better on the sporting round as Bryn and Clai took the lead. As the night segued into music trivia he finally caught sight of the woman standing in the snug and chatting with Gwen as if they were long lost friends. Celia Cartwright? What the hell was she doing here? Manx was about to head over and greet her when Amanda elbowed him sharply in the ribs.

'One for you, Old Macdonald,' she said, slowly repeating the question as if he were senile. 'Name the singer-songwriter that connects the 1978 hit 'Baker Street' and Quentin Tarantino's 1992 heist movie *Reservoir Dogs?*'

Manx was distracted, stretching his neck to get a better view. It had been years since he'd seen her, but CeeCee was the kind of woman who always stood out in a crowd. Her hair was longer than he remembered. She'd teased what used to be an unruly Afro style into submission and flattened it into a glossy, straight cut that gave her an air of maturity. She was still a head turner – some of the local likely lads were already trying their luck.

'You know this one or not?' Aled asked, impatiently.

'Gerry Rafferty,' Manx said finally, scraping his chair back. 'He wrote 'Baker Street'. He was also one of the founding members of Stealers Wheel whose 'Stuck in the Middle' was used in the torture scene in *Reservoir Dogs*, which is arguably one of the best uses of a song in a movie.'

'You sure?'

Manx threw Aled a '*are you seriously asking me that?*' look and shoved his way to the snug to find out what had dragged CeeCee three hundred miles from London to Anglesey on a Friday night.

Chapter 2

CeeCee pounded her third measure of Scotch and looked him squarely in the eyes. 'You're shitting me, Manx,' she said, angling her hand on her hip as if she were about to deliver him a good telling off. 'What the hell have you been smoking since you came here? 'Baker Street' is not the best song ever written, not even close. What about 'Save the Last Dance for Me'? Written by a paralysed man for his bride as he watched her dance on their wedding night. Now, that's a fucking heartbreak in a box right there.'

'I didn't say the best,' Manx complained. 'I said one of the most *tragic* songs ever recorded.'

'Bollocks. I reckon you're a secret saxophone solo fetishist,' CeeCee said, leaning closer into Manx. He caught a faint trace of her perfume and it reminded him of better times. 'I bet you've even got a Kenny G playlist for the long nights staking out the cow tippers.'

Manx shook his head. 'It does have the best sax solo ever laid to vinyl, but you need to listen to the lyrics, Cartwright. The man's singing about broken promises and shattered dreams, the false hope that moving somewhere new will change who you are. Self-deception, Cartwright, the most tragic human malady of all.'

'Jesus, Manx. You get all that from a song?'

'Don't you?' Manx asked, who was always taken aback when people didn't find the same depth of meaning in songs that he did. He should be used to it now, but it felt good, this bantering with CeeCee, someone who knew her music, even if it wasn't to his taste. Early Motown and funk were more her style.

'You don't change, Manx, that's for certain. Even the uniform's the same, black suit, white shirt. Still wearing the Blundstones too?' CeeCee said, running her fingers down the edges of his lapels and checking out his boots.

'Same old, same old,' he confirmed, tugging self-consciously on his pencil-thin black tie. CeeCee smiled, her lips full and moist from the Scotch. They too, reminded him of better times.

'So why are you here?' Manx asked. 'Bit out of your way.'

'Just thought I'd look up an old friend.'

'One copper to another,' Manx said, downing the remainder of his drink, 'you're a terrible liar.'

CeeCee looked around and lowered her voice. 'Is there somewhere quiet we can talk?'

'I'm renting a place just up the hill.'

CeeCee hesitated. 'Is it safe?'

Safe? Manx felt the earlier optimism of the evening dwindle away. CeeCee hadn't come here for a weekend mini-break and catch up on old times, that was for sure.

Chapter 3

hy was she doing this? PC Delyth Morris was still wrestling with the question as she took Donna Robinson's arm and guided her from the wheelchair into the backseat of her car.

'Don't want to be no bother,' Donna said, clipping her seatbelt.

'No bother,' Morris said. 'Just wanted to make sure you got home safe.' It was a true statement, but a complex one that Morris couldn't begin to explain to herself, let alone to a woman she'd spoken to for no more than twenty minutes.

'My mam says I can stay at hers, at least until I get stronger.'

'That'll be nice,' Morris said.

Donna said nothing and just looked out at the blur of hedges and fields as they drove to the east of the island.

Manx would probably give her hell if he knew, Morris thought. Manx had always warned the team not to get personal when it came to cases or witnesses. It was sound advice, which she followed for the most part, but when it came to Donna Robinson, the woman had touched a raw nerve with Morris that she wasn't aware was even there. She'd seen in Donna the *Sliding Doors* version of PC Delyth Morris – the alternative version that would have found her working a dead-end job and involved with a man like Fowler. She'd known men like him; met them personally and as part of the job.

One slash a millimetre deeper on the wrist, or an emergency call a minute too late and she wouldn't even be here, Morris thought as she drove. She was sixteen at the time, a cry for help that even to this day she couldn't understand the reason behind the act. Her parents, of course, blamed themselves and were ill-equipped to deal with the aftermath. But there was someone who was. She took Morris under her wing, cared enough to make her feel that she mattered. Now it was payback time, she thought. Her duty.

She took the woman's arm as they trod up the path towards Donna's mother's house.

Megan Robinson leaned back against the door, fag hanging from the corner of her mouth, unimpressed. She had the same harshly drawn features as her daughter, but blunted with the age. She looked over Donna as if appraising a low-ball offer she were about to refuse, took a deep pull on her cigarette and shook her head.

Delyth Morris could almost feel the desperate urge etched into Donna's face. The daughter's yearning for her mother to wrap her in her arms and tell her everything would be all right. Megan Robinson, however, found such temptations easy to resist.

'Jesus, Donna,' Megan finally said, blowing a mouthful of smoke across her daughter's face. 'Can't you fucking do anything right?'

Chapter 4

Celia Cynthia Cartwright was one of the sharpest coppers Manx had worked with. She had the rare combination of intellect and killer street instincts that had been sharply honed on one of the toughest housing estates in London's Stockwell district. She'd flown through the ranks at the Met, joining the CID in less than three years, with glowing recommendations. For a young black woman from a disadvantaged background, it was a major accomplishment, but Celia Cartwright had more than her fair share of challenges.; not least her family, most of whom had been in and out of prison for minor and serious offences for decades. *She was bucking the trend,* she would tell anyone the first time they brought it up. The second time they asked, her response would ensure they wouldn't ask a third time.

Manx had worked with her for four and a half years until she was transferred to the Serious Crime Squad – an inevitable move for CeeCee and one of the hardest recommendations Manx ever had to write. He wasn't just losing a standout copper, he was losing a good friend. They had chemistry, that was for sure, and on several occasions too much Scotch had got the best of them, leading to some awkward small talk the following morning in Manx's kitchen. He had held out the faint hope that it might develop into something more serious, but CeeCee was young and ambitious and didn't think twice when offered the position. He didn't blame her, he would have done the same.

'Just moved in or clearing out?' CeeCee asked, folding her leather jacket over the back of Manx's sofa and looking over the sparse contents of his house.

'Still debating,' Manx said, selecting one of his favourite playlists, Neko Case's 'Wish I Was the Moon Tonight', which filled the small living room.

'Nightcap?' Manx asked, popping the cork on a half-empty bottle of twelve year-old Springbank Single Malt.

'Old habits?'

'I prefer to leave change to the young and stupid,' Manx said, pouring two glasses.

'Where's your bathroom, Manx?' CeeCee asked, distractedly. Her mood had shifted perceptibly from the pub to the house.

'Up the stairs, to your left.'

As CeeCee made her way upstairs, Manx sat and let his mind wander over the case. They were closing in, he could feel it, taste it almost. After a few minutes, Manx went to check on CeeCee. There was a light on in the second bedroom. CeeCee's shadow, long and lean, flickered anxiously like a candle wick along the wall.

'Jesus. I had no idea,' she said as Manx walked in. 'I mean, you mentioned it once, but this? Should I be worried about you?'

CeeCee paced the small room, taking in the patchwork of photographs, maps, and hand written notes pinned on the far wall like an incident board. 'The Angel of Anglesey,' she said, reading aloud from a yellowed front page of the *Daily Post*, dated July 18 1987. 'Pretty,' she added, tracing her fingers along the young girl's face.

'I got this text about three months back,' Manx said, pointing at a print out, '*Miriam wasn't the only one. Find her, find them.*' Then, they kept coming, about one a month.'

CeeCee read them aloud.

'*You're asking the wrong questions. Make them pay, all of them.*'

'*Death will take them soon, catch them before the darkness comes.*'

'*They travel at night, never the same place twice.*'

CeeCee shook her head. 'Have you sent these to digital forensics?'

'Whoever's sending them is using one of those Cryptophones, end-to-end encryption, impossible to trace.'

'Listen to you getting all technical on me, you'll be programming your own VHS player next.'

'Let's not get ahead of ourselves,' Manx said. He scanned the board for what felt like the millionth time. 'It's like one blind alley leading to another, nothing makes sense, none of it. There's a connection but I'm buggered if I know what it is. Wish they'd just come out with whatever they have to say, cut to the fucking chase.'

'Maybe they're scared, Manx,' CeeCee suggested. 'Leaving you clues so they don't have to expose themselves.'

Manx shrugged and straightened a photo of his younger sister – the one he used to carry in his wallet. Miriam at eight years old, a carefree smile into the camera and a lance of sunlight striking across the ocean behind her.

'Is this even healthy, Manx?' CeeCee asked, a low tone of concern in her voice.

Manx shoved his hands deep into his pockets. He hadn't talked to anyone about this, not even his family. His mother would have clung to any news with the last cuticles of her fingernails in the hope of answers, of which Manx could deliver her none. His sister, Sara, would have dismissed it with a wave of her hand and told him to let sleeping dogs lie, it was all in the past.

'Do you believe in fate, CeeCee?' Manx asked.

'I believe in hard work and making your own luck. Some pre-ordained path for everyone? Fuck no, where's the mystery and magic in that?'

Manx nodded. 'Since coming back here it's like I'm facing my own reflection every day. And, to be honest with you, CeeCee, I'm not sure I like what I see looking back at me.'

'I don't know, Manx, you're a couple of years away from a comb over. Your dress sense could use some updating, but you're not in bad shape for a middle-aged copper with trust issues.'

Manx laughed. 'That's not what I meant.'

'Right. You're back someplace you left thirty years ago, through no fault of your own, and you expect things to have changed but in reality they haven't, not really.'

CeeCee was right. Nothing had changed, at least not the things that mattered. Despite the tourist-friendly restaurants and gastropubs, the island was still the same as when he'd left it thirty years ago: two hundred-and-fifty square miles of unreliable memories that were still chasing him down, looking for answers.

'Do you think everything that happened to me back in London happened for a reason. Destiny or something?' Manx said, not quite believing the words had passed his lips.

'Detective Inspector Tudor Manx putting his faith in the intangible, I never thought I'd live to see the day.'

Manx sighed. 'You know me, CeeCee, I'm too fucking practical by half but I don't know, recently I've been thinking about this stuff, probably way too much. Religion, all that shit. This case I'm working on, I think it's messing with my head.'

'We can find reasons for everything if we look hard enough,' CeeCee said, moving closer to Manx and taking his hand in hers.

'You'd think I'd have put it behind me by now. The thing is, I remember the before and the after, but the event, the important details, they're lost. Maybe this is my one chance, and all I've got is a bunch of texts and a wall full of shit that makes no sense. Maybe I should just—'

CeeCee pressed her fingers to his lips. 'You'll figure it out, Manx, you're one of the best coppers I've worked with. The Met was fucking stupid, not to mention out of order, to treat you the way they did.'

Silence fell. Their eyes locked as the bloom of an inevitable moment grew between them. There were no words to be said. Manx felt the soft brush of CeeCee's lips on his and the room disappeared into the distance. Her kiss was familiar, like jumping into a warm ocean where the strokes came easily and freely.

Chapter 5

Manx was stirred from sleep by an unfamiliar ringtone. Heading downstairs, he noticed a bright point of light emanating from CeeCee's handbag. He reached inside to mute the phone and accidentally knocked over her bag, shaking out her wallet.

He squatted, picked it up and stared as her official Police ID slid to the floor. He sat down and processed what he'd just read. Celia Cartwright, Detective Inspector, AC12. The Met's anti-corruption unit that investigated their own kind: police corruption across every rank and division. Manx felt a sickening churn in his gut as he flipped the ID card through his fingers. AC12 had investigated him last year – a gruelling eight months that had him questioning every decision he'd made as a police officer. Before he had time to contemplate the implications, CeeCee was standing at the door, wrapped in his dressing gown.

'So, now you know,' she said, folding her arms across her chest.

'Fucked up I have to find out like this,' Manx said, a rising tension of anger biting at his throat.

CeeCee walked slowly towards him, like she was approaching a wounded animal that might lash out at any moment. 'And how would you have preferred I tell you, Manx? Great to see you. Remember that massive fuck up that got you demoted and you thought was all done and dusted, well it's been re-opened. By the way, what are you drinking?'

Manx wiped his hand across his face. 'What do you mean, re-opened?'

CeeCee drew a long breath and perched herself on the edge of the sofa. 'Jock Sullivan, he's in charge now.'

'God's own fucking crusader,' Manx said, recalling the stocky, bilious Scot with a strict Protestant seam running through his spine.

'He's committed to investigating any case he thinks there could have been a cover-up, including Operation Ferryman.'

'So, what was the plan, CeeCee?' Manx asked, pacing the room and pouring himself a drink. 'You drive up here and relive old times in the hope I'd surrender some information you could impress your new boss with?'

'You've got it wrong, Manx—'

'Jesus, I knew you were ambitious, Cartwright, but this takes the fucking biscuit.'

CeeCee blanched at the remark. 'If Jock knew I was up here I'd be fired on the spot.'

'Jock, is it?' Manx said, his anger reaching full boiling point. 'I think you should probably leave.'

CeeCee was about to protest, but she knew Manx too well; knew that once his blue eyes had that glint of steel in them, there was no shifting him. She'd concede the battle, but the war was still wide open.

'Have it your way, Manx,' she said and turned away.

'Why now?' Manx asked as she walked up the stairs. 'Why now?'

CeeCee paused and turned. 'Seven teenage girls found dead in the back of a van. No arrests, no trail, no justice. You of all people should respect that, Manx.'

Chapter 6

Morris poured herself a mugful of tepid, stewed coffee. She winced as she swallowed it, the dark, bitter finish set her teeth on edge. Maybe she should ask Manx if the department would cough up for a cappuccino machine, but the way the force's budgets were spiralling south these days, she wasn't holding her breath. She shoved the mug aside and took another look at the pile of papers spread across the table.

She and DS Nader had been sifting through the evidence since early this morning and had come up empty-handed. None of the names cited in the original Jacob Owens abuse case matched any of the recent victims. All the minors' names were redacted, and the only other names were his wife, Elsie, and the arresting officers. The coroner had reached a verdict of death by suicide, signed 1998. It was turning into another dead end. When she re-read the site and location of death, Newborough, Anglesey, she turned to Nader.

'Says here Jacob Owens hung himself, but there was a significant pooling of liquid in his lungs. Not enough to drown, but the coroner marked it as unusual.'

'Is that right?' Nader said, preoccupied with an exhaust manifold for the Ford Cortina he'd been bidding on.

Morris stepped away from the paperwork and pinned one of the photographs to the incident board. 'Did Manx ever mention the Points Of Light Church to you?'

Nader sighed. 'Don't think so.'

'Jacob Owens hung himself in the Points of Light Baptist Church, Newborough, not the Lodge. They must be two different places.'

Nader shrugged. 'Aye, maybe, lots of old churches down by Newborough, mind you. Think the missus has her eye on a plot over there for when I pop my clogs. I told her, unless it's walking distance to a pub, she can cremate me and set my ashes on the fireplace in the Crown.'

'Might be worth checking out, though.'

'Sounds like a morning job to me, Morris,' Nader said, stretching his arms outwards as if he were about to give her a bear hug. 'Bugger this for a game of pennies,' he added. 'I'm off home to watch the telly and open a can, see if the wife's up for it.'

Morris looked up and shook her head. 'Does she know you talk about her like that?'

'Been married twenty-five years, Minor, there's nothing she doesn't know about me,' Nader said, heading for the door. 'Tomorrow's another day in fucking paradise.'

Morris checked the time. Half six. It was still light outside. If she left now she could check out the church before dark. She tipped the rest of the coffee down the break-room sink.

In the car park, the only service car available was one of the Road Policing Unit vehicles. She signed it out and grabbed the keys. She'd drive over there, take a few photos and check in with Manx first thing in the morning.

Chapter 7

His eyes fell in and out of focus as he read the list of names. He'd started with the most deserving: the ones with an immediate connection. Soon enough, the Raven Boy would be acquainted with Lucy too. He wouldn't doubt the Lord's creation then; not when he was laid prostrate at His feet, begging for purgatory over hell. He required a plan, one that would get him close to him.

Working for him, he thought would have given him access, but he barely saw him, only the once when he came to open the offices; after that, he was what they called a silent partner. He'd show him what true silence meant.

'Warrior Chief,' he said, laughing as he typed his name into the computer in the reception area. 'God did not anoint you his warrior,' he said out loud. 'I am Beniah, not you.'

'What did you say?' her voice called out from the backroom. 'Do you need something?'

He looked up, noticing the flecks of plaster hanging from the far wall and the ghostly remains of a rectangular stain.

'That picture,' he called out. 'Where is it?'

'Don't know what you mean, love,' she said, turning the volume down on the TV. She rose stiffly from her seat. The ginger tom jumped from the table and followed at her feet.

'The one that was there,' he said pointing at the empty space.

Isla Logan stiffened. 'Oh, it fell off the wall. Old thing it was. The frame smashed, I threw it out.'

He flinched. *Another lie. They always lied.* Well, they can't lie when they're dead, he thought as he brushed past Isla and climbed the stairs to his room. All except Lucy, she never lied. She was true.

Once inside, he locked the door, removed his clothes and slid inside her. She felt warm, felt like home. He wasn't working tonight, he had too much preparation to attend to if he was to snare the main prize, but still it felt good having Lucy seep into him, him seep into Lucy.

He stood in front of the full-length mirror stroking her curves and bumps, the whisper of pubic hair which he slowly reached down to touch. *No retraction tonight,* he thought as he rubbed in between her legs. He ran his fingers through her pony tails, undid the ribbons and lay back on the bed. After all the good work he'd done, God would turn his head just this once, he was sure of it.

Chapter 8

Sunday. God's day – *he could have it, the whole fucking day*, Manx thought, as he looked out over the agitated spill of ocean stirring around the bay. He'd woken up with Thor's Hammer striking at his temple. His hope that a brisk walk to the beach and a stiff wind might blow his hangover out to sea turned out to be wishful thinking. The roar of the white-chested waves roughing up against the rocks only exaggerated the pain.

CeeCee's visit was gnawing at him like a rat chewing through live electrical cable; edging ever closer to the bare, raw wire. The messages he left with a couple of old colleagues from the Met remained unreturned. He had a sneaking suspicion that, unlike CeeCee, they were keeping their distance. Maybe he'd been too hard on her, but the news had hit him like a sucker-punch to the throat.

He put CeeCee to the back of his mind, fired up a cigar and sat on one of the small, upturned rowboats on the beach. A couple of locals were walking their dogs along the cliff path. Other than that, the village was abandoned, as if an alien abduction had taken place while everyone was sleeping. It reminded him how much he hated Sundays here – nothing to look forward to but some corny early evening TV show, a tepid bath and the looming spectre of the school week just around the corner. He always imagined Sunday was the sort of day that outstayed its welcome. An uninvited relative who was reluctant to leave even after the pot was nothing but tea leaves and the cake plate nothing but crumbs.

Back when he was a teenager, Anglesey was 'dry' – a nod to the strict Protestant thread stitched into the fabric of the island. His father, Tommy, though, always found a loophole in the dictum.

Inevitably, there was a rebel landlord more than happy to pull the pub curtains, and pocket the extra few quid for a few hours of clandestine drinking. The risk was minimal. A handful of coppers were usually part of the lock-in, and later in the day, a couple of teachers steeling themselves for another week and a clergyman bored with the pious finish of the communion wine would join the party. Failing that, there was always the early afternoon ferry from Holyhead to Dun Loagharie – eight pounds for a return ticket and a free litre of spirits thrown in as an aperitif.

By eleven Manx was back in the house. It was too early to hit the hard stuff, even he had his limits he reassured himself, and slipped the cork back on the Springbank. The Pilot Arms was the more respectable option. He hid himself in the corner for most of the afternoon with only the terse exchanges of Jack Reacher and the silent peanut gallery of Toby Jugs for company.

Back home, he lay on the sofa, CeeCee's words still running rife in his mind. Had she come to warn him, or had she been hoping for a quick information grab? There was no telling with her, she kept her cards close to her chest and he had a severe lack of evidence to make a judgement either way. He'd already paid his dues, taken the rap for what went down, it should have been ancient history, but here it was again, doubling back on itself – doubling back on him. *It was just another fucking circle,* he thought as his mind churned. He fell asleep on the sofa at around seven none the wiser, but tomorrow was another day; another day to redeem yourself, another day to fulfil the promise to be a better man.

Just after ten, his mobile stirred him from a fitful sleep. The voice on the other end was light, almost a whisper. Manx asked the man to repeat his name.

'Tyler Ashworth, Second Skin Productions.'

Manx grabbed his notebook and gave Tyler his undivided attention.

Chapter 9

Twilight descending.

PC Morris pulled up at the Points of Light Baptist Church and peered at the building through the windscreen. The light had waned rapidly since she'd left the station, the encroaching darkness making swift work of the remaining sunlight.

The church looks ruined, Morris thought – like one of those monasteries ravaged by Henry VIII. The roof was intact, but the stained glass windows were pitted with cracks. Morris imagined that from the inside looking out, daylight would filter into the church like sunlight through bullet holes.

The steeple at the north of the church leant at a sharp angle. The stonework chipped and battered as if it were subject to cannon fire that had found its target but failed to bring it to its knees.

Morris reached for her mobile and stepped out, intending to take a few photographs then drive home.

No one has mourned here for decades, she thought. The gravestones had buckled into the earth like rotten teeth in need of swift extraction. There were no vases of fresh flowers or evidence of recent tears shed at these gravesides. Whoever lay here had long been forgotten.

The temptation to peer further into the grounds gripped her – just a few more photos. There had to be some connection to the case. She placed her hand on the iron gate, the frame scraping against the rough stonework. Once inside the grounds, she snapped a few different angles, the flash from her mobile fired automatically, momentarily halting the fast-invading darkness.

He was sitting in a pew to the back of the church, plotting how to best snare him: the Raven Boy. The blast of white light streaming through the holes in the window prickled the hairs on his neck. He waited, maybe his eyes were playing tricks on him. It would happen when he spent too long under the dim glow of the lantern; shapes would blur at the corner of his eyes, ghostly fragments with no substance or form. Seconds later, the same again, a flare of white flooding through the cracked windows. He reached for the knife in his backpack, crept towards the back door and stepped outside.

Morris skirted the church wall. An empty Costa Coffee cup had been discarded on the path. *Someone must have been here recently*, she thought and took another photo. Edging around to the church door, she pulled hard on the thick loop of the iron handle and twisted. Nothing. She shoved her shoulder against the wood. The door barely budged – not even a creak of submission.

He watched her. Observed the police officer. What was she looking for? Not God's forgiveness, surely? She didn't look the godly type.

Before leaving, Morris crossed the flagstones at the back of the church, just in case she'd missed something. There was little to see save a row of blank gravestones leaning against the wall, anticipating the engraving of the final eulogies.

She turned to make her way back to the service car. A sound from the peak of the steeple startled her. She looked up and felt a sudden rush of vertigo. As she stepped back to steady herself the ground snapped at her ankle; one swift bite, trapping her right foot in the teeth between a crack in the flagstones. The pain shot through the ball of her foot to the nub of her hip.

'Shit!'

She pulled harder, but her foot had fixed itself firmly into the crack.

Another sound. Behind her this time. A crackling – an animal padding over twigs.

She took a minute to compose herself, trying to dispel the image her mind was now conjuring: prey caught in a snare.

A bead of sweat fell into her eye. She brushed it away. This was stupid. She was a grown woman, a police officer, how did she get her foot stuck in a bloody hole? Nader would never let her hear the end of it if he found out.

She gritted her teeth and pulled with all the muscle strength in her leg. The foot gave, a little, but at a price. The sharp edges of the flagstones tore through her sock and into her ankle. Her knee buckled and she fell, her foot twisting as she landed, elbow first, on the ground. She could already feel the warm seep of blood trickling through to her shoe.

'Double shit!'

Another rustle in the undergrowth.

She couldn't pinpoint its origin, but it seemed everywhere, a shapeless, crawling sound itching its way around the darkness.

The first stirrings of fear pulsed through her like the hesitant flickers of a dying light bulb. She activated the torch function on her mobile. The beam out across the graveyard, shifting everything in its path into a flat, monochrome impression of itself – like one of those old black and white horror movies she liked to watch when her parents were asleep.

Her mouth was bone-dry. She swallowed, a reflex action to prove she was still here, still functioning – still herself.

'Jesus!' she needed to get out of here.

There was only one option. She folded herself at the waist, reached for her foot and began to unlace the boot, eyelet by eyelet. Her foot was swollen, pushing painfully into the tough leather as she fumbled with the laces.

The sound started again. Scratching, rustling, urging.

'Come on, come on,' she told herself, but her fingers responded slowly as she pulled at the tightly wound bindings

Another scrape, or was it a footstep this time? She couldn't be sure, but she was sure it was close.

Halfway done. She felt the boot give, the pressure slowly relieving. Another few eyelets and she'd be free.

She held her breath. The sound had stopped, stillness, save her heart slapping at her chest.

That's why people said, 'quiet as the grave', she thought – in the right circumstances, there were few things more terrifying than silence.

At the final eyelet she wrenched her foot free and groaned with relief. She brought her finger to her ankle – it was like a hot poker against her skin.

At that moment, the fragile silence cracked wide open. She whipped her head to look behind her. A thick, black shadow fell across her. She crawled back on her hands, felt the snap of downdraft across her face. Seconds later, silence. The flock of ravens had passed. She heard their mocking cackle as they sunk into the darkness.

She shook her head, cursed herself for being so stupid, and wrestled her boot from the broken flagstones.

Hobbling past the graveyard, she made her way to the car and threw herself in the seat. 'Jesus. I need a pint,' she said to herself, trying to squeeze her foot into the boot.

'Fuck it.' She threw the boot on the passenger seat and started the engine – the sooner she could get out of here the better.

She flipped on the lights and dipped her mirror.

His eyes filled the narrow frame, glaring at her from the back seat. She screamed. He wrapped his fingers through her hair and jerked her head back hard, like he was pulling on a horse's bridle.

The back of her head smacked into seat.

He wrapped her hair tighter in his fist and leant in close. His breath was warm and sour against her ear.

'What are you doing here, bitch?' She felt the cold sting of steel run across her neck. 'Confessing your sins?'

Chapter 10

The train shunted from Bangor station with a sharp judder and Manx spilled a mouthful of hot tea over his thighs. The old woman sitting across from him offered him a serviette and a pitying smile. He accepted both without complaint.

The train journey to London was a brisk three and a half hours. Long enough to re-read the case files, but too short to reach any new conclusions. As the blur of greens and browns shifted in the train window, Manx nodded off to the clacking of the wheels as they rolled southwards.

He may have dreamt. If he did, it was fitful and fragmented, a film unspooling in a projector. CeeCee had the starring role, that much he remembered.

At Euston station he grabbed himself a lukewarm Cornish pasty, thick on crust and short on filling, and called her: no answer. He left a message. His return wasn't leaving until later that evening, enough time to chase the lead and push CeeCee for more information, if she agreed to meet. He reckoned his chances were fifty-fifty at best. First, there was Tyler Ashworth's call to attend to.

He bounded quickly down the steps towards the taxi rank; the same one he remembered when he first arrived here over twenty years ago. A cocky, young PC, imagining he'd hit the big time with a posting to the Met's Serious Crime Squad. His superiors had knocked that kind of thinking out of him in short-order. Unless you were a born and bred Londoner, or your father had served his time in the trenches of Scotland Yard, earning the respect of your commanding officers was a rite of passage that you bent over and accepted with all the dignity you could muster.

Detective inspector-level entry positions were barely a twinkle in some commissioners' eyes back then. Ascending the career ladder meant long hours studying for the sergeant's exam and cleaning up the human and administrative detritus no one else wanted to touch. If you were fortunate enough to be attached to a mentor with a serious backstory and investigative experience, and who wasn't a complete prick on toast with a side plate of arseholery, you counted your blessings and sucked it up. Manx reckoned by now he owed Ellis Canton more than he could ever repay.

He jumped from the black cab outside Queen's Park station and checked the address. He wasn't familiar with the area, but could tell it was one of those London boroughs undergoing the spit-polish of gentrification. Cranes swung their skeletal arms across the skyline in a constant sweep of pick and drop; over-sized billboards with giant smiling faces and impossibly clean public spaces (that would in reality be owned by the building consortium) hung from the scaffolding. It was all carefully designed to entice the moderately well-off with the promise of an idyllic lifestyle that was within their reach and built over the festering bones of old London.

Even in the few months he'd been away, the city seemed to have shifted. Another expensive coffee shop; a moderately reviewed gastropub with some famous-for-five-minutes chef du jour at the helm; a high-end baby clothing store; a 'gin palace' offering a Bible-thick choice of cocktails.

He had to admit, he missed it all. The constant change of the place – the restless leg-syndrome that was London.

As he walked down Queen's Park High Street, he felt a familiar twinge of nostalgia. People were out enjoying the first bloom of spring; drinking outside, debating QPR's promotion hopes, the quality of the local schools and or, just like him, relishing the anonymity the city afforded. *There was no single circle here,* Manx thought, *no infinite feedback loop.* London was a series of multiple circles, all overlapping, free to be crossed and dipped into as you desired.

He stopped outside 34 Hatton Road, a compact two-up, two-down terrace close to the park. There was a skip in the driveway and the familiar sounds of construction workers – Polish, he thought.

He knocked. A few moments later a young woman, in her late twenties with a harshly drawn face, answered the door. She had the look of recent motherhood about her: eyes unable to focus on anything beyond the baby wriggling impatiently in her arms, hair in need of fresh highlights where the roots were showing, and a look that said, '*Can't you see I'm busy, so unless it's life and death, kindly fuck off.*'

'Call you back, all right?' she said abruptly and shoved her mobile into the back pocket of her jeans. 'Yeah?'

'Inspector Tudor Manx from the North Wales Constabulary,' Manx said, eager to get the words out before she slammed the door in his face.

The woman took a cursory glance at the badge, bouncing the baby on her hip. 'Wales? Long way from home, ain't 'ya?' Her accent was East London, Manx guessed – harsh, curt, ungentrified.

'I'm looking for a Mr Owens, I was told he lived at this address.'

Owens. Surnames only. It was how most of their customers preferred to do business Tyler had informed him.

'Na. Must have the wrong address, mate.'

'Maybe the previous owner?' Manx pushed.

'No idea. Might have been. We bought it from a property developer. Still bloody developing it too, lazy sod.' The woman shifted the baby onto her other arm and pointed at the sign pasted on the skip – Raven Construction. Manx made a note of the name and number.

'So you never had any dealings with Mr Owens?'

'Said that already, didn't I?' The woman ran her fingers through her hair and spoke quickly. 'Solicitor told us some church owned it, then rented it out to a single mother, she died so they sold the place. Must have lived here for donkey's years by the state of it.'

The woman paused. 'Hold on a mo,' she said, and disappeared into the hall.

She returned a few moments later with a small metal box with a tropical scene painted on the lid. It was one of those tourist trinkets – palm trees, blue ocean, silhouettes of people dancing on the beach – *'British Virgin Islands. Paradise Sweet Paradise.'* Manx's gut twitched with anticipation.

'One of the builders found it last week under the cellar. Just a bunch of old photos as far as I could tell. Here, take it or throw it in the skip, I'm not bothered.'

She almost shoved the box into Manx's hand. The baby was fully awake now, squirming to be fed.

'Worse than my husband, this one, can't leave them alone,' the woman said, reaching under her blouse and unhooking her bra.

Manx watched for a moment, unsure whether to turn his head or just walk away as the woman guided the baby's mouth to her breast.

'Hey! It's not a bloody peep show, mate,' she said, glaring at Manx. 'Go to bloody Soho if you're looking for that kind of thing.'

Manx felt the stiff breeze from the door slam across his face. Jesus! If that's what having kids did to you, he was better off out of the whole procreation game.

As he headed back to the station he got a call. CeeCee. She'd meet with him, but someplace of her choosing. But it had to be now.

Chapter 11

The cloth tasted of stale sweat and dried food. It was stuffed so far into the back of her mouth the fibres brushed against her throat. Her nose was running, rivers of salty liquid prickling at her lips. The urge to scratch and wipe was as intense as the pain still shooting through her foot and leg.

Where was she? Maybe the church, but Morris couldn't be sure. Faint specks of light filtered through the thin membrane of the blindfold. There was a thick, low roof above her and the floor was damp and carpeted with what she suspected was straw.

Her ankles and wrists were bound tight with a thick rope that rubbed her skin raw if she moved. She could roll on the floor a few feet in either direction before hitting the sides. Maybe she was trapped in a basement with a low roof, or a grave large enough for two. Neither option offered her any comfort.

The last thing she remembered was the blade at her throat, and him, dragging her from the car to the ground. She'd glanced her mobile on the grass and kicked it from his eyesight before the force of something heavy against her head – then darkness. Now, she was here, wherever here was, her head pulsating, her foot bloodied and throbbing, wishing she'd taken that one photo and left.

*   *   *

Why had the bitch police officer come? he asked himself as he paced around his bedroom. She'd complicated things; a fly in the ointment, a ghost in the machine. He should finish her off, but there was no precedent, no head-office memo of how to deal with the situation. It was off-message, outside the purview of his mission. She wasn't part of God's directive, at least, not yet. He needed to check the ledger, get her name. That would clarify things either way.

Still, there was a silver lining, a gift from God himself. After dragging her from the car he'd opened the boot, intending to pack her bones in there and await further instructions, and that's when he saw it – the instrument that would help seize the biggest prize of all. The moment he saw it, the concertina-like form, the teeth sharp as his own blade, he knew it would serve his purpose. Maybe God was speaking to him after all, he just needed to be a better listener.

Chapter 12

*U**topia T-shirt shop, upstairs at Camden Lock Market, forty-five minutes* – CeeCee's direction was terse and to the point; no opportunity to read between the lines.

As he emerged from the muted greyness of the Northern Line onto Camden High Street, the sun was tweaked to full brightness, forcing him to squint as he jostled through the tourists and punks making their way to the head shops and tattoo parlours.

He took a left after Camden Lock bridge and entered the market. He hadn't been here in years, but little had changed. There were more food stands, Manx noticed, but the thick aroma of stale patchouli oil and smouldering incense still clung to the place like an old hippy's Afghan jacket left out to air.

Shoving his way through a group of Japanese tourists armed to the smiling teeth with phones and selfie-sticks, he raced up the steps and searched for Utopia T-shirts. It was at the back of the first floor, a nondescript shopfront with a few browsers looking over their offerings. CeeCee was already there.

'Bit cloak and dagger, isn't it, Cartwright ?' he said, gesturing at her jeans and grey hoodie outfit, her baseball cap pulled down to the rim of her sunglasses.

'Fuck you, Manx, you're not in a position to judge,' she said, gesturing with a nod of her head that Manx should follow her to the rear of the shop.

'Why are you here, Manx?' she asked, removing her shades.

'Felt we left things up in the air,' he said, quickly figuring out she wasn't in the mood for small talk or banter.

CeeCee shook her head. 'I should never have come up. Fucking stupid move.'

'But you did,' Manx said.

CeeCee stuffed her hands in her hoodie pockets. 'Five minutes, Manx, tops. I can't be seen with you, understand?'

Even though he didn't, didn't understand at all what she meant, he nodded. 'Operation Ferryman. It was a done deal.'

'Was, Manx. It goes deeper. I'm not even scratching the surface and there's a stink about this that's turning my stomach.'

'Is that why you came?'

CeeCee softened. 'Partly. Look, Manx, you were a scapegoat. Someone had to fall on their sword and you drew the short straw. I don't know how far up this spreads, but I'm already getting cock-blocked at every turn. Nothing that raises alarms, but that's how these things start, soft push backs in the hope we'll eventually get tired and back off.'

'Back off from what?'

'Shit. I can't tell you, Manx, I just can't. I came to see you as a friend, now I'm here as a colleague. You know how they say everything in the universe is connected in some way? I'm beginning to believe it's true.'

CeeCee pushed her shades back over her eyes. 'You might want to answer that,' she said pointing at Manx's phone. He hadn't even noticed it was ringing.

Before he could say goodbye, or apologise for throwing her out of his house in the middle of the night, CeeCee had ducked out of the store, head bowed low, and disappeared into the throng.

Had he not been so focused on PC Priddle's mild panic, he may have noticed the reflection from a long camera lens glinting from a stall at the other end of the market and following CeeCee as she left. As it was, his conversation with CeeCee was swiftly put to the back of his mind. PC Delyth Morris hadn't turned up for work, no one had seen her since yesterday evening.

No answer at her home or her parent's house and her service car was missing.

Manx hung up. Ten minutes later he was back on the Northern Line heading towards Euston. An hour later sitting in first class, the only seat he could get at short notice.

He placed the box of photographs on the table and lay them out like the fragments of a jigsaw puzzle on the table.

Chapter 13

Shuffling directly above her, harsh grinding across a stone floor, followed by a rush of cold air. It wasn't fresh, but she'd take it, gladly.

After her first hours of panic she'd learnt to calm herself by keeping her mind occupied with short, mental jottings, like evidence in her notebook. It kept her mind from spinning out of control, imagining the worse. She listened as he moved around her. Took her mental notes.

Footsteps: heavy, probably work boots, a labourer of some sort, maybe?

Breathing: asthmatic and shallow. He was probably overweight, but not a smoker — there was no tell-tale funk of nicotine about him.

A faint tang of gas leaking from somewhere, a click of metal followed by a prickle of heat and the squeak of a screw turning.

A puff of sound, like someone blowing up a balloon? No, it was more like a camping light, one of those old kerosene ones her father kept in the barn.

She scraped her ankles across the floor to catch his attention. Nothing. She tried again, muted groans in her throat that were now dry as old bones.

He was moving, shuffling papers. He sighed deeply, slamming something on a table. A book maybe? Or his fist?

She heard the lazy drag of his feet as he moved towards her. She stiffened.

His body was inches away. She could smell him. His odour, dank and sweaty and the same sour breath leaking over her face.

His fingers were at her mouth now – fat and fumbling as he undid the knot.

His fingernails crawling around her lips. Gravedigger's nails she thought, as their dirt-ridden cuticles fumbled at her gums.

The cloth fell to her chin. She took in huge chunks of air that grated her throat as she breathed.

'Water,' she begged.

She felt the rim of a plastic bottle at her teeth and the relief of tepid water filling her mouth.

'Name?' he said.

'Erm. Morris. PC Delyth Morris.' The words caught like gravel in her throat.

He moved away. Several more minutes of pages being flipped.

'Are you saved, Morris. Are you?' he asked.

'I'm not sure what—'

'Not sure? You are either saved or you are not,' he said.

He shuffled back towards her. 'There is no room for negotiation. God does not bargain.'

His gravedigger fingernails were at her mouth again, settling the cloth firmly back in place.

Chapter 14

It was a story told in pictures, a life captured in moments. *Maybe at the end of the day that's all life was*, Manx thought, snapshots of moments, enough to fill a small trinket box then forgotten. He shook the dismal thought from his mind and concentrated on the photographs.

This was all that remained of the family now, a box full of six by fours. Marsden – at least the name was confirmed, scribbled on the back of the photos – *Marsden 5 years, Marsden 7 years, Marsden first harvest choir performance, Marsden nativity play 1983.*

There was something familiar about the boy, though he couldn't pinpoint what. Maybe he just looked like his nephew, Dewi. Maybe all nine-year-old boys with scruffy tufts of blonde hair looked alike? But there was something else about the boy, even in youth he seemed to possess a natural piousness; an aloofness that compelled him to never look directly into the camera, as if the act might rob him of something vital.

As the history of the boy unfolded from black and white to colour, Doctor Alvarez's words rang in Manx's head. *A recent loss? The death of a loved one?* If Marsden's mother had died recently, then Alvarez's profiling was correct. He'd also been right on the money with the missionary connection. Maybe he'd been too quick to dismiss the doctor's theories. If Marsden Owens was on a mission, Manx needed to figure what it was, quickly.

As the train rolled past Rhyl, Colwyn Bay and all stations to Holyhead, he looked closely at one of the more recent photographs; Marsden and his mother leaning against an old truck parked outside a field of what he guessed was a sugarcane plantation.

Mother and son looked more relaxed than when Jacob Owens was in the frame, as if his very presence drew life from them. It was probably one of the last photos taken before they fled the island. The woman's long, red hair was pulled into two bunches and tied in place with large white ribbons, her false eyelashes, long and curling.

The woman could have been Lucy in all but name.

*   *   *

When Manx arrived at Bangor station, Priddle and Nader were already waiting. His gut churned – they weren't here to greet him with good news, he was sure of that. They'd traced Morris's mobile phone to Newborough Forest. It was already getting dark and according to the digital forensics team the phone's battery was draining fast and would probably be dead in less than an hour.

'We've called everywhere she might be?' Manx asked

'House, parents' place, that's about it,' Nader said.

'Her mam and dad haven't seen her for a week,' Priddle said. 'Right worried they are.'

'They're not the only ones,' Manx said, stepping into the car and trying, without success, to stop the multitude of scenarios, each one more disturbing than the last, that were unspooling through his head.

Chapter 15

'Why come out here?' Manx asked as they pulled up to the grass parking area outside the church and walking towards Morris's service car.

'Well, boss,' Nader said, peering into the open boot and feeling a mild sense of relief that it was empty. 'She was looking through the evidence on Sunday afternoon. Reckoned the church might be connected to the case.'

'And you let her come out here alone, without a backup?'

'Swear to God, I had no idea she was coming,' Nader said, slamming down the boot. 'Told her we'd check it out in the morning. But you know what she's like, bloody stubborn, once she gets an idea in her head she's off like a terrier with a bone.'

'Aye, if that bastard's got her, it don't bear thinking about,' Priddle said, a tight knot of nervousness lodged in his throat.

Manx felt something push against the soles of his feet. He squatted and retrieved Morris's mobile from under his boots.

'Small mercies,' he said, glancing at the last photo Morris had taken.

'Shit, look at this, sir,' Priddle said, picking up Morris's bloodied boot.

The three officers looked each other, each of them feeling the same creeping sense of dread that, until now, had been an unspeakable thought lurking in the back of their minds.

'Big red?' Manx asked, turning to Nader.

Nader nodded, leant into the back seat and grabbed the enforcer, balancing its hefty weight in his hands.

'Ready and willing, boss,' Nader said, and strode confidently towards the church door.

* * *

She was at the bargaining stage, she assumed, early negotiations with God. How, if she got out of here alive in one piece, she would change, be a better person; a better daughter. She ran through a short mental checklist: visit her parents more often, be more grateful, show more charity — like she'd done with Donna Robinson. It was a start. That had to count for something in the deal.

A dull thump somewhere in the darkness interrupted her negotiations. Was he coming back to finish the job? Her muscles tensed. The sound was urgent, a deep, determined pounding that seemed to match the throb of her heart beat for beat as it hammered against her chest.

She could barely dare to imagine that relief might finally be within her grasp. She deepened her resolve with God and resumed her negotiations.

* * *

'Jesus, they knew how to make doors back in the day,' Nader said. 'Here, you have a go.'

He handed the enforcer to Priddle. He swung several times before the lock finally splintered. The door slammed open, the slap echoing through the rafters.

The stench of ancient incense and rotting wood filled the church. They took their time, allowing their eyes to become accustomed to the darkness before entering.

Manx signalled for them to split up. The church was small – fewer hiding places. They soft walked past the pews, crouching to look under each one as they passed. Empty; save for a carpet of yellowed and torn hymn sheets and the calcified eruptions of discarded chewing gum.

* * *

Negotiations halted for a while again, Morris kept her ears pricked, listening to the footsteps and voices circling above her. Fresh air was flowing into the space. They'd probably broken open the door, that would explain the hammering. Maybe she was still in the church, after all, the hunter rarely takes his prey far from its hunting grounds.

Noise. She had to let them know she was in here. She pounded her heels against the floor and groaned as loud as her sore, raw throat would allow, hoping against all hope that some sound would reach them.

*   *   *

'There's another room here,' Nader said, and gestured for them to join him at a door adjoining the vestry.

Manx leant gently on the door. It fell open easily, revealing a steep set of wooden stairs leading to what he assumed was the basement. He reached for his torch and directed the beam as he stepped down. It was more of a storeroom, he thought as his boots hit the rough floor.

In the basement, water had pooled to about two inches. It smelled of damp cardboard and rot. He shone the beam at the boxes and peered in one of them. It was stuffed with books. He took one and flipped to the first page – The Douay-Rheims Bible. Another ace in the hole for Alvarez.

'Fucking empty,' Nader said, joining him in the basement. 'Bastard must have taken her somewhere else. I don't know, boss, I've got a bad feeling about this.'

Before leaving, Manx swept the beam across the wall. The light caught on an old painting, faded and dirty with years of neglect. Through the layer of grime Manx noticed the all-seeing eye of God radiating through the clouds to the figures below. He'd seen it before. It took him a few more moments to remember where.

'Let's go, Nader' he said, retracing his steps towards the vestry.

'Where to?'

'Back to the very fucking beginning,' Manx said.

*   *   *

Her groans were clumps of sand in her throat, her feet aching and bruised. There was silence now, heavy and thickset. No voices, no footsteps. She may have heard the distant churn of a car engine and the crunch of tires on gravel but she was too preoccupied with her negotiations and fearing that she had little left to bargain with.

Chapter 16

If only he'd remembered to bring he tape and powder like he'd planned, but there was no time. It was too risky, especially with that bitch police officer finding him. They'd send more, then more still. That's how they worked, like a plague of locusts swarming towards him.

He'd lay low for a while, at least until he'd dealt with the Raven Boy. Afterwards, there would be others to attend to, then his work on earth would be done and he could rejoice in his final victory.

He lay on his back in the rear of the van, pushing the spare kerosene can out of his way, and struggled out of his jeans and T-shirt.

Slipping into Lucy in this confined space tested his faith; he was already sweating, the beads of perspiration making it hard to roll her over him. His feet and hands smacked against the thin metal of the van as he assumed Lucy's form. Minutes later, he was whole again.

He glanced at Lucy in the vanity mirror. Her face never failed to stir him, spur him on, no matter how tired he was. It would be worth it; all of it. As his father liked to preach: '*all the desires of the diligent are fully satisfied.*'

His own diligence, though, had been rewarded. *They* had deigned to whisper to him again, made *their* commands known. Her salvation would be a lesson to others, to those who had thought nothing of him, derided him and underestimated him.

No one would underestimate him again. Not in this life.

Chapter 17

Nader slammed the brakes outside the Points of Lights Lodge and cut the engine. The blood-red sun had just begun to set behind the pines, their spindly fingers crouching forward in the wind, reaching down towards the building as if trying to snatch it in their clutches.

Manx raced from the car and across the courtyard, Priddle following in his tail wind.

Isla Logan was hunched over the reception, her portable television turned to full volume. She didn't notice Manx until he loomed over her, gesturing for her to turn it down. The cat sleeping at her feet jumped to the desk and hissed at Manx.

'Remember that raiding party you were expecting, Isla?' Manx said, keeping one eye on the cat. 'Well, we're here. Now, where's Marsden Owens? And if you lie to me, I swear I will arrest you.'

Isla clicked off the TV. 'You can't come in here without a warrant, I'm not stupid.'

'If we have good cause to believe an officer's life is in danger, we don't need one,' Manx said. 'Nader, check out the barn and the outbuildings. Priddle, search the backroom and keep an eye on this one, I'll check upstairs.'

There were six rooms, three on either side of the hallway. He crept past each one, pushing gently on the doors. The first five were all empty, leaving only the door at the very end of the hall. It was already slightly ajar, a spill of light filtering under the frame. It had to be the one.

Back steadied against the paper-thin wall, Manx reached for his side baton, fixing its perfectly balanced length in his hand. Tip pushed gently against the knob, he urged open the door.

It creaked slowly open. Manx caught a smarting of cat piss and sweat.

'Marsden Owens, if you're in there, make it easy on yourself and come out slowly, hands in the air. Understand?'

Silence.

Manx edged carefully into the bedroom. It had the same utilitarian sparseness as the others, though, the bed was unmade, sheets and a single blanket drooping from the mattress and onto the floor.

He rummaged quickly through the room. The wardrobe contained a few items of clothing; nothing worth a second look. He opened the bedside drawers; they were equally sparse except for a roll of duct tape, a tube of talcum powder and trinket box identical to the one Manx had been given in London, with a beach scene and palm tree design engraved on the lid.

Inside was another collection of photographs, mostly of Marsden and his mother. Under those there was a photograph of a younger woman with striking blue eyes. She was holding Marsden in front of her, her arms wrapped tightly around him, the lodge in the background. It was unlike any of the other pictures – the boy looked happy, smiling to the camera as if he had forgone his piousness for happiness. He looked closely at the woman. She reminded him of someone – a face that was not yet haunted by whatever misfortune life would inflict on her. Manx snapped the lid closed.

Marsden Owens was their man, there was no doubt, but how was Isla Logan involved? And how much did she know? That would have to wait. If what he suspected was true, Marsden Owens had taken Morris. He'd already killed four, maybe five people. He wasn't about to let Morris be his next victim.

He ran back to the reception.

'Nothing in the outbuildings,' Nader said, panting heavily as he leant on the desk. 'Jesus, if he's got her, boss…'

'Just focus on finding Morris, Nader, everything else is just speculation.'

'Back room and the kitchen's clear,' Priddle said, walking back in.

Manx directed his attention to Isla. 'This is you, right, Isla?' he said showing her the photograph.

She shrugged. 'Could be anyone.'

'What's your connection to Marsden Owens?'

Isla Logan soothed the cat with a brush of her palm over its spine. 'None of your damned business.'

'All right, you can tell us down at the station,' Manx said.

'And if I refuse?'

'Simple, I'll charge you. Obstructing a criminal investigation, harbouring a known criminal, refusal to cooperate with our enquiries, wilfully putting an officer's life in danger. You name it, I'll throw it at you. So, unless you want to be arrested right now, I suggest you play nice with my two officers and grab your coat. Priddle, call the station and get a search party out here, pronto.'

'What about Laddie?' Isla asked.

'Laddie?'

'My cat, Laddie, he'll need to be fed.'

The cat, hearing its name, hissed again, its tail standing to attention.

'Cooperate with our enquires and you'll be back to give him his breakfast. Either way, he looks like he could miss a meal or two.'

As Manx reached for Isla's forearm to escort her to the car, the cat arched its back, spat at Manx as if it had understood the insult, and scraped its untrimmed claws across the back of his hand drawing an immediate trickle of blood.

'Jesus Christ!' Manx slapped the cat away. It ran into the backroom, still spitting at him from the floor, defying Manx to try that again.

Tempted as he was to take his Blundstone boot to the animal's hind quarters, he resisted. 'Isla, now please get into the fucking car.'

Chapter 18

The lead handler passed Morris's boot across the snouts of each of the four German shepherds. They sniffed at the item, then, scent in nostrils, pulled eagerly on their leads, their breath falling like smoke from their jaws as they stalked the undergrowth.

Behind them, twenty-five officers walked across the forest in a well-disciplined line. Their torch beams scuttled over the undergrowth and through the grey cloak of mist that had drawn down over the forest. In the distance, the steady back and forth slosh of the ocean and above them, the nervous flicker of wind through the firs.

Manx was about to head to the front of the line when a stout man, chopping his way through the undergrowth, waved his walking stick in his direction.

'You this Inspector Manx character?' he said, eyeing Manx suspiciously as he came closer.

'And who are you?' Manx asked.

The man threw back his shoulders. 'Gethyn Morris,' he said, a determined steel in his voice. 'Can't sit on my arse waiting for you lot.

She's my bloody daughter, so don't try and stop me.'

'Wouldn't dream of it,' Manx said. 'Make yourself known to the lead searcher, he'll give you direction.'

Gethyn stood to attention, wavered a little, his eyes blinking as if stopping himself from crying.

'We'll find her,' Manx reassured him, patting him on the shoulder.

Gethyn nodded and walked off into the shadows. Manx hoped he could live up to his promise.

The search party drew itself through the forest in a perfectly choreographed line.

'What if she's not here, sir?' Priddle asked, running to catch up with Manx.

'Then I'd say that's a good result, Priddle.'

'How come?'

'If she's out here, it means he got what he wanted then dumped her. So, Priddle, I'm sincerely hoping we find nothing, that way there's still hope of finding her alive.'

Priddle swallowed hard as he took in the implications.

As the final specks of sunlight shaded back into the plush navy of the night sky, the dogs had reached the dunes. They sniffed at the sand and cocked their legs at the spikes of marram grass. Noses directed skywards they whined and seemed to shrug their collective shoulders in unison, unsure as what to do next.

Manx felt a tentative sense of release. 'All right, one last pass then we meet back at the Lodge.'

Relief or not, Manx needed a better plan. He still didn't have a motive for the killings, maybe with more information from Isla Logan he could figure it out, push her buttons until she gave him what he needed. By the time tomorrow morning rolled in, Morris would have been missing for thirty-six hours; another twelve and the odds of finding her alive were fading as fast as the day's sunlight.

'Mr Morris, can I have a word?' Manx called out.

Gethyn turned around. His face was red with sweat. He wiped his sleeve across his eyes.

'What about?'

'Your daughter. The good news is she's probably not out here.'

'How's that good news?' Gethyn asked, gripping tight to his walking stick. He looked like a farmer in search of his lost sheep.

'Hope, Mr Morris, there's still hope,' Manx said. 'All right if I go back with you? There's something I need your help with.'

Chapter 19

'I've got all night, Isla,' Manx said, folding his arms. 'No place else to be, no dog to let out, no cat to feed. How about you?'

Isla looked down at her cardigan and picked off a stray fragment of lint.

'How long have you known?'

'No idea what you're talking about,' she said, glancing at the duty solicitor, a young man who looked as pleased to be there as Isla did.

Manx leant forward. 'Five people murdered, Isla, and a young female police officer missing. That's quite the body count. He's a dedicated disciple, Marsden, isn't he?'

Isla flinched slightly at the mention of his name. 'He came after his mother died. He needed a roof over his head. That's all I know.'

'So you'd never seen Marsden Owens before he turned up on your doorstep? No connection?'

'There's always shelter for the true believers in God's house.'

Manx slid a photograph across the table. 'This is you, isn't it, Isla? And Marsden Owens. You were what, mid-twenties then? Marsden maybe eight or nine. This would be after Jacob Owens fled the British Virgin Islands after fiddling a few too many little boys. The locals eventually burnt down the church. Didn't want any monuments to a child abuser. Fair judgement wouldn't you agree?'

Isla folded her arms. 'Best leave the past to rest in peace.'

'And Jacob Owens? Does he deserve to rest in peace too?'

Isla stared Manx directly in the eyes. 'The dead will be judged by what is written in the books, according to what they have done.'

Manx's anger was rising to boiling point. He was tempted to grab the woman by the scruff of her tattered cardigan until she confessed something that would help them find Morris. Instead, he sat back and controlled himself, tried a different tack.

'You know, Isla, I'm a big music fan. Love the stuff, probably too much for my own good.'

He picked up his iPhone. 'You know how many songs I've downloaded on here? Fifteen thousand, or there about. Now, there's one song that's a real favourite of mine. 'Baker Street'. Do you remember it? Back in the seventies?'

Isla shrugged.

'You should check it out, great tune, but the lyrics, that's what really got to me. On the surface it's just another pop song. Man loves woman, woman can't live with man, usual stuff. But, as I was telling a friend of mine only last week, it's about more than that. Self-deception, Isla, that's what it's really about. We all lie to ourselves, usually because the truth is too painful to face.'

Manx paused to gauge Isla's reaction. It was still non-committal. He continued.

'I reckon that's you, Isla. In your heart you know what Marsden is, but you lied to yourself, convinced yourself you were doing the Christian thing by taking him in, giving him shelter. Now, the one thing I can't figure out is why. Why are you protecting him? After all, you must have had a colourful parade of lost souls coming through over the years, why him? Why Marsden?'

Isla's face turned a few shades whiter. She knitted her fingers together in a thread of knuckle and fingernails.

'We're all equal in the eyes of the Lord,' she said, a tremor in her voice. 'I treat them all the same. Kindness and charity.'

Manx leant forward. 'Come on, Isla, there's more to it than that.'Isla directed her gaze past Manx.

'Okay, let's try a name game. Glyn Lewis. Know him?'

Isla shook her head.

'How about Kimble McLain?'

Isla's 'tell' was like a jackpot buzzer to Manx. A tap of her tight index finger on the back of her left hand. He'd noticed it at the Lodge and again now.

'Yeah, well he's in the papers all the time, of course I heard about him.'

'Right. How about I run a story past you? Not one of those biblical parables, something closer to home.'

'Will it get me out of here faster if I say yes?'

Manx scraped back his chair and paced around the room.

'A young girl, maybe an only child, is eager to see the world and joins a missionary outfit called the Points of Light Ministry. She's what, maybe seventeen, eighteen years old? She's loyal, a hard worker, but instead of sending her to spread the good word, they keep her close to home, pull tight on the apron strings. As the years pass, she sees others sent away all over the world, but she's stuck there, minding the shop, so to speak. She's still there when Jacob Owens and his family return from the British Virgin Islands. By this time, she's become close to the family, maybe too close. She sees things she shouldn't have, things that tested her faith.'

'She have a name? The girl in this story of yours?'

Manx leant his elbows on the table.

'You're the one who made the call, Isla. You put a stop to it.'

Isla's bottom lip quivered – a barely detectable flicker.

'You saved other boys from Jacob Owens. Was it Marsden? The one that finally made you take a stand and stop lying to yourself?'

Isla's voice was barely a whisper. 'His power is made perfect in weakness.'

'So you were strong.'

'No, I was weak, I found enough strength for them that was all.'

'And now, what kind of resolve will it take Isla?'

Manx slipped another collection of photographs from an envelope.

Isla sat back and smiled. 'Won't work on me, you know,' she said. 'I've seen them do this on the telly. You're going to show me photographs of the victims, hope I'll talk.' She leant into Manx, a fire in her eyes. 'I fear not the terror of the night nor the arrow that flies by day.'

Manx smiled. 'Quote all the Bible bullshit you want, Isla, but you're not getting out of here until I find my officer alive and I'm buying her a drink in that pub down the high street. Understand?'

Manx laid the photographs on the table. Twelve of them, recently removed with care and love from their frames by Gethyn and Margaret Morris.

'Twenty-four years old, Isla. Delyth Anwen Morris.'

Isla looked over the photographs.

'One of our sergeants calls her Morris Minor on account of her size. She's short, but brave, well liked. Graduated police college a couple of years ago, as smart as they come and like you, Isla, she's not afraid. We all reckon she has a great future ahead of her, parents are in the room next door right now, watching, hoping you'll find the same strength again and help them get their daughter back, alive.'

Isla looked over to the one-way mirror, then looked back at the photographs. Another life in captured moments.

'Marsden Owens is holding her, Isla. As much as you'd like to deny it he's likely murdered five people already. Now are you willing to have this young woman's death on your conscience?'

Isla passed her fingers over the photographs. 'He was a good lad. Jacob, he turned him, blighted him.'

'If you're a Christian, live up to what that means, help me find Delyth Morris.'

Isla laid her hands flat on the table.

'I'll ask you again, why Marsden?'

Isla's eye's prickled with tears as she passed her fingers over the photograph of her and Marsden.

'My sons,' she finally said, wiping away the first trickle of tears.

Manx leant forward, making sure he'd heard her correctly. 'Sons?'

Isla nodded. 'Marsden and Kimble.'

Manx felt his eyes widen and his stomach flip as she spoke.

'They never knew. I never wanted them to know, they should never know.'

'Jesus,' Manx said. 'How?'

'I was young, but you were wrong, in your story. I left home because I was pregnant. I loved him. He didn't love me. My ma and da would have sent me to a convent, made me give up the baby, this way I could still see him, at least until they took him away.'

Isla took a deep breath and continued. 'Jacob and Elsie, they'd been trying for years. Then I arrived. A gift from God they called it. They took him a few weeks after he was born. They were sent away, Goronwy thought it best that way. I didn't see him for years.'

'And Kimble McLain?'

Isla wiped the tears from her eyes. 'One of the trainee missionaries. I tried to fight him, but he was strong. They made me give up my second son too. I had no choice, nowhere else to go. Used chattel, they called me. I never saw Kimble again, well, not until a few years later when he came to one of the summer camps Jacob ran. I knew it was him right away, a mother knows.'

Manx sat back in his chair. An overwhelming wave of pity for Isla Logan flowed over him. He could almost see the etches of pain in her face as she wiped her eyes. He'd had a colossal failure of imagination where Isla Logan was concerned. He hoped it didn't extend to Marsden Owens.

'Oaky,' he said, his tone soft. 'Is there anywhere else Marsden may have taken her, anywhere?'

Isla sniffed and glanced nervously at the one-way mirror behind her. 'The church, about a mile from the Lodge. He liked to go there when he was upset, made him feel better.'

'We've already been there, searched the whole place.'

Isla shrugged. 'Sorry, there's nowhere else he goes. The Lodge or the Church.'

She began to sob, cradling herself as she mumbled. 'Marsden, my little laddie, may God forgive you. God forgive you.'

Chapter 20

Kimble McLain slapped his phone down on the desk. He hadn't heard from Glyn Lewis for three days. His mobile was switched off – an unusual event in itself. He wanted to give him the courtesy of a face-to-face confession. The police would have charged him, he had to give them a name.

But how did Lewis know about the ravens? He'd never told him, at least not that he could remember. The memories of that time still traced an outline of shame around his body that only he could see – a dark aura that defined his edges but not his whole being. He'd refused it that satisfaction.

He'd learnt to bury, bury deep. What did the child psychologist say? That he *compartmentalised*? What the hell else was he meant to do? Relive it all again; that summer? That man? His thick fingers pawing him, brushing himself against him like he was hoping something would rub off, something he lacked, was incapable of feeling and hoped he could steal from boys like him. No, it had taken will power not sharing to bury that. It was a distortion of reality; with enough faith in himself he could bend the universe to his will, achieve greatness, stake permanence on the world, a testament to the uncrushable will of mankind. Anything was possible if you just applied yourself.

But what if he was wrong and Miiko was right? There was a limit, some things could not simply be willed into existence?

As he looked over the sketch again, his phone rang. He checked the caller ID and clicked the answer button. *He* wanted to meet, tomorrow night, Newborough Beach. He hung up, scrunched the sketch and threw it onto the desk.

* * *

Outside the property wall, behind the thick foliage of sessile oaks, he turned up the heat in the van and waited. He'd come out soon, he had to. He'd follow him, figure out when he was coming back, lay out the snare ready for him.

Lucy was in full agreement with the plan. She was as patient as he was. But there was other business to attend to first. That bitch police officer. He'd save her first. But not tonight, he would not worry about it tonight. He would rest, gather his strength. *'Be not anxious for tomorrow for tomorrow will be anxious for itself.'*

Chapter 21

Manx's night had been fitful and sleepless, the minutes and hours ticking by slowly, mercilessly. It was imperative he stayed positive, visualise the best-case scenario: rescuing Morris, drinks and tall tales at the pub later, the countless re-telling of the time she was almost killed. But what if they were too late? What if she was already under his knife?

At three in the morning he threw off the covers, figuring anything was better than lying here imagining the worse.

He dragged a stool across the kitchen floor and poured himself a tumbler of Scotch. The information from Isla Logan was still burning a hole in his head. Jesus. The tragedy of it all was like CeeCee had said, *a heartbreak in a box.* He reached for the trinket box and scattered the photographs across the breakfast counter.

It would have made anyone turn from God, he imagined. But with Isla Logan it seemed to have strengthened her resolve. Marsden and Kimble, two boys, one born from passion and the other born from violence. He would have expected the opposite outcome, but life was like that, a random roll of the genetic dice that leaves us powerless in its wake.

* * *

He was back at the station at six-thirty that morning. He needed a new plan, some serious out-of-the-box thinking. As he walked into reception, DCI Canton was already waiting, his face long and grim. Like Manx, he looked as if he hadn't slept all night.

'You look like hell, Manx,' Canton said.

'Not exactly angelic yourself, Chief,' Manx said, bracing himself for the bad news he was sure Canton was about to deliver.

'Vera Troup,' Canton said. 'She's in my office.

'Thank God,' Manx said.

'Really?'

'Better than the news I thought you were going to give me. Lead the way.'

'You disobeyed orders, Manx. Very specific orders,' DCS Troup said, her pale, drawn features looking more ghoulish under the harsh morning light lancing through the office window.

'The evidence pointed to McLain,' Manx said, turning to leave. 'Now, if you don't mind, ma'am, I've got a missing officer who I'm hoping to God saw the sun rise this morning.'

'Actually, I do mind, Inspector,' Troup said, gesturing for Manx to stay put. 'Because you were hell bent on pinning this on Kimble McLain we now have a young officer in the hands of a serial killer.'

'I'm aware, ma'am,' Manx said, impatiently.

'Kimble McLain was nowhere near Liam Fowler, or the other victims, when they were killed, Manx. Nowhere near.'

'We didn't know that at the time.'

Troup leant on the desk, shoving one of Canton's plants to the side. 'Full disclosure, Manx. No omissions, no obfuscation, no maverick bullshit.'

'We're working on leads.'

'What leads? That old woman in the cells? Or this Glyn Lewis character McLain insists murdered Liam Fowler?'

'Isla Logan gave us some vital information, she'll be released this morning. Glyn Lewis is our prime suspect for the Liam Fowler murder. We suspect Marsden Owens of the other murders. He's holding Morris, which is why I really need to—'

Troup raised her finger in a *'shut the fuck up'* gesture. 'So, essentially, Manx, we're no closer to finding our killer than we were before you thought it a bright idea to bring in Kimble McLain for questioning. Here's how I break it down, Inspector.

We have two suspects, both missing, and a police officer with a death sentence hanging over her and no fucking clue as to the location of any of them. Sound about right?'

'Well…' Manx began.

Troup sighed. 'It's at times like this, Manx, I wish I still fucking smoked,' she said, pacing the office. 'What about Alvarez? I assume you saw him.'

'Yes.'

'Jesus, Manx, it's like pulling teeth with you.'

'He was right, on a few things, I'll give him that.'

As Troup contemplated her reply, she fidgeted as if she were rolling a cigarette in between her fingers.

The mention of Alvarez's name triggered an idea. 'His mission,' Manx said. 'We figure out his mission, we have his motive, that might lead us to Morris.'

'Sounds like a long shot to me, Manx,' Troup said, unimpressed.

'Better than no shot at all.'

Manx had bolted before Troup could issue her reply.

He ran into the incident room. Nader jumped from his chair – another officer with the rough baggage of a sleepless night. 'Any news, boss?'

Manx shook his head.

Nader sat back down, ran his fingers under his collar. 'I should have bloody well known she was going, bloody stupid of me.'

'No time for pity parties, Nader. You'll do Morris more good by focusing on finding her. Where are those photographs we took from her phone?'

Nader gestured to Morris's desk.

Manx grabbed them, stuffed them in his jacket pocket. Maybe there was something he'd missed, something a man like Alvarez might just notice. A long shot, Troup was right, but the only shot he had left.

Chapter 22

The scuttle of chairs across a floor. The scrape of stone on stone. He was back. The sound was different this time, though. Not the heavy drag of work boots but the brittle clicks of heels.

He placed something on the floor next to her.

Zip ratcheted open, rummaging, something removed.

His smell was different too. The sickly, dry aroma of stale talcum powder, maybe? It was almost feminine, she thought.

She heard water being poured, drips falling to the floor.

She heard the lamp igniting, the click of a lighter. Felt his hands at her blindfold, pulling it down.

She gasped. Her eyes widened. The true gravity of her situation was clear now.

A sharp breath from the unmoving lips as he spoke.

'Are you ready to be saved, PC Morris. Are you?'

Chapter 23

'These photographs, Alvarez, can you glean anything from them. Anything?'

Doctor Alvarez slipped on his reading glasses. 'Any background or context, Manx?'

Manx explained as quickly as he could what he'd discovered so far. 'You were right about the missionaries, the Bible quote, the recent loss. It all makes sense,' Manx said.

Alvarez nodded. 'Gives me no satisfaction, Manx, but I'll do what I can to help find your officer.'

'His father, a serial child abuser, committed suicide when he was exposed. We know his name, Marsden Owens, other than that, we don't know where he is or where he's taken Morris.'

'And you think I can help find him?'

'I need to know his mission, Alvarez. Is it revenge on the people who exposed his father?'

Alvarez removed his glasses. 'I'd say unlikely. These kinds of serial abusers often have a genesis in the home. The father likely abused the son then escalated his attentions to other boys.'

'Marsden Owens was abused?' Manx said. 'He'd probably be glad the father is dead, so revenge wouldn't make sense.'

'It's been said we can never truly be ourselves until our parents pass,' Alvarez continued. 'But, the father, he was a minister, correct? A Baptist minister?'

Manx nodded.

'Now put yourself in this boy's place. He's been abused by his father, he maybe sees his father abuse other boys but he's powerless to stop it.'

'So he's killing people to get back at his father?'

'No, it's more complex than that, it has to be.'

Alvarez stood at the window looking out towards the flat, grey morning as it rolled in over the Menai Strait. 'The boy's a true believer. After all that happened, he didn't turn his back on God, he's still serving Him, in some capacity.'

'His mission?' Manx said.

'If he's not killing for revenge, what the goddam hell is he killing for?' Alvarez walked back to the desk and studied the photographs. '*I baptise you with water for repentance. But after me will come one who is more powerful than I, one whose sandals I am not fit to carry.*'

'Bible quote?' Manx said, sighing.

'Book of Matthew, I think, it's been a while. Manx, did you cross-reference the victims to the Points of Light Church baptism records?'

'All destroyed in a fire a few years back,' Manx said.

'Convenient.'

'Where exactly are you going with this, Alvarez? I'm over thirty-six hours into an officer's disappearance, I don't have time for sermons on the mount.'

'Okay, then let's take the leap, Manx, together. You wanted a motive. His mission is to save. Pure and simple. He's saving souls and then delivering them to God. He's a supplicant in the service of his God.'

'But there's no connection, no thread that links the victims.'

'If you had those baptism records, I bet you a dollar on the pound that you'd find it. Think about it. His father would have baptised his flock, young and old alike. After the son discovers the sins his father committed he's overwhelmed. He feels shame, anger, maybe he even feels rejected by his father. A perfect storm of emotions would be too much for a young boy to process.'

Manx checked his watch.

'Remember that point in your childhood, Manx, when you first saw your parents for what they were? Human. Fallible. Happens to us all, a necessary stage in the parent child separation.

Imagine witnessing that, Manx, but to the power of ten. His father commits the most heinous act he could, failing to protect those in his charge and even more importantly, preying on the powerless and innocent. How can someone with that weight of sin be pure enough to save others? Because of the sins his father committed, the boy no longer sees the father as legitimate, certainly not legitimate enough to confer baptisms.'

Alvarez had a bounce in his step as he walked towards his bookcase. 'Imperfect souls, Manx. He's saving souls that would otherwise be damned from the illegitimate baptisms his father performed. He's cleansing them, making them perfect for God. That's his mission. The phials of water are probably holy water, he's baptizing the victims before killing them.'

'Fuck,' Manx said, wiping his hand across his face. 'There's no way we can find that list. And I still don't know how it helps me find Morris.'

As Manx leant down to gather the photographs. Alvarez grabbed his wrist. 'Hold up, cowboy,' Alvarez said, spreading the photographs across the desk. 'You searched this church thoroughly?'

'First place we looked.'

Alvarez steadied his glasses back over his ears. 'This is a Baptist church, there should be some kind of baptism pool. In the American South they were usually outside, near the cemetery, or they'd dip the flock in the local river. Too cold for any of that around these parts, I'd say.'

'We searched the whole place,' Manx said. 'Just a church and a basement full of old Bibles.'

Alvarez reached for a book from his shelf and flipped it opened on the table. In the chapter titled 'Churches Post 1940 Britain', he ran his fingers over the black and white photographs.

'Pools, built directly into the floor of the churches, hidden, undercover,' Alvarez said, a spring of excitement in his voice.

'Inside, Manx. The baptism pool is inside the church. You probably walked right over the damned thing.'

Chapter 24

Water. She'd give her right arm for a drop. She raised her head, ready to accept. But the water wasn't for her lips. Morris felt his damp fingers trace a line across her forehead.

As her eyes adjusted to the dim glow, his distorted features became clear. This close up was grotesque; a carnival of painted features that chilled her bones. Any hope she had of making it out alive was fading fast.

He tipped water from the phial onto his finger and ran it along her neck in the sign of the cross

Her negotiations had finally come to this. Come to nothing. God was not listening or, if he was, he wasn't in the mood for bargaining. But maybe there was an alternative, another path.

'Please,' she pleaded. 'Please. Do anything you want to me, just don't kill me, okay? I won't say anything, promise. Just between you and me, yeah? Would that be good? Right here, on the floor? I don't mind.'

The face looked at her, quizzically, as if trying to figure out what she was offering but failing to grasp the implications.

He re-attached the blindfold and secured the cloth deep into her mouth.

Morris felt a deep and endless pit form in her stomach. She had nothing left to bargain with it seemed. Not even her life.

Chapter 25

The next few minutes would pass Manx in a blur of gut instinct and controlled panic. As Manx ran from the car, Nader joined him, red-faced and sweating.

'You think this Alvarez bloke's right?' Nader asked, breathing heavily. 'Been here once already, searched the whole place.'

'We missed something, Nader. Let's go get her.'

'Without backup, boss?' Nader said, looking around.

'No time. I doubt he's armed with more than a knife, between the two of us we can take him.'

Nader nodded. 'Bloody hope so, boss.'

They pushed gently on the church door, still splintered where they'd assaulted it the day before. The faint smell of paraffin drifted from the centre of the aisle, along with a pinch of light that filtered upward through a small fracture in the floor.

The first few rows of pews had been pulled back. Manx could see it now, a slight raise and a slab of stone about twelve feet long and six feet wide, slotted perfectly into the church floor. A thick iron bar, now folded back into its slot, protruded a few centimetres from the rough stonework.

'We work fast, surprise him,' Manx whispered as they crept slowly around the pews.

They stopped at the iron bar and curled their fingers around it. Nader waited for Manx's nod. On the count of three, they pulled back on the bar and slid open the stone.

The smell of piss, sweat, and decay stuck in their throats as they looked down into the pool.

As their eyes adjusted to the light, they saw the doll face. He turned his head sharply, annoyed by the interruption. His features flickered in and out of focus under the pallid light of the lamp.

They looked at Morris. A small trickle of blood was tear-dropping down her neck, her body shivering. Manx's instincts kicked in.

He leapt to the pool floor, landing hard on his feet. Behind him, Nader did the same, landing awkwardly, with a grunt and a suspected sprained ankle.

'Drop the knife, Marsden, she's not yours to save.'

The doll face looked at Manx and cocked his head.

'Drop it, now,' Manx said. 'Let her go.'

The doll face looked back at his captive, assessing the situation.

Manx seized the split-second opportunity and lunged, wrapping his fingers around Marsden's wrists and pushing the knife from Morris's neck.

'Nader! Grab Morris, get her out of here.'

The sergeant hobbled to standing. Marsden and Manx pushed against each other, blocking his route, there was no clear pathway to grab Morris.

The doll face let out a determined growl and urged the knife back towards Manx. He was stronger than he looked. Manx lost his grip on the damp straw. As he reached behind him to break his fall, his arm swiped the lamp from its base. It toppled, spilling the kerosene over the table.

The flames caught quickly on the papers, then downwards to the bone-dry straw. Within seconds, the fire was sucking up the oxygen, laying waste to the papers laid out on the desk.

'Nader, put the fucking fire out,' Manx grunted.

He took his left hand and pressed his fingers deep into the silicon face until he could feel the hard resistance of bone.

Manx's command had failed to register with Nader. He was rooted to his boots, staring blankly into the wide, curling fingers of the flames as they caught on the straw.

'Nader!' Manx shouted.

But DS Nader was no longer there. He was back twenty-five years, trapped in the belly of the Sir Galahad, the bombs having just dropped from the Argentinian fighter planes, a ball of fire cascading towards him, burning the flesh of the young servicemen in its wake.

Manx whipped his head back. The doll face was inches away, urging the tip of his blade towards Manx's right eye. He had both hands wrapped around Marsden's wrists, pushing back with all the mettle he had.

'Nader, fucking do something!'

Nader stood motionless, his mind in his own personal hell-space.

Manx heard the wail of sirens in the distance. If he could hold on just a few minutes longer he might get out of here alive, him and Morris. The odds, though, were slowly fading as the tip of knife edged closer.

Through the blindfold, Morris could discern two shapes struggling. The heat from the flames was flickering closer, pricking at her feet. But there was as silver lining: the fire was a source of light and the fabric of the blindfold was thin enough for her to make out the outlines of both men as they wrestled.

What weapons did she have? Only her own body, her legs and feet. She twisted herself towards the shapes. Maybe if she could distract him it would give Manx some time, a sliver of a chance.

She rolled her body in their direction. Through the thin veil she could barely discern who was who, but she figured the way Manx was shouting at Nader, he must be the shape closest to her. She swooped her legs around the floor. It was a fifty-fifty chance at best.

Maybe her negotiations had borne some fruit after all. The doll face stumbled backwards as Morris's legs smacked into his ankles.

Manx took the slim opening and slammed the knife from his hand and to the floor. Doll face followed, sprawling across the floor and reaching blindly for his weapon. Manx kicked it to the far corner, then took the tip of his Blundstone and pummelled it hard into his stomach. The doll face reeled with the force, groaning and clutching at his belly.

Manx turned. The fire had caught fast on the straw and was now reaching through the floor of the pool and onto the shrivelled hymn sheets and the wooden pews.

He was running out of time. He whipped off Morris's blindfold. Her eyes were wide, terrified, but grateful. There was no time to undo her bindings.

'Sergeant, help me for fuck's sake! We need to get her out.'

On the sound of his military title, sergeant, Nader snapped from his trance. 'Jesus Christ,' he said, shaking his head.

Nader moved carefully over the root of flames and grabbed Morris's feet while Manx secured her underarms. Manx walked backwards up the few steps to the edge of the pool. They lay Morris on the floor.

Through the dense smoke, Manx saw the crouched figure grab his knife then scramble past the vestry, disappearing into the shadows.

The sirens were close now. Maybe they'd catch him. But Manx knew it was another long shot. This one maybe too long.

They carried Morris across the graveyard through the gates and propped her against the outer wall.

The firearms team had just arrived, followed closely by the emergency services.

Manx looked back. Flames billowed through the church roof, licking at the stained-glass windows until they shattered like fireworks.

'Christ,' Manx said hearing the wood blister and stretch under the heat.

Nader looked at the flames. What had happened in the last five minutes? The last thing he remembered was walking into the church.

'Help me,' Manx said, trying to undo the tight knots.

The sergeant slipped the penknife from his back pocket and placed the blade over the ropes. His hands trembled as he tried to cut the knots.

'Give me that,' Manx said, grabbing the blade from Nader's hand and slashing the bindings.

Morris groaned with relief.

'You okay, Morris?' Manx asked.

Morris nodded, swallowing huge gulps of air. Her face was smudged with dirt and grime. Manx took the cloth from her mouth and wiped at the marks around her eyes.

As he wiped, the cloth fell open.

It was a red T-shirt. He turned it around in his hands. He'd seen it somewhere before.

He slowly unrolled it.

The logo, dirt-ridden and flaked with embers, fell like a flag in front of him. Sospan Fawr – the letters were clear, unambiguous; a punch to his gut.

He took a moment to process. His mind flipped back in time.

The kitchen in his mother's house. The delivery van in the driveway. The leftover food containers in Sian Conway's house. The food deliveries to the station. The awkward, almost child-like blonde haired man. One name came to him.

Denny.

Den.

Marsden.

Manx's failure of imagination was now abundantly clear.

Chapter 26

Kimble McLain stood at the fingernail of Llanddwyn Island as the first twitches of twilight flickered through the clouds.

Below him, the Irish Sea urged itself against the rocks in short, callus punches. He looked down and felt the weight of the laptop in his hands. There was only one way to end this. He didn't have the stomach to delve into whatever Fowler had in there. It was moot now anyway, rouge code that needed to be deleted.

He took the laptop in his right hand and threw it, with an underhand bowl, into the sea. The ocean swallowed its secrets without complaint, drowned them within its vastness. He felt a sense of relief, a weight lifted, a burden laid to rest.

He watched the rush of waves for a few more minutes before making his way over the pathway skirting the beach and towards the agreed meeting point.

He was already there, waiting.

'You gave me no choice, you do understand?' McLain said.

Glyn Lewis lifted his head. He looked tired, dishevelled. Beaten.

'The project, Kimble. It was all for the project. Permanence, like you wanted.'

McLain couldn't bring himself to look at the lad. Instead he watched the orange glow of the sun, spread like a brush of paint over the horizon. Above them, an unkindness of ravens cackled over the sand dunes, flying low and fast.

'Used to come here as a kid,' McLain said.

'Must have been nice.'

'Not especially,' McLain said, turning to face Lewis. 'Some memories you'd rather forget.'

Lewis nodded and brushed back his flop of blonde hair from his eyes. 'You told them?'

'What did you expect? That I'd take the fall for you?'

Lewis dropped his head and kicked the sand under his shoes like a small child being reprimanded. 'Wash your hands in the Lord and even though your sins are bright red they will be as white as snow.'

McLain took a deep, meditative breath. 'Great. Where's your God now, when you really need him, Lewis?'

'I did it for you, a greater purpose.'

'I assume you'll be turning yourself in,' McLain said.

Lewis said nothing, breathed deeply.

McLain turned to leave. 'The sooner the better, Lewis, the press release is going out first thing in the morning.'

Lewis nodded.

McLain walked back to the carpark. Miiko was in the Range Rover, waiting.

'All done?' she asked.

McLain was tired of words. He nodded.

'Good. Tomorrow, I come with you, to the appointment.'

McLain raised a faint smile.

'No promises, just one visit,' she said, turning on the engine.

'No promises,' McLain whispered. It was all he could ask of her now.

* * *

As the sound of the car engine peeling away reached him, Lewis fell to his knees in the sand and wiped the tears from his eyes.

When he lifted his head again, the tide was already marking its territory, eager to stake its claim on the shore. Through the fast-fading twilight he saw a silhouette cut across the beach several hundred meters away, its hooves digging deep into the sand and kicking up the surf into salt-sprays that showered outward either side of its white, muscular flanks.

Was it a sign? He imagined it was, after he had committed the ultimate sin. The balance needed to be re-dressed. *An eye for an eye, a tooth for a tooth.* He removed his shoes, felt the cold snap of the water at his ankles and waded in until the water lapped at his throat then he let himself go; let God's will be done.

Chapter 27

'Complete list of all our drivers,' Andrew Davies said and sat back at his computer.

Manx took the paper and studied the names. Two thirds down the page he found the name he was looking for: Denny Logan.

'You don't run background checks on your staff?' he asked, throwing the paper back across the desk

Andrew hesitated. He was probably in his early twenties, Manx guessed. Trendy haircut – shaved at the sides and quaffed on top – with what Manx understood to be a 'hipster beard' that he kept rummaging his fingers through as if searching for a lost, ironic earring.

'We call them Delivery Associates.'

'Contractors you mean?' Manx said.

'They work when they want to. Benefits everyone.'

'Is that right?' Manx said.

Andrew offered a slim smile. 'If you're asking if any of our associates have criminal records, then the answer is no.'

'And this Denny Logan?'

'His references checked out. He worked as delivery driver in London with a dry-cleaning company. No red flags on our database.'

Manx sighed and sat back in his seat. 'No, I don't suppose there would be.'

An alert pinged on the man's computer. 'Sorry, just need to check on the deliveries.'

Manx watched as a digitised map of Anglesey appeared on the screen, a scattering of dots pinpointed around it. An idea took root.

'Do they provide their own vehicles, these contractors of yours?' he asked, leaning into the screen.

'We give them some cash upfront to get our logo printed on their vehicles, but yeah, we don't need the hassle of maintaining and buying the vehicles. Doesn't fit with the business model.'

'But you can track the drivers? See where they are?'

'Part of the contract. We fit their mobile phones with a GPS device, like a tracking app. Kimble McLain's company, he provides them, free of charge.'

'Out of the goodness of his heart, no doubt,' Manx said. 'So, this technology would let you track Denny Logan's van?'

'He's not been on shift for a few days, but if his mobile's switched on, yeah.'

Manx tensed himself as the man tapped his keyboard.

'You're in luck,' he said, pointing at the eastern edge of the island. 'Near the Cemlyn Nature Reserve.'

Manx knew the area well. It was close enough to Kimble McLain's house not to be a coincidence.

'He's there now?'

The man shook his head. 'Sorry, no. That was the last known location at eleven-thirty last night. Could be anywhere.'

Manx shoved back his chair. 'If that thing pings with his location, you call me, immediately.'

Chapter 28

'You didn't think to mention this, Ellis?' Manx said, taking a seat in the DCI's office.

'It was different back then, hell, I doubt they even had a name for it.'

'But you knew about it?'

'Of course, but the Falklands was over thirty years ago, Manx. The force was actively encouraged to take on veterans and whoever was in this chair before me saw it fit to clear him for duty and I have no reason to reverse that decision.'

'Other than he nearly got us all burnt to death.'

'Bit dramatic isn't it, Manx?'

'You weren't there, Ellis.'

Canton nodded. 'Mal can be a pain in the arse, no doubt, but he's a good copper, Manx, loyal as they come. It was a tense situation, maybe you misread the cues. The bloke jumped four feet into a rock-hard floor and sprained his ankle, I don't think my mind would be crystal clear either. Just be glad Morris is safe and put this behind you. Those two blokes, Owens and Lewis are still out there, it's time you brought them in.'

Manx took a deep breath. He could have carried on arguing but he knew Canton was right. There were two killers on the island, one still highly dangerous, the other panicked and unpredictable. Marsden Owens had another victim lined-up, another name to strike off the list; another soul to save. Manx felt his whole body tense. Finding that next victim was his sole priority. He wouldn't let another one be saved. If anyone was going to be doing the saving, it was going to be him.

* * *

The mood in the incident room was lighter than it had been for some weeks – too light for Manx's liking.

A handful of officers from Troup's extended team were sitting casually on the edges of the desks in the major incident room. Nader was leaning back in his chair, his bandaged ankle resting on the desk. He was re-telling the events of the night before for the third time that morning.

'Snatching glory from the jaws of someone else's victory, Nader?' Manx said, as he walked in. 'I'm assuming our suspects are both in the cells and offered us their full confession?'

The chattering turned quickly to silence.

'I thought not,' Manx said. 'Until Marsden Owens and Glyn Lewis are apprehended, we are not on reduced duty, any of us. No celebrating Morris's safe return with a sneaky pint at the Bull. Got it?'

A mumble of yeses was followed by the support officers shuffling back to their room.

'Right,' Manx said. 'Who's his next victim?'

'Next?' Priddle asked. 'Won't he have buggered off by now if he knows we're on to him?'

'He's on a mission, Priddle, he's not stopping until it's completed.'

Manx walked over to the incident board and pointed at the photograph of Lucy.

'This is a man who feels slighted by life. He's been abused, rejected, and lied to. Who's the person he really wants to make pay?'

As he looked over the photographs, his eyes were drawn to the happiest moment in the montage: Isla Logan with her arms wrapped around Marsden, his face beaming.

'Isla Logan,' Manx said, stabbing the photograph. 'His birth mother. He took her name but she lied to him, she's the one he wants to save. She's next on his list. Get her up here and keep her safe until he's in custody.

'Oh, she's already gone, boss,' Nader said. 'Duty officer signed her out early this morning.'

Chapter 29

He'd blemished her, that inspector, dug his dirty, ugly hands into her, distorted her perfect features. Corrupted her purity.

He ran his finger down Lucy's face as he looked at her reflection in the rear-view mirror. A thin scar across her cheek, her face smudged with dirt. He spat on his hands, tried as best he could to cleanse her. He'd bathe her, after all this was over, but first, there was the matter of the Raven Boy to attend to.

They imagined he was stupid. A little slow the teachers had said. Don't expect much in way of a career, the counsellors had advised him, best find something more in line with your abilities. But they were wrong. He was smarter than all of them. He'd worked it out just weeks after he returned to the Lodge.

She'd confessed, eventually, after he'd threatened the cat's life – it was the only way to get her to talk. The solicitor had pointed it out when he read the will. She had nothing to leave him other than the truth. They weren't his real parents. She'd written him the letter days before she passed. She was worried about him, wanted to make sure there would be someone to look after him after she was gone. There was even a name; Isla Logan. He was to go to her, she would look after him, he'd be safe there.

Of course, his birth mother was Isla – his 'angel' – it all made sense now, how she treated him like he was her own. He imagined living directly in God's love would be just like that, warm and eternal.

Then he had arrived, the Raven Boy, and suckered that love for himself. Did they think their actions would have no consequences, no implications?

He stood behind a tree close to the Lodge entrance and watched her return. A few minutes later he adjusted the strap on his high-heel shoes and walked across the courtyard.

She was in the reception opening a tin of cat food.

When she saw Lucy her face curdled, her eyes almost falling from her sockets. *Her ravens had finally come home to roost,* he thought.

'Good morning, Mother,' he said.

The tin of cat food slipped from Isla's palm. Meat scattered over her cardigan and onto the floor.

'He baptised you too, didn't he?'

Lucy stepped closer.

'You can't meet your maker like this. Unclean.'

He grabbed her wrists.

They were thin, mere matchsticks in his hands.

Chapter 30

They pulled up outside the Lodge and ran from the car.

'Check the barn,' Manx ordered. 'Priddle, you come with me.'

The reception was empty, the TV still muttering in the background. Manx reached over to adjust the volume and saw Isla Logan's foot poking from behind the door.

'Shit!' he walked carefully towards her.

The cat was sitting on Isla's body, slurping greedily at the meat that had spilled onto her cardigan.

'Get the fuck off!' he shouted, and aimed his boot at its backside, Laddie hissed at Manx before scarpering out into the courtyard.

He squatted and ran his hand over Isla's hair. Marsden hadn't had the time to bind her or perform any dissections. He probably heard them coming and ran before finishing the job. Good. It meant he was still on the island.

'Sorry, Isla, we should have known,' Manx whispered.

In the reception area, Priddle tapped on the keyboard and studied the computer screen. 'Sir, take a look at this.'

Manx left Isla's still warm body and peered at the screen.

'He was searching for something,' Priddle said.

'Or someone.' Manx peered at the search results and tweaked the brightness to its maximum.

Search:

Name meaning: Kimble – Welsh.

Great Warrior.

It was followed by a string of other results relating to Kimble McLain.

Manx's head span. Marsden's mission wasn't over. Not by a long shot.

Chapter 31

He floored the throttle and overtook the Range Rover on the Britannia Bridge. They were heading back home. He clicked on his mobile and checked the traffic. God willing, he'd get there before them and prepare everything, just like he'd planned.

Earlier that morning, he'd followed them, the Raven Boy and his pretty little wife, to a modest office building close to Bangor Hospital. It looked medical, maybe a private practice, like the one he'd tried to admit his mother to when her cancer was so advanced it was all she could do to breathe.

Money. It was all they wanted. He didn't have any. Supply and demand economics, it was how a just society worked, made it fair for everyone. He'd read an article about it, probably in one of those magazines in the doctor's waiting rooms, though, it made little sense to him. He had the demand, but not the supply. All he could offer his mother was a slow, pain-wracked slide into death. How was that just or fair?

Elsie Owens wanted to die at home; her one demand. He complied, though, those last few months tested his faith more than witnessing his father with the Raven Boy that summer and all the torment and pain that came in its wake. It took someone like Lucy to save him, bring him back into the light.

He was searching the Internet for wigs for his mother, red ones, similar to the thick red hair she'd had before the chemicals ravaged her cells. He accidentally clicked on a rogue search: a paid advertising banner that directed him to Second Skin Productions.

What he saw was kindling to the fire – a fire he was barely aware was smouldering inside him. When the saw the others, the *'living dolls'* as they called themselves, he felt helpless in their gaze. Their faces betrayed no emotion and expressed no human frailty other than the desire to be admired and gazed upon. This would be his fate. Beneath a skin like that he could hide his ugliness from the world and be loved for what he wasn't rather than for what he was. For surely no one but God could love him for himself, his father had made certain of that.

After his mother died, he'd imagined he'd stay at the house with Lucy until he too had passed. The letter had arrived a few days later. Repossession. The mortgage was in arrears by several months. It was a prime location, renovation ready, the leaflet had proclaimed.

A week later the sign was planted in the front garden. *It was like they were staking claim on a still-warm grave,* he thought as they nailed the board to the post. He looked at the lettering: Raven Construction. His blood ran as cold as winter baptistery water.

He researched the company until he found what he was looking for: Kimble Evans-McLain. A board member and investor. He recognised the photograph immediately. Ran his finger down the faint trace of a scar when he'd struck him that day, the day he christened him Raven Boy.

He understood his mission now.

He packed two suitcases, his Bible and clothes in one and Lucy in another. The following day, he arrived at the Points of Light Lodge. There would always be shelter there for the true believer. Of that he was sure.

Chapter 32

Driving back from the appointment, few words were exchanged between husband and wife. A faint lacing of hope was all that connected them. The doctor had been cautiously optimistic; more tests, a new fertility treatment, expensive but promising.

McLain felt a sense of calm he hadn't felt for some weeks. Maybe the tide was turning back in his favour. He reached over and patted Miiko's hand. She lifted her head and offered a faint smile. He'd take it.

He played his Chopin CD. The music filled the Range Rover's cabin with its soothing melody. A fitting soundtrack to accompany the bucolic scenery that streamed past the window in thickly drawn shades of green and brown. He slid back the shade covering the sunroof and enjoyed the soft warmth of the late-morning light as it filtered through the glass. Buttons of yellow daffodils were already poking their blooms through the greenery and the tree branches were bent heavy with the fresh settlement of leaves. *It was almost spring,* he thought. Another good omen: the season of rebirth and fertility.

McLain turned on to the single road leading to his house. A mile-long stretch of tarmac where he could put his foot down and feel the thrust of five-hundred horse power kick into the small of his back.

At seventy miles an hour, the front tyres exploded with an air-piercing boom, followed moments later by the rear. McLain wrestled with the steering wheel as it bucked and twisted in his hands. The two-ton missile barrelled towards the hedge. McLain pulled hard left. The back end swept by them, spinning the car around. He slammed his foot hard on the brake. The ABS engaged immediately, bringing the car to a sharp stop, the driver's side wheel balancing on the lip of a ditch. McLain let out the long breath he'd been holding in.

'You all right?' he asked.

Miiko flinched. 'My shoulder,' she said, trying to loosen the seatbelt stabbing into to her shoulder blades.

'What the fuck was that?' McLain looked behind him. Nothing but the stench of burning rubber and the outline of something that looked like a discarded strip of carpet laid across the road behind them.

Miiko groaned and turned to loosen her seatbelt. As she turned back she heard a loud slap of hands on the window.

She looked up. A long, almost feminine finger tapped its tip on the glass as if it were pointing at her, singling her out.

She screamed.

The finger was quickly replaced by a face, urging its unnatural form against the window and fogging the glass with breath that came from its full, unmoving lips. Dirt and ash smudges ran the length of the face which was barely female. Barely human.

'Kimble!' she screamed again, unbuckling her seatbelt with a notion that scrambling to the back might save her from whatever was out there before it forced itself inside.

More fingers. This time pulling furiously at the door handle until the loud, incessant clicking was all Miiko could hear.

'Jesus Christ,' McLain said, double checking the central locking. 'We stay in here, it'll be safer. I'll call 999.'

As he rummaged around for his phone, which had fallen into the foot well, the fingers ceased their urgent taunting.

They both held their breaths.

'Maybe gone?' Miiko said, hardly daring to utter the words out loud.

McLain raised his head. She was right, it was quiet – too quiet.

The rear end of the Range Rover suddenly buckled, a deadweight landing feet-first on the bumper.

Heavy boots scrambled for grip over the back window, snapping the windscreen wiper, then stealing onto the roof.

McLain looked up. Immediately, he regretted sliding back the shade. The doll face was urging its distorted features against the sunroof. He was dragging something behind him, metal scraping across metal.

McLain and Miiko looked at each other, terror like fire in their eyes. *Stay inside or make a run for it?* McLain thought. It was a bleak choice. At least inside they were safe, protected. They held each other's hands and waited.

Another brief moment of silence was shattered by the smack of metal on glass. The sunroof cracked like ice. They covered their heads as the rush of cold air and hailstones of shattered glass rained down.

The doll face peered over the lip of the sunroof as if getting the lay of the land, then stood up, legs either side of the opening and swung his weapon downwards in one, swift stroke.

It looked like a thick belt with blades attached, McLain thought as the implement bore down, its cruel grin just missing his arm.

His wife wasn't as lucky. One of the teeth ripped across the back of Miiko's head, removing a large chunk of flesh and hair. Blood spurted from the wound, covering the cream seats in sprays of red.

'Run. Just fucking run,' McLain shouted.

Miiko didn't need the second command. She flipped the lock, kicked open the door and ran, not daring to look back.

McLain felt the lash of a blade against his shoulder, followed by the grip of strong hands under his armpits and pulling him through the jagged edges of the sunroof, which tore at his body as he was hauled onto the roof.

He lay there for a second as the dol face loomed over him, his breath sour and warm as he spoke.

'Are you ready to be saved, Raven Boy?'

Before McLain could register the significance of the remark he felt himself being rolled from the roof. He landed, shoulder first, on the hard tarmac. Then darkness.

Chapter 33

'What the fuck?' Manx shouted, as Nader almost ploughed the service car into the backend of the Range Rover. They ran out.

Tyre marks were etched like charcoal marks across the road. All four tyres were blown, blood sprayed on the interior, blood dripping from the roof and onto the road. Spots of damp crimson on the road, trailing off into the distance.

Manx followed the red traces until they stopped directly outside the security gates at McLain's house. Miiko was there, unconscious, her head matted with blood, her body splayed on the floor.

Manx put his fingers to her neck. It was still warm, but only just. 'Priddle,' he shouted. 'Get emergency services out here. Make it quick, I've barely got a pulse!'

Manx stood and contemplated his next move. Was Marsden in the house? Somewhere close? They needed the code to enter, the gates were too high to climb.

As he debated, his phone rang – Andrew, from Sospan Fawr. He'd had a ping from Denny Logan's mobile half an hour ago. Britannia Bridge, then Cemlyn Bay Nature Reserve fifteen minutes later. The signal had been dead for the past twenty minutes, but the last ping came from Llyn Rhos Ddu — Black Heath Lake — on the borders of Newborough Forest.

Manx hug up and ran back to the car.

'Change of plan,' Manx said, watching his sergeant limping slowly across the scene and scratching his head. 'Nader, you stay put. Call an ambulance for the woman and radio for the firearms unit. Tell them it's about as urgent as it fucking well gets. Priddle, you're driving. I'm not losing another one, not today.'

Chapter 34

Kimble McLain's face smashed, bone on metal, against the side of the van. Warm blood oozed down his cheek.

He was bound tight, like a trussed pig on its final journey to the meat market. Had the other victims died the same way? He tried to recall the details but his mind wasn't going there – maybe there was a good reason – the less he could imagine of his fate the better. Instead, he focused on Miiko, hoped she's made it back safely, had called for help.

They turned sharply on to one of the hundreds of pencil-narrow roads that connected the island. Minutes later, they came to an abrupt stop that sent him careering into the back of the seats.

A flood of daylight streamed in as the back doors fell open. The doll face leant in. McLain scuffed his body back along the floor as if a few centimetres of space might save him, but the doll face wasn't interested in McLain, not at that moment. Instead, he reached for his implement, dragging it behind him as he walked away.

The engine churned again, followed by the harsh crunch of gears. They'd crossed to new terrain now; rougher, more undulating. The tyres buckled and bounced as they dug into the potholes and dips.

It was several more minutes before they stopped again.

The doll face threw open the back doors, looked down at McLain, and secured his hands around his ankles

McLain dropped from the van like a sack of bricks, his head smacking violently on the lip of the cargo space. Another blackout. When he came round again he was moving, dragged by his feet across the ground where the stones and rocks scratched their names deep into the bare, small of his back where his shirt had come loose.

His senses were shot. Eyesight blurred, hearing muted, smell blunted, touch numbed, taste…? What was the taste that filled his mouth? Fear? Fear of death? Or just death itself, settling thick like a gout in his throat?

The doll face stopped. McLain could hear his laboured breathing as he rested. Where was he? The roll of grey clouds above him gave little clue. The doll face moved closer, stood over him with his legs either side of his waist, his grotesque features, like a mid-afternoon eclipse, swallowing all light and life in its path.

McLain was quickly hauled to standing. He blinked, taking in a featureless expanse that bore no determinable shape. He looked down. His feet were wet. Cold water seeped over the tongue of his shoes and through to his socks.

He blinked, his eyes slowly recalibrating. It wasn't a featureless landscape, it was a lake, oil-black and calm with a curtain of stubborn dawn mist.

'Why?' It was the only question McLain could think to form.

The doll face grunted and returned to the van.

McLain shivered. The cold nipped through the thin layers of his expensive light-wool suit and deep into his bones. He could do nothing but stand there, vulnerable and at his mercy. Mercy? The thought reverberated through him. Maybe if he talked to him, pleaded, presented a persuasive argument as to why he should be allowed to live, he would grant him mercy.

The doll face returned and urged the full weight of his body into McLain's back. His breath whispered around his neck and throat. He reached his arm around, proudly displaying his knife to McLain. The grip was solid, confident. No hesitation, no mercy.

McLain swallowed hard, keeping the tart bile of death in check. 'Please, I've got money, whatever you need, name it.'

The doll face grunted and bought the blade closer to his eyes. McLain suddenly realised his desire. He required a witness, someone to confirm his triumphs that were smeared in dried blood over the blade.

The doll face urged the knife closer to his lips.

No, McLain thought, revising his earlier conclusion. His desire ran deeper than that, it was crueller, more visceral.

'Lick it,' the doll face said.

He wanted McLain to taste his triumphs. McLain shook his head. He felt the cold steel press urgently against his mouth, carefully prising his lips apart.

'Lick it,' he repeated.

McLain stiffened and complied. His ran his tongue over the knife's edge. If he had ever wondered what death tasted like, it was there, set on the blade of the knife – metallic, sour, inevitable.

The doll face laughed, or was it a groan of pleasure? McLain couldn't be sure. He pulled the knife away quickly, as if he'd given McLain enough of the taste of death to feast on, at least for now.

'It's you, isn't it? The boy from the mission?' McLain's voice was trembling, dry to the last word. 'The one who hit me with the rock. You called me Raven Boy.'

The knife was back, now settled across McLain's throat where he rocked it back and forth, barely breaking the skin.

'Tell me. Is it? Is it you?'

No response, other than the removal of the blade. But there was little time for relief. McLain felt the pressure of strong, determined fingers claw around the nape of his neck compelling him to drop, knee-bound, into the water

'On your knees, give thanks to your God, boy, or I'll bend your bones myself, understand?'

McLain's knees buckled.

With a hard, wilful push on his neck, McLain's face broke the surface of the water.

The doll face urged him under, held him there for what felt like an eternity, before dragging him back into the light. His voice, preacher-like and sincere, seemed thick with the tomes of ancient history. Words uttered from time immemorial.

'I baptise you in the name…'

Chapter 35

Priddle flat-footed the accelerator as he drove. Manx was communicating as clearly and quickly as he could with the Police Air Service. As he talked, he was suddenly thrust forward in his seat, his head narrowly missing the lip of the dashboard. The car swerved as if it had hit a patch of ice.

'Christ, Priddle,' Manx said, tugging on his seatbelt and groping for his radio that had fallen between his feet. 'Trying to kill us both?'

'Bloody tyre's blown,' Priddle said, getting out.

Manx followed. 'A stinger?' he said, examining the front tyres. 'He must have got it from Morris's service car, then used it to nab McLain. Twisted fuck.'

Priddle shuddered as he examined the police-issue device and the blood smears on the teeth that had dug deep into the tyres. 'Aye, we had training a few weeks back with these over at the circuit. Stop anything with wheels, that would.'

'And the bloody rest,' Manx said, remembering the deep gouge on Miiko's head. He looked east, towards the lake. 'What do you think, half a mile or so?'

'About that,' Priddle confirmed.

'Let's put those lanky legs of yours to work, Priddle,' Manx said, grabbing his radio and setting off.

Chapter 36

'In the name of the Father, the Son, and the Holy Ghost.'

McLain was hauled from the lake for the third time. His lungs were sodden, his throat raw. He gasped at the air, inhaling large mouthfuls before the hands urged him under again where all was black, cold; deathly.

When he rose for the third time, he heard a sound to his left. His ears were too water-logged to hear clearly, but he was sure it was a another voice, shouting.

'Marsden, put the knife down and move away from him. If you understand me, raise your arms.'

'Marsden.' His mother was the only one who called him that. To everyone else he was Denny, had been since they'd moved to London. What else did he know, this inspector? The same one that had taken it upon himself to blemish Lucy.

'Marsden, do you understand what I'm telling you?'

Understand? Yes, he understood. He understood the inspector was godless, just like the rest of them. That day when he'd talked down to him, threatened him, he had displayed his true colours; the colours of a non-believer, the colours of one in need of salvation.

The inspector too, had underestimated him. As if money had any importance to him. He'd deliver him to God too, after he'd finished with the Raven Boy.

He shoved McLain's face deep into the water, pulled him back up, and settled the knife at his throat; solid, calm, steady.

'Put the knife down.'

This time the voice was coming from his right. Another police officer. He didn't recognise this one. Maybe they were everywhere, the plague of locusts finally coming to devour him.

'Don't do it, Marsden,' Manx called.

The doll face pressed the knife closer to the skin until he could feel the knot of the Adam's apple rub against the blade. In the distance, he heard the flutter of raven wings. He looked skyward. A whole flock of them, death-black, chopping at the air.

'He's your brother, Marsden,' Manx said. 'Your blood brother. Isla told me before she died. Now, put the knife down and we can all walk away, alive. You and your brother.'

More lies? He couldn't take the chance, but what if it was true? What then? He needed time to process, time to confer before making his next move, a backup plan.

He dragged McLain back towards the van, knife poised at his throat. He reached inside for one of the spare kerosene cans and unscrewed the top.

'Think about it, Marsden,' Manx shouted, taking short, slow steps towards him.

'Isla Logan had two boys. McLain was sent away. If you want to be angry with anyone, blame the mission, your father Jacob, your grandfather. Isla was young, Marsden, too young to know what she was agreeing to. It's too late for her, but not for your brother, you can still save him.'

Brother? More words polluting his mind, confusing him. He looked up at the flock of ravens, their black, amorphous form swooping in an ever-decreasing circle towards him.

Manx's radio crackled.

'We've got a clear shot,' the pilot of the Eurocopter EC 135 voice was confident and efficient.

Marsden looked again at the black form circling above him. They weren't ravens, he could see that now. The only raven was here, in his hands, the one with a knife pressed against his throat.

Was he really his brother, the Raven Boy? And if he was, what did it matter? He too would be unclean, like the others, in need of salvation and the mercy of God's forgiving light.

As he lifted the knife, ready to plunge it deep into McLain's throat, the marksman guided the cross-hairs of the sight and pulled the trigger.

The bullet ripped through the air, burying itself deep into the Marsden's kneecap. He collapsed, the knife falling from his hand and into the undergrowth.

Marsden struggled to his knees and lunged towards the kerosene can. He reached inside his jeans pocket. A click of metal. A spark hitting the butane. The flame ignited, taunting Manx as he ran. He stopped dead in his tracks.

'No!' he called out. 'Don't do it, Marsden.'

The helicopter circled low, its search lights burning into Marsden's eyes. Another gunshot. This time the bullet burrowed deep into his shoulder. He spun one hundred and eighty degrees and dropped to the floor. The lighter slipped from his hand, the flame catching on the dry scrub where the liquid had spilled.

Manx could see the damp run of kerosene on the ground, a direct line from Kimble McLain to the van.

'Now,' he shouted at Priddle.

Priddle received the message loud and clear and ran at McLain. He grabbed his feet, dragging him from the spread of flames and onto the shore of the lake.

Marsden stumbled to his feet. The flames had caught on his shoes where the kerosene had spilled.

He looked down as the trail of flames danced in ribbons of bright yellow and red around him.

'You can still come out of this alive, Marsden, if you surrender now. Last chance.'

Surrender? Isn't that what he had done all his life, surrendered in some way? And what was so special about life anyway? Compared to what lay beyond, it was overrated, a suffering to be endured so the fruits of heaven would taste that much sweeter. Did that inspector really think that life was that important to him? No, the final victory was not life. The final victory was death. He took a step back towards the van.

Manx was about to run, make a grab for Marsden, but pulled back as the downdraft from the chopper sent the flames flickering under the axel, and directly to where Manx suspected the petrol tank was located.

He pulled back just as the explosion rolled like thunder through the morning.

Black smoke, thick and swirling, shot skyward. The helicopter dipped its beak, then pulled up hard to avoid the heat. Manx stepped back, shielding his face with his arms as the metal debris skimmed past him like incoming shrapnel.

Marsden looked up, hoping for a sign from God; a divine beam of light that would take him in its warm embrace. But there was nothing but the slash of helicopter blades and the swirl of blackness enveloping him. It wasn't for him to question. Maybe this was the fate God had ordained for his Beniah. A fate better than life. His own baptism would not be through holy water, but through fire. A just and noble death – a warrior's death.

Like Lucy, he understood what was required now. No more questions, no more doubt. He stood calm in the heart of the fire, arms wide as if preparing to receive a benediction.

As the downdraft from the helicopter blades fanned the flames it cleared the smoke for a few seconds. It was enough time for Manx to witness and standby helpless as Marsden Owens accepted, without complaint, his fate.

The flames caught first on the artificial hair, which crinkled to nothing as the heat seared at the fibres. The ribbons followed moments later, burning to ashes and floating away like embers.

Folding around his neck with its nimble fingers, the fire licked at the silicon and rubber compound until it blistered and melted, fusing to Marsden's face. Skin was now plastic, plastic was now skin.

A surge of peace rejoiced through Marsden Owen's soul. Maybe this was God's love after all; warm, forgiving, eternal.

His skin felt alive as the doll suit welded itself to every particle of hair and every pore of his body. But, it wasn't his skin, not any more, it was theirs, his and Lucy's.

They were united now, just as God had promised. They would share the final victory together.

Chapter 37

Kimble McLain and Manx stood over Glyn Lewis's hospital bed. The machines keeping him alive beeped and breathed with brusque efficiency.

'I never imagined,' McLain said. 'Not Lewis.'

'He was lucky,' Manx said. 'A bloke exercising his horse saw him, dragged him out in time.'

'Lucky?' McLain said, turning to Manx. 'When he recovers, what's next? Life in prison, most probably, where's the luck in that?'

'Better than dead,' Manx said.

McLain offered a non-committal nod of his head.

Manx shrugged. 'Did he ever talk about his plans for Fowler to you?'

McLain turned towards Manx. 'Do I need my solicitor?'

'Not unless you think you need one.'

McLain groaned. 'You don't like me much, do you, Inspector?'

'Don't take it personally, I'm an equal opportunity sceptic. I don't take to most people until they prove me otherwise.'

'Not a great humanistic trait, Inspector. What about the benefit of the doubt?'

'Unworkable,' Manx said. 'At least for my job.'

'I'm not sure whether to be impressed by you or pity you,' McLain said, turning to the bedside table and adjusting the expensive spread of flowers he'd sent. 'I expect you'll need me to come in and make a statement.'

'Par for the course.'

McLain eased himself on the edge of the bed, groaning. Every part of his body screamed with pain. 'I had no idea, you know,' he said, 'that monster was my brother.'

'Isla Logan wanted it that way,' Manx said.

McLain rubbed at his shoulder and groaned.

'Your wife?' Manx asked. 'How's she fairing?'

'She'll be out next week, no permanent damage. At least not physically.'

'Did she know about you and Sian?' Manx asked.

McLain let out a small, throaty laugh. 'I need to go through this all again for you, Inspector? It was a legal, binding contract. Six months from now, we'd have been a family. A real one.'

'And your wife would be none the wiser?'

'What are you getting at, Inspector?'

'We got the DNA tests back yesterday on Sian Conway's foetus.'

McLain blanched. 'You have my DNA now, so no doubt it will prove I'm the father. What difference does it make now?'

'Yes, you're right. But the maternal DNA was Sian Conway's.'

McLain stiffened.

'Which is odd, because if Sian was your womb to rent, then the only DNA would be that of the mother and father, yours and your wife's.'

McLain felt a small bead of sweat form on his forehead.

'You were having an affair with Sian Conway. There was no surrogacy, McLain, only a pregnancy.'

McLain kept his gaze fixed on the machinery, concentrating on the bleeps and hallow breaths.

'That's why you met with Liam Fowler the night Sian was killed. He was blackmailing you, not about your past or about the surrogacy, but about your affair with Sian. He had access to all her communications. She did leave you a message that night. She confirmed the child was yours; yours and Sian's. Glyn Lewis got his wires crossed, didn't he? He thought Fowler was out to ruin you, so he acted to protect you.'

McLain looked over at Manx. 'Will she need to know, Miiko?'

'It'll probably come out in court, so for the sake of your marriage you should probably at least give her a clue, eh?'

McLain slumped, snapped open his pill box and downed another pain killer. He glanced at the thick, bound Bible on the bedside table.

'He was a true believer, probably what got him into this mess,' Kimble said, running his finger over the gold, engraved cross.

'A true believer in the Bible or in you, McLain?' Manx said.

McLain sighed heavily and tuned the Bible face-down. 'Probably both.'

Chapter 38

Donna Robinson twisted the key in her front door and entered.

The familiar smell of home greeted her like a warm hug.

Three weeks with her mother was enough; probably too long. She would fare much better in her own place, fending for herself, and away from the constant fag smoke and bitterness.

She picked up the pile of mail from the floor and walked it to the kitchen table. It was mostly bills; probably overdue and final notices. In the centre of the pile, though, was a parcel stamped with the returned address of Bangor University.

She opened it carefully and reached inside – a flash drive, from him, Liam. Her stomach churned. She held it between her fingers. She guessed immediately what was on there, but she didn't need those memories; she was stronger now, more resilient. What she really needed was a drink. She threw the drive in the bin and poured herself a tumbler of vodka, lightly diluted with flat tonic water.

By the time the night had fallen, she'd drunk five of them, each one corroding her willpower not to look at the flash drive. As she downed her fifth vodka, that willpower had eroded wafer-thin. One more drink and it would disintegrate entirely.

Liam had at least lived up to one promise. The videos he'd taken of them together. He'd compiled them for her — their Greatest Hits. He must have been thinking of her just before he died. If he'd lived, maybe they could have worked things out, he'd have taken her with him.

The thought warmed her as she poured another drink and slipped the drive into her computer. Something to remember him by. It was almost sweet, she thought, as she pressed play on the video file and selected full-screen mode.

A dimly lit room. It didn't look like her bedroom, no curtains or a lamp.

She kept watching. Sian's face filled the frame.

Donna bought her hands to her mouth. 'No,' she whispered.

The sound of her own voice crackled through the speakers.

'I better go, he don't like the smell of it on me.'

Donna held her breath, not daring to move, though she knew she should. Should switch if off, walk away. But something compelled her to stay, something beyond her understanding.

A woman's face behind Sian's shoulder. A flash of steel. Sian's final scream as she was dragged, blood seeping from her neck, from the chair.

Chapter 39

The roof fell with a loud crash, followed by the walls, which cascaded in a hailstone of brick and cement. The bulldozer moved in quickly, making fast work of the rubble, shovelling the debris into its jaws then into the back of a lorry.

An hour later the Points of Light Lodge was dust. There was nothing left now other than the memory.

'Need your autograph on this, confirm it's all done,' the demolition foreman said, handing over the clipboard.

Kimble McLain glanced over the paper work, signed it and handed it back.

The foreman removed his hard hat. 'Holiday flats, or a hotel?'

McLain thought for a moment. 'Still up in the air,' he said.

The foreman nodded. 'Shame, though, not many of these old places left on the island. Thought this place would be around forever.'

McLain breathed deeply and looked over to his wife, Miiko, who was sitting waiting for him in the car – a brand new Lexus four by four, deep crimson with black leather interior.

'No such thing as permanence,' McLain said, and walked back to join his wife.

A flock of ravens nested in the pine trees ruffled their wings and cackled loudly as if echoing his words.

Chapter 40

Nader booked the lounge bar at the Bull's Head for Thursday night. PC Delyth Morris was being released from hospital that morning. It had been three weeks since they'd dragged her from the church: it felt like a lifetime ago. It was the least he could do. The guilt had been gnawing at him for weeks, maybe this would help ease the burden.

By six forty-five, every team member who wasn't on duty had arrived. Morris walked slowly through the doors just after seven to a thick round of applause and a loud chorus of 'For She's a Jolly Good Fellow,' Nader's overbearing baritone leading off the proceedings.

Morris blushed as she navigated her way, leaning unsteadily on her crutches towards the table which was covered in unopened cards and a box the size of a football in the centre, wrapped with bright red paper.

'Not looking too shabby,' Nader said as he pulled out a chair for her to sit on. 'Couple more weeks and you'll be back on the Tinder, eh?'

'Lost none of your charm then, Sarge,' she said.

Manx walked over and settled a pint in front of her.

'First of the night, always medicinal,' he said. 'Doctor's orders.'

Morris laughed. 'Had enough of bloody doctors, thank you very much.'

The team cheered as she downed half of her pint in seconds. She put down her glass and smiled. If she had her way, she would have cried. Not because she felt sorry for herself, but because this moment was all she had thought about when she was his prisoner. Now she was here, in the middle of what she'd negotiated for and been granted, it was overwhelming. She held back the tears as best she could.

Truth was, the entire team shared the same desire, though none of them would dare admit it. Those kinds of displays of emotions weren't required. Being here was enough. Morris was smiling, they were buying her drinks. For now, that was as good as it got.

'What's that, then?' Morris asked, pointing at the box.

'Got you a present,' Nader said. 'Nothing fancy mind.'

Morris looked at him warily. 'There' not a bloody severed head in there?' she said. 'I've watched *Seven* five times, still gives me nightmares.'

'Only one way to find out,' Nader said, sliding the box towards her.

She undid the loosely tied ribbon and slowly tore at the poorly wrapped paper. She reached inside and smiled.

It was her own boot, spotless and spit-polished until it gleamed like wet coal under the pub lights.

This time she couldn't hold back the tears.

'Hope you didn't throw out the other one,' Nader said, feeling a catch in his own throat. 'Took me ages. Army training. I can polish the enemy to death if needs be.'

Morris laughed and wiped her sleeves over her eyes. 'Thanks.'

Manx felt a lump in his own throat as Morris held the boot in her hands and lifted it to show the team. Another loud cheer.

Manx turned around as someone laid a hand across his back.

'Didn't think you'd make it,' Manx said, shaking the man's hand.

Daniel Alvarez smiled. 'It's raining, I'd be in some pub or other, so may as well make it this one.'

Manx turned to Morris. 'Morris, this is Doctor Daniel Alvarez. Don't think we would have cracked the case without him.'

Morris looked up and shook his hand. 'Thought I'd told you I'd had enough of doctors,' Morris said, smiling as Alvarez dragged a chair next to her. 'What kind of doctor?'

'Theology and lately criminal psychology. I worked as a profiler for the FBI then moved here on a whim. Ten years later, I'm still complaining about the weather but can't find it in me to move back.' Morris's attention had stopped at 'FBI profiler.' She pushed the boot to the side, listened to the rest of Alvarez's preamble, then took the opportunity to pounce on him.

Manx moved away, sensing Morris's evening was set as Alvarez, always fond of the sound of his own intellect, began to talk.

Manx ordered another pint. Ashton Bevan had just arrived. He was sitting at the bar drinking a double Scotch and looking over the proceedings as if he were observing wildlife in its natural habitat.

'Manx, the man of the hour! Another criminal bites the dust, eh?' Bevan said, raising his glass.

Manx guessed he was already a few doubles down, his eyes glassy and blood shot.

'You're only ever as good as your last case,' Manx said. 'Could all change tomorrow.'

Bevan ordered another. 'No such thing as a reputation in our business, being assigned another case is the best we can hope for.'

'You all right, Bevan?' Manx asked.

'Nothing a lottery win or drink won't cure,' Bevan said. 'But you'd know that better than anyone, right?'

He smiled at Manx, and raised his glass.

God, it was a damn ugly smile, Manx thought.

'To tomorrow, and whatever the fuck it throws at us.' Bevan downed his shot and walked out.

Manx shrugged and returned to the team. No matter his feeling about being back on the island and the memories it stirred, this was a celebration of life and the saving of one of their own. He could find solace in that fragile sense of peace, at least for a night.

An hour later he made his excuses and left. As he walked through the bar, he glanced up at the television. The news was just starting. He'd grab the headlines and drive home. He gestured for the barmaid to turn up the volume.

Manx felt a flutter in his belly as the newsreader reported on an incident near Ladbroke Grove, London. There were scant details, but the words *'one of their own'* sent a shiver through his bones – it always did.

His attention was directed from the stream of text running across the lower portion of the screen. Instead, he focused on the photograph that had just been superimposed over the newsreader's left shoulder.

He sat on the stool and held onto the bar to steady himself. CeeCee's face, smiling and filled with promise, stared back at him.

THE END

Acknowledgements

I'd like to thank Detective Superintendent Iestyn Davies and Chris Walsh, Digital Forensics and Cyber Crime Investigator, both with the North Wales Police, for their expert advice in writing this book. Also, a big thanks to Iwan Evans, Head of Legal Services at Gwynedd County Council for his expertise and steering me in the right direction.

Finally, to my beta readers. Your insights, as always, made for a better book.

Hugh Jones, Cynthia Nooney, Gloria Flores-Cerul, Laura Russell-Jones and Justin Fawsitt.

Lightning Source UK Ltd.
Milton Keynes UK
UKHW011343051219
354824UK00001B/104/P